BARE LIFE

BARE LIFE

Book Three of the Eldorado Trilogy

DONALD MENGAY

SADDLE ROAD PRESS

Saddle Road Press
Ithaca, NY
saddleroadpress.com

ISBN 9798990054356
Library of Congress Control Number: 2024953046

Design by Don Mitchell
Cover image by Donald Mengay

Books by Donald Mengay

The El Dorado Trilogy

The Lede to Our Undoing
Ojo
Bare Life

v.1.1

For Hrvoje Slovenc

1

WHAT IF GOD WERE MATTER, a body rude, expansive, and with a certain kind of mind? What if matter just is, divinely? Bare and eternal. If what it isn't is what we try and make it; bodies generally—no matter how we try to shoehorn them, they evade us, shoehorning being the problem. The way they tried to shoehorn me.

A stranger told me, That big-bang thing. . . . Even if you buy it as a concept it fizzles when you realize it had to come from somewhere, by which he meant someone. As though someone created in our image is capable. As though the thingness of being isn't enough; the only thing we can count on; the brute, diaphanous, flowy, inscrutable, lean boneness of nature. As though everything else we come up with weren't a fairy empire, sugar castles in the sky— gods and saints; genders and nations; heroes; borders and hierarchies; all pulled from the minds of humans.

Yet we dream on.

Closer to earth, feet grounded, grass beneath, we're given a choice: make do or make off. To the underworld usually. The underbelly of society. Some things we have no choice of, two parents and the need to eat, shit, stay warm or cool, depending. Beyond that you gotta make your own wiggle room, figure out how you'll get by in the straightjacket they call life.

When a bigot rules, the bigots are ecstatic. They talk a good game about bliss, though I'm not so sure. Borders;

drawing and policing them. This side and that—they love a hard line—as though the options were reduceable to two. That is to say they obsess about a geography of bodies; who can do what; what with whom; with themselves; and when; pinning everything on god.

For christmas I wish them a moment of self-doubt. Regarding things as they are, things as they used to be in some glittery-age fantasy—you gotta question anybody who wants to make the country better again.

As though things were ever good.

For whom?

A philosopher once said that stones have no world; that animals are poor in world; and wonder of wonders humans are rich in it. Just don't tell that to a rock or a gopher, humping to get by. They may not take kindly to it, especially given what humans have done to the place, the actual, physical world—you could call it rich in a sense. In fact rocks and gophers may have a thing or two to say about philosophers, and philosophy generally; kin to religion.

It all depends on where you stand, not what it says in some book. They have meaning in lots of ways, books, especially in a history of ideas, growing in complexity since writing began, a thing fascinating in itself; beyond that you have to take them with a grain of salt because we're moving, or trying to. Look around! I hate to inform you but things have shifted in flight from then to today, over eons, no matter how much some want to set them in stone. There ain't no firmament up there; no ether; we're talking an ever-spreading universe; a fullness; the very opposite of a void.

How can anything go wrong in a place called Eldorado? Which is where I live; in the wake of so much passing, Tomás, Jacob, and Toby; Wren and Donald; Cinthia and Debra; and several others? The ancients you meet—they're by and large all ancient here—not only do they not fuss about what or who preceded the big bang but quite frankly don't care. They left those musings behind, along with philosophy, religion, and gainful employment. Books too—I heard yet another declare just the other day, I'm too old for that; books that is. I can't read anymore. I don't wanna do anything where I gotta think. Or: I only read for pleasure these days. In fact pleasure seems to be the mantra here, a resurrection of the motto, Do your own thing. Whatever blows your jeans up. If you were to bring up rocks or gophers in a context other than Nuisances You Gotta Remove they'd look at you sideway, take a step back, as if to say, Is it the covid?

It's not that Eldorado is free of bigots, them or the occasional young person, relatively speaking—on a walk just the other day I saw a guy my age, yanking his dog and barking, Sit! Sit, damn you! [*Several hard jerks on the lead.*] SIT! [*Several more hard jerks.*] As though pleasing the guy were her *raison d'etre.* As though she didn't have a mind of her own. It took everything in me to keep from running up to the thing and shielding her, like some thinker on the verge of madness, halting the beating of a horse. If it weren't for Serge, I might well have.

They're here, bigots, the way they're everywhere, though most people are too busy doing nothing to think about them. They found a place where bigots don't do well at the polls, so why worry? There are churches here, though not the bigot kind. They pray to the great spirit, to love and such. My mother was into it; when she was in town she went. Her and Cinthia, Debra too, but not my dad or uncles, god forbid. To an unchurch in a sense; where they talk and sing about acceptance and to the joys of no-creed.

Just like in the Garden there's yardwork in Eldorado. The difference is that in this place, as in most of the City Different, you hire it out; in part because you couldn't be bothered, in part because you're above it; and in part because there's an army, some say, that made it past la frontera that's clamoring for work. For that reason the majority shell out cash; a not-immodest fee. Eldoradans earned it, by dint of birth and nation both—that's the feeling you get. You never have to wipe a window, scrub a bowl, mow a blade, or wield a brush. You rent that out because there are paperless who'll leap at the chance, in a language of gestures.

My uncles missed the memo because on any given day you would have found one or the other shaded under the brim of a hat in an unblinking sun, pulling spurge or fox grass, Russian tumbleweed or purslane. As for them, my first memory was that time we traveled west from the Forest City to the Monuments, after which we visited them in Ojo. I was in another body then, captive, braced, and not myself, so things are fuzzy, but I do remember spending time with Jake and Tommy, his future husband—amazing to recall it now. At the time they were mere furniture in the house of relations; that and old.

Jacob was far from famous then; far from it. And truth be told my father always regarded him, since I was a little—boy—I think inconsequential would be the best way to put it. A fact to file away; like foods listed alphabetically; common as ants or mosquitoes. Jacob wasn't as bad as Just Another White Dude, but close. Boring as white guys for sure, and clueless; which is not the same as ill-intentioned.

That was before anyone envisioned, he and I especially, that we'd end up living in the same city one day, breathing the same air, first in The City then the City Different, including Eldorado. To be honest I don't think I thought much about him, period—it was Tomás who made the impression—I liked him better. Tall and handsome, for one. And similarly different. Or is it inly?

Like I say Jacob was like house clutter until my girl, Shoshana, in a room in Morningside Heights, until she and I got into that game of Who You Know? She made a fuss when I outed the blander-than-bland fact that Jacob and I are kin, as though I were talking about a soda, pitched on an ad outside the corner bodega. It was she who remarked, Are you fucking kidding me?! Bitch, you're joking! We just studied him in art history! I was like, Whaaaat? Not that piece of untoasted Wonder Bread. Not only was he Just-Jake then, but in all honesty I found it a waste to think of him at all. In part because I saw him and Tommy so rarely. Whether my father felt the same I don't know, but from where would it have rubbed off? In a sense my mother didn't count because everyone matters to her, not the least of course her twin. It was my father I turned to for a discriminating eye.

Anyway there I was on the edge of Harlem, Mecca to my daddy, after I made my grand escape from the Forest City, my newly-blended family, body too, the one my mother birthed and clung to, having always wanted a daughter more than anything in the world, or so she took to saying a time or twenty. Times twenty. The physicality I was born in was so—Midwestern. Harlem was a chrysalis from which I emerged other, unrecognizable to Wren most of all; though not unrecognizable to the former me. My uncle and his mate had a front-row seat as the thing emerged, wings unfolding. They even claimed they saw, or pre-saw it, ages ago; like I existed to them. I hated them for that, knowing before me. They said they understood the deal as far back as that time we visited in Ojo, when me, Wren, Donald, and Skye caught them fucking in the middle of the kitchen floor— my dad tipped me to it when I was old enough to get it. By the time they arrived in The City my uncle's name and fame were undergoing a transition in a different sense, so he was preoccupied, and, trust me, I was happy to fly under their radar, on the other side of the world from Brooklyn where they lived. It didn't hurt that on the handful of occasions I saw them I swore I'd kill them if they breathed a word of what was going down, to my mother most of all.

I was walking the halls of Allen, Jack, Lawrence, and Lucien, at my alma mater, on my way to class, but more important Alicia, Eudora, Langston, and Zora; my spirit animals. It was their steps I tracked. What's more, I was at the center of the universe. To me, my uncle, no matter where he lived, could never be anything but a born-and-bred Laurentiner, just like Wren; a whole other realm than the one I inhabited. I couldn't help but see him that way, as anything but related by accident; otherwise he'd never be in my life; let alone be flesh and blood. My father used to say, in ear-shot of my mother, I wouldn't trust anyone from there, meaning Laurentine. He used to refer to their father as Harry Hitler. And as with most things that age, it stuck.

So we were in The City, my uncle and I, and Tommy; Serge too, though we were on separate planets. Granted, Tommy was a different story like I say. I always felt a kinship, and ultimately with Serge with all his shape-shifting.

For most of my life I lived in fear of the twins, the bond that money, time, nature, god, politics, and the elements can't sunder. I knew that my mother, far away, was struggling with a loss, and I was sure that Jacob couldn't help himself, couldn't help telling her what was going down, no matter how vehemently he protested he wasn't; on the bible of Uncle Walty, the Gospel of Grass; he brought it out and we went through the ritual of laying hands on the book. Was there anything he and my mother didn't share across the miles whether they spoke or not? I was cocked and loaded, ready to blame him for any leaks because I wanted to do it my way, and he could only fuck it up. I made him swear fealty to his only blood relative in The City, namely me, whether either of us liked it or not, because there are some things you just can't undo; like a baby out of wedlock. I made him swear because I knew there was no light between the two of them, him and Wren, especially at their age— damn, they were annoying! As though my mother had a spyglass named Jacob trained on me, twenty-four-seven. As though she were in The City with me, in my dorm room, through him; at the doctor's office; despite the fact that I fled the Forest City specifically to get away from her and her million declarations regarding the joys of having a girl. I fled to daddy's Mecca, his occasional stomping grounds where he used to come on business, offish and unoffish.

2

In hindsight I realize my uncles could a cared less—they had their lives; it's just I wasn't able to believe it at the time. It's true too I wasn't keen on white people. Again if I'd thought about it for a minute I might have thought otherwise, but I wasn't much for thinking. Fearing most of all. Wondering how to protect a me that was shaky; vulnerable. Which is how it should have been, me concerning, presenting me. Two-Point Oh.

Tell that to someone in the middle of it.

It's all shot by now. The goose has flown, like all of them—all gone. Everyone but Serge. They live a different existence, each in their way, in memory. We have photos, journals, and a house to recall them by, a slew of canvases worth many more times the adobe. There's the archive, which, in his function as sole executor and heir, Serge turned over to the big museum, a hop-skip across the park from my alma mater, my uncle insisting that under no circumstances would the bulk of it end up in the city of his birth; with the exception of a handful of pieces he painted specifically for the place, including one of a row of sycamores. It wasn't my decision to make about what work went where, even though I'm the official next-of-kin, the only blood survivor—Jacob saw to that.

Fair is fair. Relationships are windows on old houses that need to be tended; otherwise the rails need to be propped. Nothing makes up for inattention, an opportunity once missed, and given my behavior he intuited my eye to back off. So everything passed to Serge, to the guy Tommy used to refer to as the other husband, and only half in jest. Life has its terms, such that you can end up without a thing and with it, like a detachable body part.

What no one planned is how high Jacob's star would rise after he passed, so much so that my alma mater reached out to yours truly, of all people—how the hell did they find me, all the way out here?—requesting that I do my best to procure a piece or two for the school, and because the place mothered me in a way I tried to oblige. I mean were they tipped off or did they follow the bread crumbs from Serge, who'd taught there for a while? Anyway when I floated the idea by him he didn't poohpooh it; the idea of the school getting a piece; that the main body would lie in The City; that some would go to the Queen City and City Different; and that—yes—some to his birthplace in the spiritual sense, that beaux-arts beauty in the Forest City; not far, I was told once if I was told a thousand times, from where Molly was interred. So that my uncle's body was divvied up through the work; scattered like ashes in the wind; resting in places across the continent, the points of which Serge and I visit from time to time as often as we like; never mind in The City we pay our respects to a box, a series of them; acid-free, unlike ashes. Work lives on the walls here too, in the house next to our casita—when we're next door I see the way Serge takes them in, touching them the way he does, filling me with questions I never ask.

It took some doing to pack and haul everything from la casa aquí, a museum in its own right as all homes are, a house with its duo-curators and visitors in one. Although we could have plunked the whole shebang on the market all at once, in a single fell swoop, Serge determined to part with Jake, and Tommy, in dribs and drabs, so the change is less noticeable; mainly things remain as they were the day the two passed.

It wasn't as though Tommy and Jake ever thought of it as a shrine. On the contrary, they drove the place like an old Fiat, into the ground, complained about wanting to get their acts together and move all the clutter. The many canvases stacked in rows, shrinking the floor space, encroaching on the kitchen and even the portal in front, peering toward the mountains. Anyone who had the yen could have walked off with a work that'd go for a fortune today, and given what I see popping up on the market, canvases we didn't inventory, I reckon some passerby or delivery person did just that, as though they were free for the taking. Either that or they're out-and-out fakes.

There are days we feel the two skulking around. A pair of beer bottles gather dust on the counter where they were left, their nightly ritual for over half a century; a single beer imbibed at night, though at some point they switched to alcohol-free; maintaining the ritual power of the thing. Given my uncles' love for the place, and given their feelings for him, Serge determined it best to leave everything where it lay. By the time their resting papers were written Jake had already turned his back on a city or five, beginning with Laurentine. He knew full well that Serge and I planned to stay in The City, that it had tattooed itself on us, our souls and skins; plus I knew as much as he did that Serge had no plans or even hope of returning to his country.

The final step on the part of the museum—you might call it a browbeating—was not the fact of housing the archive there but what went in it. The principle of the thing we'd already established; the difficulty rested with particulars, including which documents—I'm talking letters to friends and family, galleries and museums; writings, including his own, and those of his great-grandfather, which in a backward reading sheds light on my mother's father, a document I was almost sorry to encounter because it meant I had to rethink that side, my grandfather most of all; my mother and uncle too. To Serge I'm grateful; it's been harder for him than me, though the fact is we're orphans, albeit in different ways. The letters, journals, sketchbooks, canvases of course, emails and texts—they're all there is to verify the Laurentine group ever lived, suggesting in a way that eternal life is nothing more than artefacts. Concrete things. Bodies. Graphia of one sort or another. Brute matter.

The museum wanted all of it, though commitments to other institutions made that impossible. Bottom line the museum got a chunk, though not all. The one proviso was that Serge and I retained not just full access but rights of first reference, which is to say we maintained the ability to present the material as we saw fit, without any institutional filter.

There are books on the market that are pure gobbledygook, almost laughable; about characters unhinged to the ones I knew; volumes that would have surprised Jacob given his certainty, when he first heard the word, that he was anything but an influencer. Not only would he have laughed his behind off if he ever saw them but he didn't give a hoot about the idea; convinced as he was that popular culture was a very shallow stream, in fact the shallowest; motivated by one thing and one thing only; that he preferred flying under the radar so he could work. The only way to do it honestly is anonymously, he used to say, a state he came to prefer once he left The City, thinking of the trailer in Ojo—The work I did there was the best in my life, he claimed—I'd say falsely. He craved anonymity after the debacle early in his career, unlike the museums, the MO of which is to create gods of influence. How can you draw a crowd without divines? Unless you construct, fabricate deities, ones that sell tee shirts, mugs, posters, postcards, and what have you. Would people tolerate standing in a line around the block in January if not to ogle the output of a god?

It was museums who invented influencers in the first place, Names and Bodies-of-Work. Genres and Periods. The endless slicing into eras and micro-eras, like the moods of a drag queen. Movements. The untouchables that devotees defend so strenuously, the way bigots do their despot in the sky. Dare to point out that one of them was imperfect, creatively or technically, then sit back and watch the fur fly—Jacob made the point often, goading people by questioning, for example, the great *David*. It worked every time. He used to shoot me a wink, then he'd suggest to a group that not just the nude dude but the mother and child were immature works, out of perspective and out of whack, and boy did that put people's blood in a boil, every single time. Claim the *Impression: Sunrise* guy wasn't aging well, that he tended toward the saccharine, Hallmark side, or that the *Untitled* drip artist had grown a bit too drippy, then sit back and watch the roof blow. It wasn't even that Jacob copped to those views—though it's true he preferred the later, unfinished and freer, works of the *David* sculptor to the earlier output; instead what interested him was how veins popped when you suggested that the art deities were human after all, not perfect in the ideational or technical sense. A touch heavy-handed and possibly overblown, as all worship is.

But it seems people must do it, create gods and adore them, beings greater than them, and Jacob had his own as well. The Dutch guy, for instance, who he never soured on; whose name was created by his sister-in-law, Jo. The Bohemian writer, who owed his memory to his friend, Max. And others who were unknown and never sold a thing in their day, relatively speaking. Were he to appear out of the blue, morph into an apparition, Jake might have chided Serge and me for the way we disposed of him, which is to say his body in the work. But as I say he left it to Serge to decide, maybe because Jacob didn't trust himself; his instincts; not in ways he trusted Serge, in a sense burdening him. The long and short of the museum's argument was, What good will it do if everything remains in the middle of nowhere, as one of the reps put it. As though Eldorado weren't a real place; one with skyrocketing real-estate; populated with folks who boast of benefitting the museum itself. At least here at the center of the universe, she seemed to imply, the works'll be available to anyone and everyone to make of them what they will—wink-wink. They'll be guaranteed eternal life—that made both Serge and me laugh. I took that to mean the deification would commence the day the truck arrived.

What never occurred, to me at least, was that in my tour of so much material my uncles would come to life in a way they never had, that I saw them and came to know them better, to whatever degree that's possible, in death. Or maybe death is what allowed us to finally make an acquaintance, especially with someone I found too close to get a bead on while he was living. In some odd way my uncle had to die for us to know each another. He's no longer a moving target, him and Tomás both—they're set, morphing and shape-shifting in a different way. The dead, like deities, change with the living, as they have over millenniums, even though devotees swear to the contrary. The reality is that relatives, like gods, shift in death as we do in life.

3

It's a mind game, to come upon an archive. Like looting a grave. An archive's a crypt, and cryptic; bursting surprises, things you didn't expect or want to come upon; things you don't want to know. An archive indicts you, the culture you inhabit, under the guise of dead documents that wallpaper a life, paper over it, like I say in journals, emails, texts, and scraps, envelopes torn and scribbled on, in a rush to free things from the confines of a skull. There are studies; half- and fully-executed works; canvases; small ones Jacob resorted to working on after rejecting monumentality; a form of masculinism he argued, machismo, no matter the gender of the maker. Setting a giant boot on a space. Artists and curators obsess over size like sophomores in a locker room. He even broke form and wrote an article, mainly overlooked, about the power of small, small works and small visions, an argument that carried no weight at all.

Among those dwarf canvases are some Serge deemed too personal to put out there. He argued at first it'd be better to destroy them—The bastards ignored them anyway, he complained. I persuaded him to keep a few, then all of them. They tell a truth I can't consider long or out loud, having led to one of the few out-and-out arguments Serge and I ever had. What I said in the wake of Jacob's passing was it was too soon to make a decision, that he—we—should wait, see how he felt in a year or twenty. They could remain privy to us, and maybe a handful of others, never to be duplicated—

working on them could come with an ultimatum, a legal injunction, which is funny when you consider how Serge saw this country and its obsession with suits.

What he said was, Never to be reproduced?! Are you kidding? In a country of millions of lurid, prying eyes, malevolent tricksters and pranksters, lascivious nosybodies—leaks, tips, and pay-offs—smart phones and dim intentions—a world in which nothing ever isn't without a price, sold, traded, or commodified? A world in which privacy is deader than Jacob and Tommy, and only because the power of a buck—pound, ruble, euro, yuan, or yen? Are you *kidding* me?!

At which point I backed off. But if he won the battle, I won the war, because the smaller works remain still. Ten times more impactful than any of the wall-sized jobbies at the Met—sorry, people. They force you to draw near; become small; lower your head before a low door; look and look some more; gaze at bare life. I'd love nothing more than to talk about them because they haunt me more than Serge, who's clearly spooked. In a sense it makes my efforts more difficult, having to craft a slant point, never getting at the thing directly the way I'd like. But then again is there any line that isn't slant? Including intimacy between beings, stones with stones and people with people. Some of which I'll leave to others to expound upon in the assemblage that follows, cast in their own words, stones excepted. Serge has sequestered the images god-knows-where, though occasionally he pulls one out just to look. I stumble upon one from time to time. Who knows what he'll decide, whether they'll ever see the light of day or go with him to the grave. After all he's mastered the ways of this country, if I may put it that way, more than most native-borns—he knows what's up. I'll just say the miniatures are eye-openers, though not in the way you'd think. They reveal something about masculinity that even I overlooked, a subject I've been tracking since memories began tracking me.

Serge aside, my uncle possessed more catholic tastes than I knew, given the array of bodies and types, and so many unhealthy. Wracked. Or just plain different. He sought the kinds of bodies pontiffs blab about embracing, but only on Good Friday. Goddess knows they scoff at them as subjects of art, labeling them illicit. In-your-face. From eighties, plague-ridden bodies to those poxed in the twenties. As though the conventional—the hegemonic, normal, and salutary—were anathema. Were he not my uncle, had I felt differently about him when he was alive, I might have sat for him—he asked and I refused. Several times. He argued it could be—I think he used the word repairing. At which I burst out laughing. Nothing is going to repair this ship, I blathered, blasted by believers, politicians, and the medical establishment, backward-gazing culture most of all. But that was before I got to know Serge, who's done more than all the heartfelt approval of Wren and my father could have, Wren who pined for a me that was for all intents and purposes stillborn at birth. A being that never lived. A coinage of her brain.

Had I known what I know now, had we perhaps not been related, I would have done it for sure; sat for Jacob—I would have fit right in with his pantheon of freaks, as I like to lovingly say; ungods as he called them. Modern undivines. His heroes.

I'm an exhumer, the obverse of a grave-digger, unearthing figures, including my uncle's, uncles' plural, which is not to say resurrecting them. Let the dead lie. Jacob would've hated the language of revival, not believing in revivification of any kind, which is not to say rebirth or renewal. If he said it once he said it a million times that the problem with the world is the mania over a body coming back from the dead, literally; cheating death or, god forbid, conquering it; as though death were a bad thing. Including the christian-pagan version most of all; ascribing power to anyone in such an antique, threadbare sense; the worn-out notion of a demigod, getting a purchase on the underworld and mastering it; that mystery of mysteries that he preferred to live with—he didn't feel the need for that kind of myth, one he said people took literally. Like fairy tales for adults they never stop to question; because they don't dare. No doubt he would have been the first on the Resurrection Train were he to think for a second that people were clever enough to understand the tale in figures—tropes—but perhaps that's where his philanthropy, if that's the opposite of misanthropy, came to the end of the line. It was easier to wreck the whole idea, which is one of the many forms we parted ways, given that I know a thing or two about the subject, resurrection; transformation; transition. Coming to life, finally—call it what you will. Anyway it was lost on him, the will to turn ideals into idols. Stop it people! he used to shout at the TV, or at a dinner party after a rare drink or two. Stop it with your god-making! It makes both you and your gods small, and in a bad way!

Hateful.

As a palliative he preferred flaws. Blotches. Glitches and kinks; defects and deformities; disfigurements and imperfections; irregularities, abnormalities, and malformations; blots, blurs, and spots; stains, taints, and weaknesses; failings—peccadillos even. In short, messes, such as we construe them, without any god to forgive or form a fake positive; like a being from dead clay. He had this thing about things in flux, which he said he learned from Molly of all people—for him, first and foremost, the person who finishes a work is not the same as the one who started; the process itself being transformative. We only have that, never stasis; a flawed maker. A dabbler. Putterer or imbricator. To which, again, if in some real way I missed the opportunity of knowing my uncle in life I've had the chance of making his acquaintance in death, presented here as best I could. In fact I'm not the same person offering this second edition as I was when putting out the first.

Although my goal has been to make the writings public, how to present them has always been the rub, given their haphazard nature, the choices I was presented. If it comes across as a monster brought to life by a zap, a bolt to a figure that is part human and part animal, then so be it. I, Will, will it. Plus for this edition the goal has been to include materials not available for the first—in fact I knew nothing of their existence when I began the project. The initial go-round was rather loosely organized but was nevertheless helpful, hopefully, strictly by what it offered in terms of content. Including an insider's view of the machinery of the market and how it catapulted Jacob from obscurity to recognition at an early age; the inner mechanisms of the industry; and his subsequent— he would have argued merciful—return to obscurity and disrecognition. It featured his reflections on The City and the move from there; to (un)retirement and his ultimate (un)doing; a journey back to his, but more important Tomás's roots. It dealt with the most fertile time of his life artistically, and may I say institutionally speaking, including some of the relationships he forged, rewarding and fraught. He listed his place of birth alternately. Ojo Caliente. The Queen City. The City. Even the Forest City. But never Laurentine, which is unfortunate because I'd argue he was a Laurentiner through and through. It's The City that most credit as his true birthplace, spiritual in a sense, a place where climbers go, something Jacob was rotten at. As I say it was difficult for me to think of him as anything other than a boy from Laurentine that I only vaguely knew; a transplant everywhere else.

Either way it's important to keep in mind that he lived in The City longer than anywhere, including the City Different ,where his flame both cooled and heated, depending on your point of view. In The City he lived in a spotlight that burned brightly for a short time, a fraction of time compared to the anonymity that followed. Conventional wisdom says that an experience like that is bound to sour a person, given the competitive nature of the world, and The City most of all; a lab experiment of eight million rats within the borders of the boroughs, and twenty million in the metro region, which over sixty million tourists invade each year like a solar wind. Having been birthed or liberated there I can attest it's a place of unique, some would say difficult people, not welcoming to shrinking violets from the heartland. Folks scramble for sidewalk space, grips on subway stanchions, and essential services. A job worth having attracts a mob, from every other Laurentine in the country and around the world. People learn quickly to sharpen their elbows and tongues because without them you'd be toast.

4

To CIRCLE BACK, I'd be remiss not to point up the way los intolerantes, as Tommy called them, tarred and feathered Jacob early on, especially Senator Bradford; who was not unknown to Jacob from what I gather and who accused him of every manner of impropriety; who cast his work as vile and of the devil, after my uncle won the taxpayer-funded grant. As though the work were a form of sin; an offense against god and country both. They, reporters for the tabloids, owned by the Methodist from Down Under come to foist his protestant ways on us, just as we were unshackling ourselves from bonds millenniums old—his tabloid labeled my uncle The Diabolic Dabbler, Painter of Perversions, and Prince of Peccadillos—Prez Sez It's Mezzed Up, said one of the headlines.

In the lurid, overheated minds of the Senator and the papers' journeymen, the morality police, opiners on everything that happens in the behind-doors lives of the country, a relationship like Jacob and Serge's was enough to cause a meltdown. Serge, whom los intolerantes labeled a Rotten Red, a Socialist Sociopath, a Commie Insurrectionist Out to Destroy the U.S. of A.; the beloved moral fiber of this blessed land, from the inside; like a spideress injecting its prey and jellying it out. In the early days the right-wing press had a field day, casting Serge as Atilla the Homo, implying all manner of things between him and my uncle. Panting, flushed, and feverish headlines from the rag pilfered by the Aussie, the once-respectable middlebrow paper that he promised the former owner he'd leave as is, until the bill of sale was signed and it immediately began its descent to the bottom; to depths no one thought possible in a paper; an abysm of populist pap; replete with photos of the two in what was alleged to be compromising positions, plastered on the covers; painting the two as a danger to the state and hardworking taxpayers most of all, never mind The Children. To the point that the crusty—single—senator from East Shagaran, by that point over seven hundred and sixty-eight years old, raised his skeletal finger in the middle of a congressional session then brought it down, mumbling condemnations, which his interpreters claimed he had never, ever seen in his many centuries of sucking air on the planet, never mind expectorating in the senate air while holding forth—he had never seen anything that got his moral ire more aroused. Years later when the bigots' bannerman, Crumm, fell in love with a real red, a gnome named Vladdie, or Baby Bear as some called him, a fierce devotee of Old Whiskers, licking his—hand—the way Crumm did Vladdie's, another pussy-grabbing macho—rather than take Crumm to task for kissing the backside of a Red the faithful renewed their assault on Serge, and my uncle, even labeling Serge a turncoat to Baby Bear, declaring my uncle guilty not of association with a Commie but turning Serge against his own country. In short the two could do no right, to the point that they even painted Tommy as the victim-wife!

I'd like to say what follows neither attempts nor in fact does set the record straight on that score, other than in passing, because it would imply that Jacob, Tomás, or Serge cared what the bigots thought much less said about them, charged them with or implied, because the only bite that hurts comes from one you respect. As Wren used to remind Jacob, You know who you are, and what you're capable of. One thing any of them refused to do was give "their side" to the press, an industry obsessed with both-sidesism, as though truth and lies were partners on equal terms; as though the public needed to hear from the Führer and Mother Teresa both, in order to keep things balanced. In fact the media gave generous shrift to the zealots' fantasies, even inflamed them because it sold papers, though that's where things died as far as Jake and Serge were concerned; Tommy too. Having said that, such is the nature of fiction and its ability to rile people to belief, which if Jacob were here he'd argue—I can hear him plain as day—that the only true history is fiction, a story of one not making grandiose claims; everything else is the record of loudmouths, here in Puritania most of all, as Serge calls this country; where everything is bent, twisted, and distorted by belief.

5

THE PLUNGE DOWN and spring up. The sudden shot into a world at speed, not toward the stars but depths, a drippy world where death lurks if you don't watch, but—screw it!—this is a coming. Naked, whirling, shooting, and descending; the arms windmilling to move me this way and that; an awkward if purposeful locomotion. The beauty of a liquid. Endless fluidity, cool, wide, and deep, that doesn't stop or constrict the way air does. A bobbing. Floating. Paddling. Luxuriating. You're an aquanaut of the abyss down here, unburdened; by gravity; weight. The heavy fluidity buoying you up—you have to work at sinking.

To grow gills and morph into a native in this vastness, colonize without dominating, ruling, displacing, or dispossessing. To be native and foreign, enjoying the perks of your watery citizenship, the skin sluicing, volumes invading my chest, armpits, thighs, and asshole—nakedness at its best.

A hugging.

Welcome to wetness.

I want to: somersault, breech, or backflip, not to mention dive, because Peacoat, I know that you're down here; that you transitioned here decades ago; reconnect with Wren in this womb of all wombs, the two of us back where everything, we, began, in a fluidity, swimming around, into each other; celebrate this Dodgson of a lake where Tommy and I jerked each other into existence, a sloppy, pissy, deluged start to our life together, a flowing in so many ways; slam slant into Serge, here in this ozero not far from the family dacha, rented but real, the two of us in the night, stars exploding white and milky on the surface of the water, glopping and covering the jut of physicality, ours, the one that religious quacks revile, but—

Jacob?!

I try to respond but my tongue locks, void of saliva, the lips resist an opening; cracked. The only thing I can do is try to spit, eject what dust has found a way in—

Are you all *right*?! Are you OK, Jacob? What in the world?!

Who is this bruja—do I know you?—robbing me of water, depth, and pleasure. A past. Freedom. Constraining me on this rock, this mesa. I struggle to get back to that other, lacustrine world, the way you do after the fog of an operation, waking on a scene of discomfort. Toby whines, tongues my cheek, looks up—

Do you think I should call an ambulance? An ambulance! Do you want me to call someone?—I don't know what to do!

I plunge back in the wet with my loved ones, avoid the mistake of our fishy ancestors who took a chance on land, only to find there was no going back. Instead of a riverine realm though, what I spy is a table world, a broad bottom, of what was, hundreds of millions of years ago, an inland sea—now a hard, cruel line—inflexible limit between up and down, the very antithesis of a fluidity, incapable of waves, wavelets, or full-on breakers, the kind you marvel at on the coasts when the winds are up—I'm atop a floor basically, an unforgiving solidity, flat as a hospital ward but trying to get back to the center of the earth, moving we're told, but imperceptibly to someone whose life spans no more than a century.

And even then.

It's obdurate, the soil here, bone dry or just bone. A clay boneness you can hardly get a shovel in, so sere you have to scrape what you can and then add water, just to penetrate a few more inches, until such time you need another bucket, slopped in an indentation in the top crust, seven thousand feet up, until, repeated several times—you finally have a hole. Nothing akin to the vastness I'm in.

Jacob, I'm worried about you! What are you doing on the ground?

I don't—. Words are loathe to come, and after such a volubility. Still my eye swivels here and there. A portly man just there inches his car from the garage down the drive, aside a mailbox, then stops. He jacks the door, hunches around the headlights toward the other side while swaying his arms behind; he extracts a stack of envelopes then retakes his seat behind the wheel. Slowly he backs the vehicle back to the garage, sets the thing in park, then disappears in the house with the speed of a tumbleweed on a day without wind.

6

THE FUSS OF THE MEDICS and Toby's agitation. The triage nurses buzzing. I thought we'd lost you there, worries Debra. Tommy phoned to say he'll be here soon!

You can't go home until we run some tests, remarks the doctor. It isn't normal. That an otherwise young guy like you would tank like that—where was it, Miss?

It was on Descanso.

Young—ha! What would I know about young? I want to check myself out—

This nice lady here—the nurse is talking so loudly I gather he thinks I'm on the verge of slipping away—she said you were out cold. That your companion here was distraught—what's her name?

His. It's Toby.

She said it took some time to get you to come to. Could be a number of things. Heart, liver, brain—

(I'll make it easy for you: all of the above.)

Beyond the to-do, all I could think of was a certain kind of green, which in this south-western world is rare as water. Not the kind in your pocket but the leafy, deciduous kind. In some ways I'm reliant upon it given where I'm from, but too bad for me because green-green is a nonstarter in these parts, sliding to yellow to orange then scarlet come fall. That kind sucks up too much water. The green you carry, in your pocket, in The City most of all before currency became digital and paper obsolete, the kind you can never get enough

34

of in a world where green rules, especially post-pandemic when everything is rocketing into the stratosphere—I'm thinking of that green too now given the copay on tests, much less a real ailment—I gave up a salary years ago, me and Tommy both, and we're now wards of the state, old farts waiting for monthly hand-outs, for the duration in our current, embodied state, me and Tommy, who's jonesing for our past life in The City more than me, and now here we are in Eldorado, watching ourselves and the world dry up. Green most of all.

The candles on the ponderosas beyond the glass flop in the breeze, a type of needly jauntiness. After a lifetime of living on or near water, a great lake or reservoir, river, creek, or ocean, it's an adjustment to exist in such dryness. Cracked clay. A rock, exposed. That is until the monsoon shuffles in in mid-summer, almost always late, to the point you want to bargain with the sky, scream your head off, or curse. Beg Skye to have her primo come from Santa Agata pueblo to do another dance. Anything for a drop.

It doesn't help we're in a thousand-year drought, Skye remarked, the kind that must've chased her relatives and Tommy's, the Chacoans, from their roost, centuries ago; aligned with the moon and stars. Here in Eldo, earth takes flight in the form of dust, as though you were in Zambia, among constant gales, effacing the mountains in the distance, flattening them like construction paper, cut and glued to the sky. Tossing the peach and cherry trees that I insisted on planting, the apricot and apple—as if the basic fact of dryness wasn't enough, that it needed wind to amp it, rob the landscape even more. You'd tank too on a walk if it were you.

Yet natives thrive, unbothered; unlike some transplant from the East. Tommy and Skye—they thrive in a world the color of dun. The kangaroo mouse, packrat, and jackrabbit; road runner and Cassin's finch, canyon towhee, and thrasher; grama grass, prickly pear, and cholla—what do you mean dry? Dun, or done, as in just right, like a casserole at Navidad: this is our home now. Among chamisas in their variety. Snake bush, salt bush, and winter fat. Sage. Slithering gopher snake and red racer; prairie rattler and whiptail lizard—Por favor, señor, que significa seco? Many gringos don't make it past two years, the time it takes to come to the conclusion, Oh no. No. No, no, no. This won't do—how can anything survive here? Any*one*? Skye would beg to differ. Tommy too. And yet in the aggregate the gringos are winning, and have been for years, altering the place the way gringos do, everywhere they go, from Peru to Palestine and the hundreds of thousands of other places they've colonized, pushing out; displacing; and much, much worse; turning a foreign place to their likeness, imposing Gringoland, going back centuries, here and elsewhere, honing then celebrating the art of dispossession, expropriation, and, let's face it, murder.

I wonder if it's a sign? I mean if I'm going to succumb like that, maybe I shouldn't be here. Debra replied as we were leaving the hospital, Don't say that. If you don't then god knows neither do I. But it's your people who came first! I countered. Came is the thing—past tense, she replied. As in many thousands of years ago. It's funny to think about, ain't it? Which was true. Spend time in one of the pueblos in the Land of Enchantment and you realize the quote-unquote new world, all of North and South America, are Asian lands. You see it in the most obvious, quasi-racist ways. You realize that from the tip of the land bridge to Cape Horn they were first, that these are Asian continents, unidentical twins, where everyone else is a freeloader—tag, you're it! Persons who can't manage to offer a drink

to a migrant, that or a bite to eat, for all their stentorian,
bloviating christian faith, though there isn't an inch of this
or the other continent that isn't Native land.

7

WHOA! SHOCKS DEBRA. Are you kidding? Why would I do that? wonders Serge. So you're actually from there? she wonders. As in: as-an-adult? I am. Are your parents here? —Were you a *Pioneer*? Does the pope wear a dress? quips Serge. Debra asserts, I came here too young to have the pleasure. My sympathies, I'm sure. Are your parents here? queries Seth. They run a restaurant—of course, wheezes Debra. They did everything they could to keep me out of it. Be gweilo, they said—all the time, like a broken record—be gweilo. When I went to the convent they weren't thrilled—I mean, me being the only child. Lee ain't a name on the verge a extinction, remarks Tomás. Ha! They understood the idea of a female monk—they had them back in China, or did in the old days, when my parents were young—I don't know about now. Nuns don't work in restaurants, so it wasn't all bad. They consoled themselves by saying there'd be no fourteen hour days for me, seven days a week, like for them. How 'bout your folks, Serge? Factory rats of course. Though they're retired now. I watch as Serge lifts his glass and sips. For us there's no such thing as retirement, comments Debra. What would that mean? Free time; time to take it easy—are you kidding?! Death is our retirement. Lucky them, asserts Serge. My folks didn't have a choice— at some point you're pushed out, to spend the rest of your life luxuriating in all the time you don't want, on a pension of three hundred bucks a month. If that.

Can you imagine? muses Charles. That's a meal here, in a so-so restaurant.

One where you end up thinking, I could a made that better myself, adds Seth, sitting opposite Charles at the table.

How do they do it? wonders Beverly. It's not as hard as you think, assures Serge. People've been surviving on nothing for centuries there. They know how to milk the system—one. But also how to live on nothing, unlike here; with a little help from the black market. Which is better than the above-board kind—I mean you can get anything, and cheapy-cheapy. Also they're not in terror of bare life the way people are here. Though that may be changing. What does that even mean? inquires Seth. They read, informs Serge. I watch as he takes another sip from his glass; it's something about the way he doesn't guzzle like most people. What's that got to do with anything? challenges Tomás.

Unstructured time ain't their enemy.

That doesn't begin to capture the situation in this country, asserts Risk. Terror of unstructured time is more like it. I'm mindful of how pretty they, Risk, is—pretty in an unconventional way, but by the standards of convention as well. Youthful and confident.

Terror of what? queries Beverly. What Serge calls bare life, returns Risk. Does bare life even exist in this country— can it possibly? Serge sets his glass down. Can it possibly in a culture that created fun and is infatuated by it, twenty- four seven? I think the Amerkan constitution states that every citizen has the right to the pursuit of liberty, freedom, and never a dull moment. Could people handle it if someone pulled the plug on any of the million ways people run from bare life? But from what exactly? wonders Tommy. From nothing, basically, Serge replies. Land and sky. Getting by—life in my country. Me suena horrible, putting it like that, remarks Tommy. I'm only saying we're—my folks—

are used to it, not that they don't got their—y'know. It surprises me when I go back, or used to, how accustomed they are to nothing, how little they go on. Like I say, they're readers. Accustomed ain't exactly right, opines Jacob. I'm noticing the way he looks at Serge, his gaze lingering. They seem happy, to me at least, he continues. That's way too strong, old man, counters Serge. Content then? Only slightly better. Resigned? More like what choice they got? Serge pieces at a crust of bread, dredges it through olive oil, nabbing in the process a rosemary leaf. They manage—it's such an American comment—They seem happy. That all you got? What does happiness got to do with anything? The idea had to've been invented here—happiness. And like I say, fun. Diversion. No wonder so many commit suicide—I mean, the pressure. To put all that on a person, like life ain't bent enough. My folks at least don't have that, not like Amerikans.

No, gracias, intones Tomás. You can have that life there.

Maybe it's a generational thing, asserts Beverly. We were raised reading—but you young people?—Sorry, kids. Speak for yourself, contends Risk. Comics don't count, quips Beverly. Ha! blurts Kenney. Does fantasy—count? Goth—does it count? Sci-fi? I'm not sure it does, insists Beverly. The very thought of reading makes Tomás sweat, remarks Jacob. Whenever someone asks me, What are you reading? or, Have you read X? or Did you see the review of X in *X*? For him, es una pesadilla, a nightmare. I get it, Tomaldo, sympathizes Skye. These pretentious bastards. She peers at Beverly, her partner, then Jacob. That's funny coming from you! chides Jacob. You read more than most. Still. Why parade it?—I mean, there's reading and reading. I watch as Serge's face flushes, first pink then scarlet.

I never said that—

—No one said you did, returns Skye. So no worries.

I'm talkin' about my parents. When you ain't got nothin' reading's something. Plus, they enjoy it; don't ask me why. They read everything. More than people here ever could. They read more Amerkan lit than Amerkans. Amazing to think they're younger than me, muses Jake. What are they, fifty? Jacob, no one's as old as you, returns Serge. Toby jumps in his lap and curls in a ball; Serge begins stroking him softly. I'm sure I could be their father too, laments Seth. You could be Methuselah's father, asserts Charles. One thing about his folks is they're resourceful, informs Jake. In ways people here ain't—it takes a certain smarts. No wonder people come here from god-knows-where and kick butt. Ring money outta rocks, saving while earning air for wages. Sending their kids to Yale. If we weren't so good at keeping them down they'd run the place—

—Better than Crumm!

He and his gang of thugs would all be run outta office—

—Or jailed, affirms Charles.

Waaaaay too rosy, opines Serge—you got Crumms in every country, including my own. If your nose is in a book you get to escape a while. Spend time in the banya with friends. Hunt mushrooms in the woods. Stop about reading already! protests Tomás. It ain't all that. No different than any other escape, affirms Charles. And it sure is cheaper. So long's you got a library nearby. Books are mother's milk there, Jake contends, glancing at Serge. Unlike here, counters Charles. Especially in this city, where a reader is a lone tortoise, like the one on the Galapagos; unless you like fluff. Where he's from—I catch Jake stealing another look at Serge as he speaks, his gaze lingering there—every kid learns the Tradition, the whole thing, going back millenniums, and not just the popular, the home-grown. That's changed, old man. After '89. I never said I was like them, a book lover. He glances toward Tomás. Is it a thing anywhere nowadays? ponders Debra. Or is it the enemy? Too much unfiltered information. Something you do alone, without anyone telling you how to think—it's dangerous these days, isn't it? Reading; and thinking. Isn't that why the zealots wanna ban books? Debra hazards it was the computer that eliminated the love for books; at least real books, the kind Jake is referring to. Do your own thing has come into its own, pipes Charles. It depends on whose thing you're doing, quips Kenney. The table explodes in laughter. True that, responds Risk, unsmiling. You don't get to pick apparently, including what you do with your body. In that way we're going backwards. I think it's a lot easier in the EU, asserts Kenney.

That's because the EU is godless, asserts Jake.

Godless my ass, counters Serge. I can tell he's avoiding looking Jake's way. They're as bad as here, maybe worse. The zealots there just get drowned out, unlike here where the press gives them the floor. To every bigot. But in the EU tradition is god too. Architecture. Art. History—that and their superiority over Amerkans—about that they're sure. Debra replies that everything—god, tradition, religion, family, and apple pie—are forced to bow to a different god here, and that the entire rest of the world is following suit. Tell it, sister, follows Kenney. The whole world bows down to the same god, the almighty buck, agrees Jacob. An American animal. Founders worried about factions, the tyranny of the few, especially where money's involved. When things come down to that your goose, and god, are cooked—sorry for the metaphor, Jake, remarks Beverly. Jake's goose is never cooked, quips Tomás. Créeme, believe me—. Still—we got factions! wails Charles. When the zealots marched to the steps of the capital and declared war on the country, in the name of god! Waged an insurrection, in Crumm's name, every hater poured from the woodwork.

When the zealots declared war not just against the idea of us but anyone unlike themselves—

Cinthia opens the door without knocking and I get a thrill. In many ways she and Debra are more my parents than my parents. Sorry I'm late, she pleads. What'd I miss? You missed Crumm. Oh boy. Pozole too. Tamales. Rice and beans. Ain't tamales a no-no? I mean—manteca. You're safe, assures Risk. And it tastes? Like the real thing. Evil genius, remarks Cinthia, embracing Jake after he's made it to his feet, intent on preparing her a plate. She limps to the unoccupied seat, set aside for the living and dead who couldn't make it to the meal, and waits to settle before letting out a huff. I'm Cinthia—she takes Charles' hand next to her. Again, sorry I'm late—I'm eager to try everything! Say that after and not before, Jacob comments while rubbing her back. Just be sure to wear a hat, warns Charles. Or your head'll blow clear off. Gracias a Lita—she taught him how to cook, comments Tomás. Jake adds, So if you're gonna blame anyone, blame her; with her there was only one level of heat and that was hellfire. I'll brace myself—I'm Cinthia—I gaze as she reaches her hand across the table toward Seth. Is this your first time? You'll get used to it, hopefully. Over time. A gringo who learned from the best. You may find yourself craving it. But don't tell him that.

In the diminutive kitchen, perpendicular and open to the living room, directly overlooking an empty space that Tomás and Jacob couldn't agree on what to do with; and which after many dead-end arguments decided to do nothing with; Jacob ladles a bowl of pozole— hominy, carrots, jalapeños, and so on, everything but meat—he squeezes a wedge over giant corn simmered for a day, just as Lita showed, with a few adjustments for Señor Sincarne, the Loco Gringo—the dried kernels exploded like popcorn in the broth. Jacob pulls a pair of tamales from the steamer, still in theirs husks, and spoons on a ration of arroz y frijoles pintados. He sets the cup among them, then places the plate in front of Cinthia, who remarks, Did you ever think that night on the beach, after you had your breakdown or whatever it was, the night we discovered Peacoat—did you think we'd end up here? You serving me this? El plato gringo, interjects Tomás. Pero igual de picante que el mi abuela.

Jake, tell the story about Tomás's gram! I think we heard it enough, complains Tomás. I haven't, remarks Charles. Jake doesn't need coaxing. She was brutal, he explains. His grandmother—he glances toward Tomás while resting his hand on Cinthia's wrist, there on the table, her spoon hand bringing broth to her mouth. I mean, here's this little woman in this little house in this little town in the middle a nowhere, where it snows well into May, wedged in the mountains. A place I'd never been literally or figuratively—geographically, psychologically, culturally, aesthetically, you name it—I mean, I didn't know places like that existed in this country, a whole other world, not to mention language—and she serves this chili, except she's gone out of her way to make it without carne or caldo de carne or all the stuff she's used to—so I gotta eat it. No excuses. Whether I wanna or not—I mean, I was raised on boiled and bland, potatoes and carrots, cabbage, cooked within an inch of its life, flavor and nutrition boiled away. Now here comes Lita, dropping a bomb—and she's eyeing, watching as I eat. Observing. There were tears in my eyes. I wanted to grab the hose in the yard to put the flames out in my mouth, but I didn't wanna give her the satisfaction of callin' me a lightweight—You mean a gringa, quips Tomás. You shush!—so I'm sitting there, thinking to myself, I'm gonna die. After I kill this guy—that guy—right there!—for putting me through this, which he was clearly enjoying. He had the most annoying smirk, eating the same as me and totes unfazed. Did you do it? asks Kenney? Do what? Finish it? I had to—out a sheer spite, but in a niiiice way. Estúpido güey, asks for more. That's sick, comments Cinthia. I ask Lita, Why aren't you eating? And she goes—get this—she goes, Porque está pinche picante—because it's too damn hot. After that he was in, sorta. Most important test a your life, assures Cinthia. Which, by the by, I am sweating. Like I gotta run outside. Rip my clothes off.

It'll subside . . . by midnight I'm guessing, comments Charles.

Tomorrow, however . . . warns Beverly.

Here's to living for now, enthuses Kenney.

In the moment, adds Risk.

8

We lived in The City for decades, a whole other world than where I grew up, different than Ojo most of all, but the City Different too. Even after we decided to leave, Tommy bucked the idea, there at the end, after having insisted on booking in the first place, relocating back to the turf of his parientes, with me in tow—it's ironic given he didn't want to move to The City in the first place. In fact he was a spastic mess the night before we set cross-country, all those years ago. I'd never seen him so unnerved, shaking even, shedding tears and complaining I was asking demasiádo, too much, that it was mean of me. To force him to leave the Queen City, weeping memories of our chosen family, most of which by then were dead. What followed was a decades-long journey.

We weren't in The City a year before I was saying, I'm good; we can go back. But by then Tommy had spiraled down roots, unlike me; so, near the place where some of my clan migrated, and where many, I'd later learn, hunkered to live in Brooklyn after fleeing the famine, a world away from where la gente de Tommy had come here, through the back door as some say, before there ever was a country, or a back door. It was a surprise to see him claiming The City in his own way. I learned he's a tree that doesn't like transplanting, not often; unlike me. What's more, Lita flew from Las Nieves, her first time on a plane, to suss the situation for herself, not once but several times, as though the two were colonizing The City in a reverse gesture, putting their mark on it, and Lita with her limp. Down the subway stairs and along the platform, pressed in the crowd, jammed in the car, then up a series of flights on foot because the escalators were always on the fritz; then along the crowded streets and back again on the train to Smith Street, hiking up the three flights to our flat, narrow and rickety; then crashing; out cold on the couch; fully clothed and unresponsive to several shakes until the horns began to blare the following morning, as Smith Street shook off sleep; swelled with cars on the way to Brooklyn Bridge.

Lita set her imprimatur on the town for her jito, who didn't need but in a sense lived for it, Lita's imprimatur. She put her stamp on me too, which was curious given she still entertained doubts, I'm sure, about her jito's gringo, su novio. In The City she and Tommy leapt, like off a cliff. Plunged into a town that never stops giving, day or night, like a whore working overtime. And in fact I think in retrospect Lita rolled the way Tommy did, or the other way around, because like I say she returned, often, exhausting herself in the process not just in the rudiments of getting around but in the way the two never paused, stopped back at our place for a bite or a nap, un café or un té. Instead they left early and dragged back late, taking a world in a day. As though Lita were indulging some kind of urge that to me didn't jibe, what with what I'd seen on my handful of visits to Las Nieves.

She and he discovered omakase and Korean barbecue; Russian tea cakes and pupusas; ban mi and poulet fricassee; dobos torte and mille-feuille; muffulettas, churrascaria, cuy, and bistek; choucroute alsacienne; steak frites and gnocchi; paella Valenciana; aloo gobi, biryani, and rice pulao; shakshuka, rqaq w adas, momo, and dim sum; shabu shabu hotpot, and an endless array of other dishes, during which her jito patted my knee under the table, looked sad-face as I picked through the menu for something to eat; something my conscience allowed; while the two of them chowed to their heart's content, time after time, in neighborhood after far-flung neighborhood, micro neighborhoods and personal haunts, all around The City.

I often wondered how a person from Lita's background squared such diversity, coming from a pueblo no more than a hundred or hundred-and-fifty strong; falling into The City like a lynx in her native lair, as though the transition from place to place were seamless. Tommy followed suit, fell in love, leaving me to wonder if I'd created a monster, as though I had the power. I only knew there was no turning back whether I liked it or not.

So we stayed; three decades. Long after Lita moved on to La Gran Manzana in el Cielo, the Big Apple in the Sky—I used to think those trips to our apartment were her way of prepping for an eternity in which the options, major and niche, never ceased. We stayed, whether I wanted to or not, which is to say until Tommy, rebranded Tomás somewhere along I-80 between Omaha and Fort Lee; during the move there; just before our tires ambled over the GWB; before Tomás decided he was ready to leave.

It's interesting in retrospect that when we first arrived he was loathe to quit our flat. On the heels of a crash, after the president told The City to go fuck itself, it wasn't the safest, and Tommy hailed from a feedlot after all, on the outskirts of a town called Loveland. So he spent the first month holed up in the apartment without a TV, the windows draped with sheets. He wondered aloud how I could bring him to a place where he was afraid to go out—I mean what kind of locura was that? Insanity. In the weeks after we first arrived I returned the rental truck, shopped the greengrocer, waited in line at the post office, phone company, and cable outfit;

purchased and pocketed tokens; met with Cap at the gallery; fetched take-out at Sahadi's—I took care of everything that required leaving.

You're used to urban squalor, he argued.

It's true he'd glimpsed the Forest City while we were still in our trailer, including when we pulled the van into Wren and Donald's drive during the move. Given that, his association with urban life was the Forest City; Wren's block and neighborhood; the park along MLK, né Liberty, Boulevard, which were nowhere then the way they are today. All of which he considered forms of eastern urban decay, like our Brooklyn neighborhood when we arrived.

It wasn't until he saw with his own eyes that I returned unharmed at the end of each day, for days on end, that he ventured out, after which it became more his than my city like I say, his bitch as the kids say, that and his home, while I morphed into the perennial out-of-towner. But it was a month at least before he muscled up the nerve to spread his wings, never mind submit a job application.

Those were the days when looking for work you still pounded pavement, door to door, from one establishment to another, though Tomás made a beeline to one location only. Applying for work was like Smith Street to him, long before it was gentrified, namely foreign turf, especially for someone who'd had only one job to speak of; who was set for life if only he were interested. He never had to submit to the process before, so he was unused to it. Finally he trekked all the way there, filled out the paperwork, then returned and declared, That's done. I pointed out that most people compiled a list of potential employers, from To-Die-For to To-Hope-For, all the way to What-I'll-Settle-For, a chit with at least ten names but ideally twice that, anything to ensure you'll hit at least one, hopefully; but again he asserted he'd done enough. While I ran back and forth to town, arranging my first show, he took in the afternoon line-up on TV once cable arrived, having never in his life had the luxury of watching in the afternoon. I wondered if it wouldn't be an imposition on his viewing time when the company called to say he got the job.

9

In fact I was irked that his system of nonapplication worked; at his confidence and lack of concern; given how many rejections I'd received over the years. I remember one shop I hit in the Queen City, where the owner didn't bother handing me a form. Instead she did a once-over, studying me from hairtips to shoeslaces, which she peered at imperiously, given they were a little worse for wear—and that was that. Did you get the job on your good looks? I demanded. Your magnanimous personality? Your last name?—I was envious and grabbing at straws. Again I'd put in many dozens of applications in my day, at a less-than-twenty-percent success rate, if that, and now here he comes banging the bell the first time.

I remember the day he went in. He luxuriated in the shower, not just drying but talcing after he got out. He took care to press his briefs and undershirt; slowly sliding each on, just so, smoothing them before proceeding to the next item. I said I was going to jump him if he didn't hurry and cover up, which didn't speed the pace. When I did approach him he pushed me away, complaining I was gonna cause a wrinkle, in his outfit and chances. So I sat watching from the side of the bed and observed as he manipulated the buttons on his dress shirt, one by one, after which he again smoothed the fabric against his chest and stomach, then threaded the tails through the band of his briefs, tugging them so they rested against his thighs, and in so doing flattened the fabric like a fitted bedsheet, so the trousers would retain a pressed look. On they went, past the ankles and calves, dark and furry; over the knees and up to the waist; the creased fronts and backs lining up along an imaginary center line of the legs; drawing the eye from the stockinged feet, upward where he ran his belt through the loops like an arrow sailing through hoops. He tugged the belt taut but not tight; fed the prong through the penultimate hole; then inserted the tip through the frame of the buckle and smoothed it. I watched him do the necktie dance, that extended tongue or phallus of male attire, its jaguar spots popping against the gunmetal gray of the jacket after he finally snugged it in place. It was a magic show; the way he swagged around; drawing shoes from a box, swathed in tissue; the emerging pair buffed and shiny as on the day they were purchased— if I were to take the box from the closet today, decades later, I'm sure they'd look the same; spitshined and unscuffed. He fit one then slipped the other foot in, unhurried and unrushed, until finally, after what seemed an eternity, he pronounced himself *there*, ready to take on the world, I thought to myself, with that look, though not without a mist of fragrance first.

After which I shed my night clothes; threw something on; and we left.

On the subway, before we parted at Broadway-Lafayette, me from the subway car and him to ride further uptown, I glanced back and spotted Tommy checking his reflection in the glass, insuring his hair was in place; the jacket unmussed; creases aligned. Indeed he was a sight, one that turned heads in the crowded car. With no place to sit he rested against the door, and after I schooled out of the car with the other fish, leaving an eidetic image of him in my brain, I thought him off to the great Sodom. I peered again over my shoulder—a tear fell while gazing at him, as though he were a stranger, wondering what would happen to both of us in a world of eight million looky-loos, half of them gay.

At times I thought he landed the position at such an iconic firm because of how he presented, as though the HR person understood the second she saw him, that, no matter his backstory, anyone with such an eye for detail could do no wrong. As though he embodied his resume, the paper version of which HR possessed no need to peruse because he bodied out the document. I found it hard to square the Dodgson-Reservoir Tommy, the horizontal, unclad, feral version clad in sweaty, hirsute flesh, with the Tannery-and-Co. Tomás on the subway that day, tipped to the nines. Though, granted, those weren't the resume-mania days like today, when you come out of your mother with your CV in hand. Back then a handwritten sheet would do, in cursive, that and an up-and-down look. Whether they even bothered to glance at the lines regarding his experience—to wit, First Vice-President of Loveland and Sons Cattle Co.—I'll never know. I couldn't help but think of the time I first visited that facility, unable to believe my eyes, or my nose especially; siblings wading in shit; shifting cattle from pen to pen; the father grown portly on a surfeit of beef that others bought; unbothered by or unnoticing the offense to the nostrils, his and the cows'; in knee-high boots clomped with manure and piss.

Whether the HR brass ever learned that the name was a fancy version for stinking, fattening pens, just before the animals were shipped to slaughter, I'll never know. Or if they, in that famous concrete-and-glass structure, were capable of imagining the air in an around a place like Loveland and Sons, for miles and miles along I-25, smelling to high heaven. Tommy neither said nor did they inquire, I guessed; nor did they seem to care. Bottom line, he got the job, hired on the spot we later learned, though it took half a fortnight to get the official call because in The City you never let a body know they killed it. On the contrary, it was better to make them sweat, which of course Tomás never did except when naked, one-on-one or one-on-two, stacked or twisted.

After hearing the news we went to eat, traveled the subway then headed east, to Alphabet City. If I was surprised, and quite frankly elated, for reasons I'm still not aware, that Tomás knew by osmosis or intuition, basic belief or a hunch, that he'd nailed it—I never let on. Main thing was he landed a position at not just any place but an Institution; one that emitted its own mystique; inhabited its own zip code; featured its own fragrance; subject of literature and film; with a familiarity not just in The City but around the world, including Las Nieves. I thought Lita might be clueless about the place—are you kidding? Her attitude was por seguro, jito. Of course. I wanted to hit him and jump for joy at the same time, knowing what I brought in wouldn't be our only income in a two- and preferably three-paycheck city like that.

When he phoned Lita she sounded as if to say, Tu estúpido. I knew that. As was the case with his parents when he contacted them. No one queried, What company is that? Or, How did you manage it, coming from here? Because they knew. His mother couldn't help asking what kind of job his roommate got; if the güey was pulling his weight; and if what he brought in would at least match Tomás's salary. She knew I wasn't his roommate, but she insisted on calling me that because that was the only way she would square the situation. I could hear her through the line given our flat consisted of only two rooms, and Tomás translated for me later the parts I didn't get—Just make sure you don't get screwed by the guy—I mean, I don' know what you two are doin' down there in the first place. When Tomás failed to respond she remarked finally, You just make sure he pays his share—his half—that's all I'm saying. Even if he has to work a second job, or third—don't let him get away with not paying—no matter. That from a woman who hadn't talked to her son in some time; his father either. Who had not that long ago disinherited him from the family business. Having overcome that bump in la paz familiar, they were on to the next chapter, and it was as though he'd landed an executive job at GE; the only concern was his freeloader-roommate, whom their son had given up the world for, the vice-presidency of a company, to accompany him on a wild-hair—all she knew is he'd better not get stiffed.

In fact for many years my roommate status dogged me; the way I was compartmentalized despite what they knew; because they insisted on squaring the situation, round as it was, in a way that squared with their religion, unlike Lita who saw us with raven's clarity. Especially after the I-do's in Polly's room which they refused to witness. They knew, but preferred not to. They weren't interested in washing things another way than sexlessly, pegging me as the perennial roomie, one of two güeys checking out La Gran Ciudad. Whatever the situation, Tomás went with it. Es lo que es was his attitude. Is what it is. One thing I can say is his madre's attitude made it abundantly clear I'd married up, no matter how much Tommy tried to reassure me after those Sunday calls that their uppity attitude was a coinage of their brains.

They run a goddam feedlot, he commented, after setting down the handset, after I complained. I think your father's factory job ranks higher.

Still—in their minds. And with their money?

Their minds. Do they even think? And why do you care in the first place? We're here, niño!

In time I learned the feedlot business passed down through the family, not through Tommy's father's but his mother's side. It was supposed to go from father to first-born son, but as it turned out el hermano mayor, Tommy's maternal uncle, after whom he was named, had no interest in baling hay or shoveling—anything—even if someone else was charged with the task. So he begged off and went into banking where he made a bundle. The same with otros tíos, the other uncles, thus devolving the operation to Gabriela, Tommy's mother—or her husband to be more exact, in a transfer that bequeathed the *de jure* title to Gabriela while her esposo, Tommy's father, Quique, performed the duties of *de facto* head. Which is to say she called the shots while Quique superintended his sons over hundreds of acres.

It turns out that fattening cattle afforded the family quite a lifestyle, which Tommy enjoyed growing up, he and his brothers both, so long as you could blot out the smell. As for Quique, hailing from Las Nieves, the lone child of a sheepherder, he was used to being around animals and everything that came with them. Lita and Pop saved enough to send their son to college in the Mile High City, where instead of a degree he earned a wife, and prosperity, compliments of Gabriela, thereby removing a giant question about what he was going to do with his time on earth, sheepherding and staying in Las Nieves not being an option.

Despite his background, Quique was in no way rough around the edges—on the contrary—though to hear Gabriela tell it you'd think he were an unshod bumpkin. She never stopped reminding him she'd married below herself, a Spanish woman, unlike Quique, whose line had mixed with Natives.

Le enseñaba a dirigir una maldita empresa, she complained to me one day on a visit back to Loveland—I'm the one taught him how to run a goddam business—she was referring to Quique. She discovered I was able to understand more than a little of her conversations with her son, so she went with it. He didn't know shit so I had to show him. How to stare a gringo down, dead in the eye while shaking hands—he would peer up at the clouds when I met him. How to speak so it didn't sound like he was always asking a goddamn question. How to drive a bargain with a half-smile, so that everyone thought Señor were doing the gringo a favor—I taught him all that. Would I do it over again had I known then what I know now? Para nada! Not at all! I tried to change the conversation but she persisted—He told me when I met him he was gonna be a doctor, and I thought, bueno. That'll do. He never told me he meant a vet—that's no goddam doctor. What the hell do they make? Same as a car mechanic—probly less. I only learned that after I tied the goddam knot.

When it became clear where her son had landed a position, she was sure it was she who'd endowed him with the touch of turning any- and everything to gold, or, her favorite, la plata, silver, which I'd never not seen on her. The only thing able to mar the sheen of his success was the burden of a plain-jane roommate nowhere near as gifted. At which point Tommy heard enough, declaring I wasn't his roommate. Well then your amigo. Pal. Friend. Whatever. Just make sure he pays. When I finally peeked past the door into the bedroom, I could hear he was about to go off on the subject of him and me, and I began gesticulating, motioning, shaking my head and finger both, anything I could to keep him from doing what he did best, tell the truth, because for him, there was no other option.

After he hung up he chided me, What were you doing, reining me in? Why couldn' I say what I wanted? You an' me—estamos casados! We're married, no matter what she or the state says, the damn country! She needs to know that not every gringo is after her sons' dinero. Does she really, I asked, think that? What if things don't work out? I queried. I was thinking of the looks he'd gotten from the other riders on the subway, gauging my chances in the face of all the competition in a city where people put the moves on other people's spouses while you're standing right there, next to him—What if she ends up being right? If we end up roommates sooner or later, if I don't measure up? Wouldn't that prompt her to say, See! I told you!? So we dropped it, leaving me in the role of son- and family-wrecker, an open question not just for Gabriela but for me too.

What I came away with in those early days in The City, in hindsight, after Tommy and I'd been together for years already, in those early days in a city that made a boatload more demands than the Mile High City ever could or needed to, was that somehow Las Nieves; Loveland & Sons Cattle Co.; and god knows what other ovine and bovine concerns before them, going back generations before Tommy was born, had produced a son able to stroll into not just any operation but one so celebrated, and proceed to command a position as though ordering a shot of tequila. His background prepped him for it, going back generations, though exactly how I still don't know. In contrast, for what did the Forest City ready me; Harry and Florrie; Geist Manufacturing; and Laurentine? How does shoveling shit compare to doing piecework in a factory, one where you slept with the owner's son, ironically named Romeo? Does the former set you up in a way better than the latter? I mean, what was it? I suppose it's like comparing armadillos and jackdaws, but I couldn't help myself. I mean, where did it come from, what I saw that day he put in his application, after having never seen it before? Tommy became a stranger, a wizard, appearing after the others in the subway car emptied out, not a few heads turning to take in the apparition along with me. What did I unleash, on myself most of all? I mean, where in the world did that person come from? He turned not just their heads but that of the HR person, sure as she was on the spot that he was one of their own.

Only one hurdle remained, and that was for Tommy to sit for a polygraph, him of all people given his incapacity for untruth, because he didn't quake before the Great Calculator in the Sky, the Recorder of Peccadillos, the one we were taught to fear in our youth, that Perennial Peeping Tom; meanwhile Florrie with all her devotions was incapable of airing anything straight. Tomás, if left to his own devices, as unspiritual as the animals in Florrie's religion, Gabriela's too, the cows in the lots, could never do otherwise than tell it like it was.

In those days, before they were challenged in the courts, lie detectors were *de rigueur* in hiring for companies like Tanner, a firm with a thing or two to lose. I've often wondered if the point wasn't so much to prove a thing as to test who'd balk at the challenge. Tommy marched in, knowing he moved in one mode and one mode only. If the company had been on a mission since its inception to discover The Last Truth-Teller Alive they hit the jackpot, especially without me to shush him.

Investigator: Have you ever stole anything?

Tomás: Of course.

Investigator: Was the value over a thousand dollars?

Tomás: You know, to be honest I'm not sure. It felt like a thousand bucks, I can tell you that. How much is a box a Laddie pencils? I took it from Fabiola Maestes in third grade, though I realize it only after I got home—I borrowed it in geography and when I realize what I did I try to give it back the next day; only she weren't there. Like I says I done my best. I remember it was a really hot day, and I was burning up inside, fevery, wondering where she was—I'm sweating like a mofo. Then one thing leads to another like I says—she gets sick or moves away—I try and try but I never do find out what happen—and there I was stuck with the stolen goods and no way of findin'—

Investigator: Do you do drugs?

Tommy: Doesn't everyone?

Investigator: Do they?

Tommy: Everyone I know. OK when my sissies were alive—don't you? Most a them are gone now. That was difficult, I mean I thought I was gonna lose my shit. I didn't even wanna visit Polly in the hospital, I couldn' face the thought a her not lookin' her queeny self, givin' people hell the way she did. It was Jake got me there finally, arranged our marriage at sissy's bedside, just 'fore she pass. Took me forever to get over Polly's going, just like that, so fast, faster than I was able to process what was going on let alone what t' think of any of it, including how I could a tried to save her—and all my sissies. At least they were there when Jake an' me got married—we said our vows before a ordained minister, or ministress—is that a word? It was Jacob saw t' that, with all his reservations about getting hitched, and with so little time to spare—we had a bang-up celebration right there in the ward. Anyway t' answer your question I'm in control of my drugs.

Investigator: Your husb—. Bedside wedding. I think we're done here.

Granted, the company stood to lose millions from a schemer, the very kind of person that kept Gabriela up at night, wondering if one of hers was being taken by a gringo. But a self-described pencil-thief, or pencil-forgetter, wasn't on their radar. Nor was the casual imbiber of illegal substances. In that way Tommy's post-bovine career, or as he put it his post-shit life, was set for decades.

I often wonder if the investigator didn't pack up after that interview and quit; after observing the needle stand stock still, dead or paralyzed for all intents and purpose, a doe caught in bright lights—Like what the heck is this now?—as the graph paper paced by. Had the technician ever seen that in his career; pegging for a company as enormous as that with its hundreds of employees at the flagship alone; with so many hopefuls jonesing for a gig, day after day? Did he want to gift Tommy with a trophy or oversize teddy, or enshrine him in the Smithsonian for having been the first person ever to break the machine?

Anyway after Tommy's first turn of actual work, for which he primped meticulously—I pestered him, Any crowned princes, sheiks, or home-grown royalty gliding over the sales floor? But his day had devolved instead into something far more low-brow, namely a training session in the basement of the famous structure, where he'd be spending the next two weeks. He was vocal from the moment he hit the buzzer two flights down, after a hot and sweaty ride on the metro—his least favorite thing in the world, sweating, as I say, except in bed or on the dance floor, both of which involve disrobing. He opted to buzz instead of use his key, complaining after that that his pants were sticking—I mean, I can't even! he complained. Once inside the flat he removed his monkey suit, as he called it—We were so jammed in the car—with no AC!—I mean why do people have so many kids?! I had to stand the whole way while the little brats hogged the seats!

He then went on to wonder how such a poorly run establishment as Tanner & Co. ever made a dime. How it managed to open its doors in the morning was a miracle given how poorly it was run—Does it all come down to that movie, a morning meal in a place where meals are never served? And the train! It's more a zoo than transportation—worse than a cattle car—the way they pack you in!

He opined he had to endure all that after sitting through a totally bass-ackward presentation—I mean they really need to revamp how they do things there because it's very confusing. Not just how they try an' explain things but the entire system. In general. Tommy barked that if he were in charge he'd a set everything up night-an'-day differen', so that it actually made sense to people; so it was a lot more easy to comprehend—he made a point of telling them flat out. When I suggested he might want to wait to set them straight, for the time being at least, until he was a bit more established, he replied, Oh no! They need to know! For their own good! Which became a pattern, day after day, year after year in fact, stretching decades, during which Tommy returned home only to apprise me of the assorted failures of the operation, after passing on the information to anyone willing to listen, a diminishing subset in an enterprise as set in its ways as the pontificate, and nearly as monied; after that first day it was always news to me, and even a revelation, one that took place nightly as Tommy removed his other self, the one he would don thousands of times in the years he humped for Tanner & Co., dressed for success, showing items to rust-belt tourists searching for the restaurant; looky-loos; and what his colleagues labeled BLTs, Browsers, Lookers & Touchers; them and the Bridge & Tunnel crowd; along with a torrent of silver-screen hotties, including, wonder of wonders, the very one whose name is practically synonymous with the place, having breakfasted there, a company that lacks the facilities for service; in the early or any time of day. But there he was, the person with whom I got shamelessly naked, there on the side of a reservoir in the middle of nowhere, ten thousand feet in the air—he was standing at attention, so dashing, waiting on the breakfasting actress, a diminutive woman, trailing smoke from her cigarette despite the no-smoking signs, which they ignored for her only; drawn as she was to Tommy like a moth to a flame; while the other staff salivated, ready to serve if he failed; though I only learned about it weeks after the event from his colleagues while downing a series of drinks. They filled me in, not Tomás, from whom I usually had to shoehorn, pry, or wheedle whatever bits and bobs of gossip I could get.

Was it really her?!

She's just a person, Tommy countered. She ain't no goddess.

Blasphemy—she's a goddess indeed!

Tu estúpido.

Stupid or not—what did she say?!?

Wha' d' you mean?

I mean what did she talk about???

She wanted a silver pin.

It was over drinks with his colleagues that I learned most things Tanner-related, events at which he chided me for looking a little "schleppy," a word he learned behind the counter, while talking about the Bridge & Tunnel crowd— it was only over a martini or three that I discovered that she, the goddess, seemed to be quite taken with him, my man, and that she small-talked him for an eternity, such that one of the women gushed, She was flirting! The eyes of everyone on the floor were trained on them both! Business practically came to a halt!

Pffft. No es verdad—that's not true.

It was! chimed the chorus of associates on the banquette across from us. She liked him—everyone could tell! She was making eyes!

Señor America continued to deny it the whole ride home as I continued to drill him—I mean Florrie would a blanched and required smelling salts if she ever found herself a hundred-yards of her—*of all people!*—a woman whose movies never failed to make her gush a lake of tears; a person she was sure never spent a day on a diet. If she could un-be herself and inhabit anyone else it would be her, hands down; so svelte, so classy, and now, come to find out, so into my man—we were married after all, the government be damned.

As soon as we crossed the threshold of our flat, before we could manage to ease the door shut, I was undressing him. In fact we never made it past the kitchen, if you could call such a tiny indention that—definitely not as far as the bedroom, or bed, or any cushioned surface. I had his suit in a heap and he met me, his back to the floorboards.

I'm her, I remarked, unable to shake the idea of someone, anyone, famous or not, having designs on what I fantasized belonged to me. In retrospect I realize it was no different than saying that Fifth Avenue and Crumm Tower belonged to Crumm.

No eres ella, gracias a dios—Jake you're not her, by a longshot.

It's Jacob to you, mister—and thanks a lot. I was struggling to catch my breath.

Niño, you're just Jake. And I'm just—

After that day he began amassing a collection of suits, first run-of-the-mill then designer, a collection that grew until it shouldered me and my clothes out of what was originally a shared closet, rendering my clothes homeless and insuring for practicality's sake that my wardrobe never amounted to more than a pair of jeans and a single pair of pants for going out; a modest exchange of shirts, which I wore until I wore them out; rendering them fodder for quilters; even as Tommy's stash of shoes, shirts, slacks, caps, and bags mounted; to the point that after Lita passed our bedroom became his private walk-in; forcing us to sleep on the pull-out in the living room where Lita used to doze.

10

IN THE DYSPEPTIC AIR that Crumm created, after he slaughtered the poohbahs of his own party; after they bent the knee like a conquered army—kowtowed, groveled, and yessired, abetted and amplified his lies, ones even my grandfather was too savvy to fall for; after gathering at his feet every bad hombre in the country; after that it seemed good news had gone the way of the bison. I mean it was nightmare on nightmare in Crumm country as we watched what was purchased with so much blood, over so many centuries, dissipate in thin air, after so much straining and shouting in the streets, outside admins, in the face of so many hostile elements, billy clubs and rifles, armor and water cannons, at the expense of so many bodies and lives— we watched things take a mammoth step back, disappear like dust after Crumm wrecked the high court that rolled over like a poodle; like the rest of Crumm's party; on the high court and in congress; in brown-shirted lock step— in the middle of that mess, those dismal and dispiriting realizations that your country was run by a government of bigots—after all that unsettlement a document came into my hands, hand-written, after my uncles' passing and out of the blue, from the daughter of a daughter of a woman I never met, a great-great aunt named Catherine. The family had been sitting on it for some time, she said, in fact many decades. It'd been bequeathed to her when her mother, also named Catherine, passed, who got it directly from her father, my uncle's namesake, Jakob, with a K. The woman who contacted me, already beyond middle age and whose name was Sarah, said it'd taken her ages to track me down, which she did via social media at the suggestion of her granddaughter—she'd seen my name mentioned in the obituaries as the only surviving blood relative. It's a flinty business, trolling those pages, which I've taken to doing the older I become—in a grim way I get why people do it. I mean I would've never come by the manuscript had she not been one too, a death troller.

Anyway, she tracked me down after seeing my uncle's name in bold letters, a name unlike most of the others listed there, Smiths, Browns and Whites, for sure, but more likely Gorskis, Kowalskis, and Wojciks; Novaks, Jelineks, and Svobodas; Grgics, Babics, and Radics; Bacius, Ionescus, and Nicolescus— the vast range of surnames you find in the death notices of the Forest City. In fact my mother used to tell me she was always teased about her name growing up, because it was so different from the usual Forest City fare, what people refer to, still, as her maiden name, because it had a funny resonance, akin to some deep-penetrating salve, ointment for what ails you, for common aches and pains, which the other boys, and girls too, couldn't help aping; switching it out for the real thing, the actual name, the way a person might toy with Fuchs or Gaye. Anyway she used to grow embarrassed about her name, to the point she couldn't wait to trade it once she wed.

Until I received the document from Sarah—is she my second, third, fourth, or is it fifth cousin? The irony, or paradox, was not lost on either of us when I paid her a visit on a trip back to the Forest City. She opened the door and immediately tried to close it in my face, though I'd learned when ringing a white person to brace my foot at the toe of the door, in lieu of my shoulder higher up, to prevent the hatch shutting; or worse.

I'm Will, I remarked, and added, but you probably were expecting Billie, which is what was in the paper. She continued to pull the handle toward her until it dawned on her—Oh! Billie! You're my—. I was—

Long story.

Is it really you? How can I be sure?

As much as cousins can ever be. I went through the litany of my maternal grandfather's family.

They're the right names alright. Her grand-daughter came to the door and enthused, Oh—hi! This is so cool!

To think we're kin, mumbles Sarah.

To think.

To think we're *kin*! remarked Cate, Sarah's granddaughter.

And kin we were, me and these white folk, from a world I knew nothing and all too much about. With a family history that not just I but my mother, uncle, and I'm guessing grandfather too were clueless about. To think that someone sat on the story all these years; avoided sharing it; until Sarah saw my uncle's name in the paper; the same as hers until she married, learned for the first time that he was a Someone; on the coast at least. My uncle Tomás could trace his roots back millenniums in the world where I live today, as far back as Skye, so we're talking the arc of continent time, but on my mother's father's side we could have been birthed from a zucchini yesterday for all I knew, given the farthest back that we were aware of was Harry; Ruby and Miss Glasby on my mother's mother's side; beyond which no one seemed curious enough to ask. About my grandfather, though, no one knew diddley. For that reason it seemed my mother's line was on the verge of extinction, that or rot; unlike my father's.

Bottom line, the document, a memoir written in pencil in a considerably shaky hand, changed the way I viewed not just my mother and uncle but grandpa too; his father and grandfather; and the entire clan, circling to me of all people whether I liked it or not. It didn't, could never have, excused anything, but it did shed light; on Harry mostly, a monster in a sense—sorry, grandpa. I started to wonder: If we can understand the etiology of a physical disease can we trace a familial cancer too? Can we create a space for rethinking how we view the categories perpetrator and victim, if they can be referred to in such a vulgar way, again, without excusing behaviors and attitudes that don't just appear out of thin air but have a history, a source—an etiology—like a medical condition, to the point you've got to suppose you might have ended up with a whole different animal—family and culture—had conditions been different. Which is to say that Chance—talk about a trans-entity—intervenes in all our lives. Sentient and non.

11

When Vati, oder mein Vater, was young, Zimmi took him to the kirchweih. Why was that strange you ask. Because boys were suppose to take girls to the kirchweih, the November harvest fest, and Vati was a boy. Mutti, meine Mutter, told me Vati was primped in a dress and wore a babushka, which made the people roar with laughter. They'd never seen anything so outlandish in Frühling, a farming village in the middle of nowhere. Kleinbauern, Mutti called them, spitting the words. Damn peasants. Which was strange coming from her. When she was in a fit she called them all kinds a things, I can still hear her after all these years, now that I'm old and understand a little more about her, people too. I see the saliva jump from her lips—Verdammte kartoffelköpfe. Damn potato-heads. Idioten. Kohl Gehirne—cabbage brains. There was a lot worse, but why set it to paper? It brings tears to my eyes to remember her in one of her snits; to remember her at all. Going on about this and that around Frühling. She always had a thing to say. More than I wanted to hear most times, including about my father, Vati, and Zimmi, which started the night at the kirchweih, or soon after from what I could piece together, though Vati never talked about it ever. What I know I got from Mutti.

I wasn't that old when I left Frühling, or when I was pushed out, you tell me. At sixteen. Old enough by then to say it must a been a sight, to think a Zimmi following the age-old tradition except in one respect, namely when it came to stealing someone three or four years younger it was a boy Zimmi dragged to the roadhouse dance, reserved for the youths of Frühling while the adults looked on—a boy and not a girl, which was usual. Had anything so bizarre happened in that dorf in the middle of the Banat up til that point, especially in Frühling with its love for tradition? Wasn't that what made Frühling Frühling? The fact that nothing never changed, that customs went untoyed with like the clock outside the rathaus, given the way people loved routine, and stories of course. They gave the town a good one, story that is.

After those rocky years early on, going back to the 1700s when the place was founded, after the villagers were lured there from Swabia, the Old Country, hundreds of years ago, before Frühling became the Old Country for me— Swabians were lured to a wasteland, coaxed by the empress Maria in order to keep the Ottomans out. They were living shields like the Mexicans in this country, also hundreds of years ago, brought up from Mexico to keep the Indians in check, and they'd seen enough of change right off the bat in the form of raids, but also typhus, cholera, drought and fire, which wiped out a third of the town. Changes in the official language too, not to mention the flags flying over the rathaus. So it's no surprise that routine was their thing, honored like ein gott.

And now here comes Zimmi, was he three or four years Vati's senior, bowing and offering his hand before escorting Vati to the dance floor, mixing with the normal couples, the adults looking on half amused and half aghast. They must a been in shock, but the way Mutti tells it the whole thing was so outlandish all people could do was crack up, nervously at first and then falling auf den boden. Never mind that Zimmi was total serious, which is how he played it, making it all the more toll or wild to people, who took it as a joke. No one could stop pointing at the clowns, the way they saw it, lisping across the floor like a cock and hen in the yard, feathers fluttering.

From what I understand the two were the last to leave. They waited for the boys to abduct the girls as custom demands on the first night of kirchweih, before returning them to their parents three days later at the end of the fest. Mutti used to suck her teeth and swear, shake her head while commenting, no wonder girls are forced to marry at vierzehn, fünfzehn, sechzehn—14, 15, or 16—if they're lucky! Hell if they can even make it in time to the verdammte altar before their term was up! And plenty didn't. Make it. To the altar in time. When the bun slid out of the oven early the girls were blamed. The kid was called sucio or sucia in the register, depending on the gender, in the record book that Vater Feri kept. Dirty. Tainted they were called. Well then, why the hell do they let the boys steal the girls and keep them three whole nights in the hay, under the roof of the barn behind the house, under the moon most of all, rolling around like schweine, hühner und kühe? Pigs, chickens, and cows. Letting them get up to gott weiß was god knows what. No wonder they gotta make a beeline to the altar, just in the nick a time, though that was never the case with Vati and Mutti, my papa and mami. They were ancient when they wed, in their twenties, the age when people raised an eyebrow and started to question, though it was more normal for boys than girls. Which was another of Mutti's pets, that the boys were told to wait and have a good time, after stealing eine menge von mädchen, a bunch of unmarried girls, after they finally decided. While girls were told to snag the first boy they could. That Mutti waited caused no small amount of abuse from the kleinbauern, until she and Vati decided they better go for it, even though they weren't racing any clock.

Go for it is what Zimmi and Vati did the night of the kirchweih, I was informed one night. I must a been about ten. In the same way Vati informed me one day, From now on you're gonna hafta learn Hungarian—we all gotta. Apparently I'd been asking too many questions, not just about Vati and Mutti but Zimmi and Trina too, our housemates, at the point it usually becomes impossible for a kid to ignore life around her, especially when it becomes clear it's different from other people. I mean I had enough friends to realize our arrangement was a little off. I think I probly came close to even blowing the cover, which is why Vati, Zimmi, Trina, my brother Nikolaus too all left, and Mutti sat me down. She made donuts, that's how she lured me. Though to be frank I wanted to run because if Mutti sits you down you're in for what-for.

Why I'm even saying these things and worse writing them down I can't say. I guess I feel I gotta or I'm gonna bust, and at my age, over eight decades since all that took place, since I was last time in Frühling. The misses ain't interested in discussing it any more, claiming all the talk in the world won't change nothin or bring it back, which I would give a limb for if it was possible. But Maria come from a normal home unlike me. Will it help to put it on paper, she asks one day, and I really didn't know.

12

I already feel better I guess, in part because I haven't seen Vati, Mutti, Trina oder Zimmi in so many years and know I never will. Writing puts them beside me again, like me across from Mutti that time at the family table, stuffing donut after donut in my mouth and not getting called a schwein for once. Doing my best not to run outta there like meine hose were on fire, that or cry. I can see the kitchen or parlor or whatever that part of the house was called, it being all one room, walls decorated with Mutti's paintings applied to the plaster. People used to bay at her brush work; her ladies with flowers; horses, cows, and houses; all silhouetted in black. I'm sure her art stayed long after Trina and Nikolaus were forced out, after we all were, all Swabians, after we were shipped to the camps in cattle cars to the reservation. Whatever their fates it was as though the kleinbauern from the Old Country never stepped foot in Frühling, after they were driven out, a story I hope to live long enough to tell. As though hundreds of years of turning swampland into the bread basket of Europe never occurred. I mean they invited us then took it all away.

Gone. All of it. My people, including Vati und Mutti. No crying over spilt milch, though when I do cry nights on my pillow, tracked by questions when the memories blow back, Maria does her best to console. Mami tried to comfort me too the evening with the donuts. When stuffing my face didn't do it tears popped against my will, I don't know what come over me. I was living a reality, day after day, my whole life, ten whole years, a decade when everything was going good, until Mutti spelled things out in words that changed my life in a instant. Like everything you lose that you love, you can only think of getting it back when it's out of reach. Or maybe it's because when something unsaid is said, even when you sort a knew it in the far back of your head, you can't ignore it anymore or wish it away. It's splat like an egg on the floor or a cowpie under your shoe. The fact you know for sure what before you only feared: the people you love and depend on are strange. Or different. It felt violent, the way words like truth can hurt you. Worse than the times Mutti slapped me with a look. How do you face people after that, including your own Mutti und Vati, knowing for sure what was once unsaid, and not able to unsay it; not being allowed to say it outside the house?

Words are wicked.

They invent the thing you fear.

Anyway it started that night, Vati and Zimmi. At the kirchweih. I had a hard time looking at Zimmi after that, for months and years. Because of what he did to my daddy before I was even born. It didn't matter that other boys twice his age were taking girls Vati's age, I just couldn't help but think Zimmi made him that way, into a girl. It never occur to me that Vati was that way too. My Vati. Der mann der mich erschaffen hat, the man who created me. Mutti assured me herself it was true, said she'd swear on a stack a bibeln if I wanted. Vati was my Vati, sicher. For sure. It's just he liked Zimmi the way Zimmi liked him.

I think it wasn't until Zimmi was out of the picture, when talking to him was no longer possible, that I began to go a little easier. As long as we lived together though, after the donut talk, I felt cold. Though funnily enough I didn't feel the same toward Trina or Nikolaus. Instead I just felt sorry for them, like I felt for me, Vati, und Mutti. If it weren't for Zimmi we would a been two normal families and by that I mean able to be open. Instead Zimmi nailed Vati that night after the roadhouse dance and shut the door on our lives.

Mutti didn't use that word, nailed. She didn't say Zimmi *nailed* Vati, I learn it here in this country. Truth be told it took me a while to comprehend when I first heard it in English. I knew what ein nagel or nail was before I come here, but I didn't know you could nail someone like that, that nail could be a verb like that. To nail. Look it up, it says to copulate. Like vieh, cattle. I only was able to put two and two together recently, enough to say finally that Zimmi nailed Vati. Like the romans got Jesus, but in a different way. Held him down and nailed him. So it was—what? Vati lying on his tummy with Zimmi on top, is that it? Or did Vati lay on his back and lift his legs so Zimmi could look him in the eye, the way Maria and me used to do it.

Did the two kiss—do boys do that? Did Vati like or hate it. Did he cry and squirm the first time the way Maria did? Was it like the cows in the yard? Soft or rough, like two men fighting, or ficken as we germans say, the source of another word in Englisch.

This is the first time I allow myself to ask these questions, why is that. In the donut talk Mutti used the words liebe machen, quaint and old as chopping the tannenbaum and lighting the candles of the advent wreath on Sunday evenings, singing songs—the words liebe machen made me laugh and spit out my tea. Liebe machen—lovemaking— ha. As if that were possible with boys and especially two men, I mean everyone knows only a man and woman can liebe machen. Or so I thought, no matter what I'd seen til then. I don't even know what I thought before the plausch with Mutti. I guess I thought here we all are, sleeping in the same room, me and Nikolaus in one bed, Mutti und Trina in another, and Vati and Zimmi in theirs. I don't know what I thought really, maybe that we slept two by two like animals on the ark. You may not believe me, fine, but I thought it made sense, boys sleeping with boys and girls with girls, until Mutti informed me the words schlafen zusammen, sleeping together, had many meanings, that only Nikolaus and I were paired in the way I thought it meant.

As though we were the odd balls.

13

IT USED TO GET THEM, asserts Charles. What did? queries
Tomás. The readings. I mean I was there almost forty years
and it happened time and time again. What did? Students
would write letters at the end of a semester; something along
the lines of, "When I first took your class I was a believer.
Now I can't even." Can't even what? asks Donald. Believe,
returns Charles. From a single course? Bro, how you achieve
a miracle like that? marvels Donald. Dude, it weren't hard.
I didn' even try. All we did was read the stuff written before
the bible. That all it take? It was the wholesale copying that
got them—the flood in *Gilgamesh*. The demigod who goes
to Hades and comes up again, times three hundred, in all
the ancient works; tongues of fire on Ascanius's head—
my students would protest, He stole that from the bible!
referring to the author. Try the other way around, I used
to say. The bible stole it from him. It was written like a
century before the new testament account. Virgil remarks
how strange it was that Ascanius and the others didn't get
burned from the fire, just over their heads. The haloes. It
got the kids thinking, about plagiarism most of all, a thing
they never stop hearing about, the evils of it. And there it
is in the bible, many times over, in passage after passage,
though no one talks about it. For millenniums the ancients
specialized in half-gods who went down to the underworld
and come back up again—in fact you had to do it in order
to be a hero. It didn't matter if you were a king or a poet

77

going down to fetch your love—that or a carpenter's son. In the ancient world you had t' do it to be godly.

So what you're sayin'—

What I'm sayin' . . . the ancients' number one requirement was that a demigod go down to hell and beat death—they had to resurrect, and it happened from story to story to story. Soun' familiar? Are you saying the christian god is a run-a-the-mill deity? ventures Wren. I'm saying it was stock storytelling, completely conventional—and people still get woo-woo about it today, as if their version were unique. In fact there were hundreds of Jesuses floating around, and how the "real one" was picked was random, never mind political. Surprise, surprise, asserts Wren. Basically the men shut the women down, explains Charles. I think I'll keep him, gushes Seth. It gets better, insists Charles.

Not s'prised, replies Donald. Why would we expect otherwise?

The people who drank the Kool-Aid were a cult. And it stayed a cult for centuries until the emperor converted, not because he was a believer but because it was expedient. So he makes the cult official—again we're talking Romans—nothin' more t' say. It didn't take long before he starts sacking the temples—and bodies—of the non-converted. Commencing a reign of terror. Big shockaroo, I commented. Why are none a us surprised by that? piggybacks Risk. Toby leaps into Serge's lap; he sits as if in a trance, following me with his eyes, as in a daydream. The marriage of terror an' religion, fear and hell, the way they wield them at you. Vicious, concurs Kenney. And people talk about Stahlin, pipes Serge. There's a monster for you, declares Jake. How many'd he kill? Only about twenty million. His people took care of another ten mill, at his orders. But bible thumpers killed more than that when you consider the crusades, inquisitions, several reformations, slavery, the holocaust—don't forget the führer was a christian—

Bingo—is that the word, intones Serge? Add them up and we're talking tens of millions, remarks Seth. All in the name a god. Stahlin was an amateur, avers Serge. It was another kind of religion, though, verdad? queries Tommy. I guess that's my point. Your students—Serge motions toward Charles—they hung their hat on something someone else told them. On dime-a-dozen stories from the old days, completely recycled, returns Charles. Tell that to a class at the beginning of a semester and they'll report you; a student tells that to a class at the end, though, after they've had a look-see for themselves—you don't hear a peep.

Well I still believe, declares Wren. Heeeere we go, I whined; I couldn't help myself. Will, stooooop! Lemme speak—y'all had your chance. Wren, you believe in what? asks Seth. Not in Jesus. I do. B'lieve. In Jesus. Heads swivel this way and that. I believe in Jesus—I said it. Though not the monster the crazies invented—Jake you knew 'em well, from the inside, even though you soured on 'em. Jake starts, to see his twin so riled. She continues, They're hateful, without any connection to the real Jesus, if he existed—I grant you, Charles, we don't know for sure. The bigger point—you ought a know this as a professor—is that a figure was either memorialized or invented—think about it! I mean the main point comes down to one thing, nothin' more. Which I'm guessing had to be radical in its day, I mean as an idea, in a world where honor ruled; patriarchy; the rule of revenge; and vengeance. I don't have your education, Charles, and maybe I'm wrong in wanting to believe in a character, real or imagined—call him what you will, including an allegorical figure, or any of the highfalutin terms people grab at now—great spirit—the universe—teacher—creative energy—all the offerings on the smorgasbord of belief—but for me at least there's one figure in those stories that's useful. From the brutal world of the Romans kindness emerged.

Tenderness even. Love for the outcast—and should have flowered, ever after. Among believers at least. None of the hate we get nowadays in the current incarnation of Jesus Inc. I grew up in that tradition; Jake and me had a front-row seat. But—Jake—those brothers at St. Andrej's, the nuns I had—they peddled a different version, not the usual creep the bible thumpers and politicians invoke, people mixing politics and religion. Anyway, I grew up—I can't believe it was that different from the world you grew up in, Charles—Seth, you and Beverly both—and you, Kenney, in yours—which is not mine but in another way it is—they all are—it doesn't matter if it's all plagiarized, copied, so long's the message's right. If Jesus is just another demigod like the Greek and Roman versions—so long's the message's right—and in a way the christian myths are better than the Greeks, which is as it should be given they come hundreds of years later when hopefully they'd learned a thing or two, about the limits of the honor code—revenge. Patriarchy. Even if later christians can't help trying to reinstate them. Even if it defines what it means to be off-message.

I was startled to hear my mother go on like that, without alcohol to stiffen her words; insisting on getting it out; like how long had she been sitting on it, after all these years of never saying a thing remotely similar?

Here's where we start to sing kumbaya, deadpans Donald.

Go 'head—make fun, mister. I'll say it again—I don't give a damn if the bible was plagiarized or not; whether there was a historical Jesus; that that figure we call Jesus has been hijacked by haters—and they are haters, the majority of them. What matters is we focus on the message and not the million do's and don'ts the haters concoct, pulled from their own behinds. Who's in and who's out—there's only one rule; and it's affirming.

Silence follows, the way it often does after someone carries forth like that, as though the conversation slid in a ditch, until Charles pipes up finally, If you're gonna go there I'll repeat that it ain't like there's one Jesus, which is to say one writer. There were different authors, and they all present a different dude. The only-love Jesus is one of many.

Well, that's the one I'm going with.

A hummingbird approaches and lands on the feeder, just beyond the glass, flashing emerald, then scarlet. In and out the tongue darts, slurping nectar. Will! Check it! shoots Donald. Emerald and ruby! Tomás remarks—Well I never bought it ever. Weren't you raised religious? inquires Risk. A course! But that don't mean I am. I liked the statues. The pretty colors; las flores; the pageantry. Candles. All the gold. To me—. —He was in love with all the stuff's that's irrelevant, cracks Jacob. Me too, concurs Seth. Though my folks were cultural, not doctrinal believers, we did engage in our share of ritual. Ritual's the thing, asserts Tomás—I could see an expression steal across my mother's face, like a tree-shadow, raking across the landscape at sundown; as if to say, I give up. Mis padres were into it, continues Tomás. I mean era una locura. An insanity. But I spent summers with mis abuelos, my grandparents, and for them religion was otra cosa, something else altogether. They used to go to church—in a town as small as Las Nieves they had no choice. But when the priest was caught pants down, going after un monaguillo, a boy, they were the first to use it as an excuse to split—actually, mi hermana—Tomás peers at Wren—I think Lita was a believer like you. The opposite of a fundamentalist, though I don't think Pop believed in anything but sheep. Maybe a few cattle. I think it's why you were the only two in la familia—Tomás glanced toward Wren again—that stuck with Jake and me, because you weren't stuck. The rest stopped talking to us, including Florrie, who couldn't cut Jacob out of her life fast enough—That'd be for decades, Jake interjects. I was there, remember? informs Tomás. Anyway, Lita didn't give a hoot, after she thought about it por un minuto caliente as they say in English, a hot minute.

Just like this guy. Serge lifts up Toby, jarred all of a sudden. He don't give a hoot either.

No one's as christian as Toby, returns Tomás. Point is, I had no faith in religion, religious types especially; apart from you, mi hermana, you an' Lita.

Which isn't to say Lita was a saint, Jacob adds.

She had her moments, god knows. But if modern religion is about no, she was all yes, just like you're saying, mi amor.

Which is all the more amazing given where she's from—I mean, if you could see the place. Jacob, we have, I remind him. Well then I mean those who haven't. Point is, explains Jake, a place can speak, form and shape you; open you up or shut you down. Well, when I was young, continues Tomás. Spending time in Las Nieves, I can report, they lived with animals, in a good way. Talk about bare life; is that what Serge called it? They could teach us a thing or two; taking what you need and no more. I mean they had their shit, no pun intended. I only know that it was fun there and hell in Loveland where the church breathed down our necks—which by the way, Jake, that world was also animaled out, a lot more than Las Nieves.

Well you're the one told me they were your friends when you were a kid, protests my uncle. Doomed as they were. I'd argue by the time they ended up there the animal part had been humaned out of them. I mean unlike Pop's cows, his sheep, who he loved like family according to you, señor. By the time all them cattle ended up in Loveland they had dollar signs on their heads. They were no longer thinking, feeling beings but money in the bank, if they ever were ever anything else in that world.

Well they mattered to me, insists my uncle. How would you know Mr. Smartypants?

14

THEY WERE KIDS when they made me, too young to know what they were doing. I'm twice the age they were then, and I still don't have a clue. I guess you can get away with it in your youth, being clueless, acting without thinking consequences, because thinking and knowing paralyze you. If they thought at all it was to consider their actions noble, sticking a pin in the puppet of culture. Saying fuck you to categories, binaries, gross and inaccurate. As though they had any relation to life.

You can say a thing doesn't exist, fine; that it has no ontological status; until you leave your door, where you discover it's as real as shit and smells as bad. That's the power of culture, even though it's invented; and random.

I learned it early, starting with the kids at school, talking about their grandparents. They had four and I had two, Grandpa Lloyd and Grandma Delma, who were an active part of my, our lives, though not Harry and Florrie, who were only names to me; without bodies. I must have been six or seven before I connected dots between them and my mother, though I'd heard my father harangue against them when he thought I wasn't listening. I made the connection just about the time I began to discover evil in the world, though not the kind the zealots go on about, about the most inocuous things.

If my mother had her druthers I think we would have left the country, to which my father always harped, Where to? As though Eldorado actually existed. She would have preferred we never had that conversation that my father insisted on, him and me, to prepare me, though I don't know if my mother poohpoohed it because she was embarrassed, overprotective, or if she thought it would create the very problem my father hoped to skirt, trying to spare me from the realities stemming from their own actions; a problem they only slowly came to realize.

The questions from my classmates started early, including not Who but What are you? Fish or fowl, redfish bluefish, black or white, in a world where responding both or none is not an option; a world where you gotta pick; A or B.

As far as A was concerned the message was clear: You ain't one a us. With B it was in a way the same, but different in that they took me in, adopted me anyways, in ways A never would. Where would we have been without Lloyd and Delma, who grandparented a half-breed like me—they even used the word, half-breed, in a lively-jocular way— they took in me, but more important my mother, given the reverse was out of the question, the very idea of Harry and Florrie taking in my father, never mind their own daughter, who they eighty-sixed before I was even in the world.

That was the landscape then. The culture since has maybe moved slightly off that dime, though not by much, if at all. Or maybe it's a mixed bag. You still gotta be on your guard when white people act all "I'm above that kind a thing." Often you don't have to dig deep, be around long to discover, There it is; the devil themself. Hiding behind liberal smiles. Because bigots have a million faces. More like billions.

15

I inhabit a world of color. I've been chasing it my whole life, though I'd like to unremember much of the journey; the way living undoes you; who you're moored to; what you hoped for; because the naysayers come for you. Life reaches in, extracts your guts, twists, then shoves them back, along with a parting fuck you. You ain't all that; what you imagined; and by the way no one cares. Luck did drive my way, but as with so many things there was congestion on the road. A professor at the university, Bank, turned me on to a gallery, or rather she turned the owner, Cap, on to me. One of my fortunes was to have Bank as instructor. Our work diverged in lots of ways but shook hands in a desire to say something off-track. Even back then the work was out there, with a rawness that Bank was drawn to. I learned from Cap years later that I nearly missed getting in the program, at a school that fashions itself the Harvard of the West of all things; were it not for Bank fighting, for me of all people, a factory worker and framer—to the point she threatened to file a suit, up the ladder to the board of trustees, if I wasn't brought in. Which is to say it doesn't hurt to have, and in many ways you need, an angel willing to go to the mat for you; if you're not trading in convention. She succeeded in getting no's to yes because Bank was no pushover. In fact if she believed in you, you could expect things. She bragged of being the only faculty whose students were in the Centre Pompidou, Hamburger Bahnhof, and several MOMAs—

her quarry was work that delivered a Zen slap. Which I guess is how we took to each other. If I ever hesitated her response was, Stop being such a pussy and go for it!

It did cross my mind, stealthy as a coyote, that she might be trying to undermine me given the questions in my gut about where to draw the line—that slippery, shifting boundary just shy of which your work strikes a chord and a nose hair beyond which dooms it to a closet, that or a knife. In fact it seems like it's all about romancing that line.

16

The work was out there. When I fretted about it I recalled Ginny's response to the image of Dan; her comment that she'd never seen anything like it. I didn't intend it for eyes other than his, but she got a glimpse and was intrigued. So against my gut I went with Bank's urging, channeling Ginny. And, accordingly, when it came time for the final show there was hell to pay. Bank contacted Cap in The City to fly out and take a look. He came all that way from the center of the universe, to an erstwhile cow town, hub of rustled cattle in frontier days, clomping into cars from feed lots like Tommy's, to a beef-obsessed nation.

The powers-that-be determined it was best to sequester my work in a room away from that of my colleagues—I wonder in retrospect if it might have been Bank's colleagues who insisted on it, especially after the federal case she made of including an image that the higher-ups deemed controversial; in that way a series of monumental canvases ended up in a room a fraction the size of what my colleagues enjoyed, capacious and cavernous, because the administration feared it would offend not the general public so much as the trustees, who had been enlisted in their capacity as donors to the school. They argued the paintings didn't carry the appeal Bank insisted, and the one canvas in particular; featuring a male couple with clearly diseased bodies; replete with lesions and exhibiting serious weight loss, in the act of more than an embrace—it troubled the sensibilities of the mucky-mucks, or so I was told. I volunteered to remove it but Bank insisted I leave it in, and she even hyped it as the one must-see canvas in the entire shebang. Fuck those puritans! she railed. What in the world do they know? It's your best piece!

It was a semi- or fully-expressionist portrait of Tommy and me, ridden with the disease that took our chosen family, the frailty they succumbed to, distilled in an image that is almost too raw for me to contemplate still, decades later, regarding a time when rumors about the disease were rampaging like a dust-dealing herd across the country; the whole country in a panic. A time we couldn't swim in a public pool; give blood; or hug a person; let alone kiss.

The canvas in question started life as a diminutive work; one I thought powerful enough despite the size; one I also think in retrospect might have sidled by the censors, in that format, given the way people overlook anything short of monumental, as though what gets their knickers in a twist is the possibility of interposing themselves among the figures, life-size like them, including on a rickety, old bed. Bank suggested, which is another way of saying she insisted, that I treat the original not as finished work but a study, for a larger painting in mural dimensions, which is no mean feat given the translations required. What works on a small panel demands rethinking when bringing it to scale. A few strokes in the smaller might need hundreds in a larger; in fact whole areas needed to be reworked, a project that nearly made me loco and that quite frankly I would have abandoned had Bank not keep saying to the point of shouting, Shut up for once and just do it!

Not a year and a half later it sold for a very pretty penny at Cap's gallery in The City, though I still prefer the smaller version that hangs here in Eldo, which several collectors have tried to get me to part with but which I can't bring myself to do because it would mean opening the lid on a trunk stuffed with delicate things, memories, regarding Tommy and me in the early years; our chosen family; those we lost most of all. In the early days of loss we were clinging to each other given everyone falling around us, like a herd drove off a cliff, the universe approaching an end, belying the scene on the canvas, two bodies, dearly joined. You could argue we were newly in love and with death all around, causing no small alarm, a status broadcast in the treatment of skin, so like our loved ones before they flamed out.

As circumstances would have it, the show took place at the height of the panic about the "gay disease." Could anyone catch it? The disease—and gayness? I used to wonder: Could anyone stand and look at it for any amount of time? At a work so in your face? Asking who matters and who doesn't; the dangers of being us; disease or no disease. Who gets treated and who withers away. They were open questions then. Nowadays when we're in the throes of a pandemic of a different kind, which experts claim is the first in a century, it's difficult not to reply it depends. On where you lie.

I'm still pacing around that post, the way lookers paced around the senior show. What I found interesting was for such a small space, my own private idaho within a larger country, it sure attracted a crowd. A mob even. To the point I felt bad for my colleagues because it seemed to suck the air out of the larger space. Label a work unviewable—ban it, basically—and it's like declaring free drinks to undergrads. A giveaway of paper-products during the recent pandemic. People will stop their cars, triple park, to get in on it.

Which is to say that if numbers are your measure, the show was a smash; if critical reception is your yardstick, however, then it was a bomb. The two newspapers in town panned it, or my portion of it. One averred that no one needed to be let in on the sordid goings-on in the sordid bedrooms of the city's underbelly; like the apartment on Josefina. Which is to say he attacked the work on the front I was concerned about most. The reviewer for *The News* chalked my work up to a contrived device intended for one thing and one thing only, namely to shock. He carried forth about how that urge was the enemy of Art, and thus contradicted every line that ever trailed from Bank's mouth. The reviewer for the *Mile High Ranger*, younger than the more traditional critics at *The Post* and *The News*, did his best to find value, ending on a pithy note along the lines of, "Despite the artist's efforts, the mammoth canvases nevertheless came up short." Bank's response was, Men! Wha' d 'they know? And in fact it was only the reviewer for *Out/West,* a woman, who had anything halfway kind to say, in the form of general comments about "The Community" being able to see itself in a public exhibit, even if it was viewed in a closet. But she failed to comment on the aesthetic merits, including the painterly manipulations, tonal choices, compositional decisions, or any other elements related to craft.

To be Tommy-honest I liked the work. I appreciated Bank, the way she got it out of me and not just for her stylish good looks, her bob and red lipstick, the three-piece suit; the way she harangued me; the place she brought me, kicking and screaming at times. It's true the administration wasn't happy with the panning in the papers; the bad publicity. One accused me of ruining the show for my colleagues, to which Bank argued they had only themselves to blame. In fact they're all faring better than I these days with their conventional careers, while I wallow in obscurity—that's where convention gets you. My friend in the program, Vittoria, was offered a one-woman show at Eye; one of the new galleries on Wazee. She had mixed feelings about the hoopla then but conceded it wasn't entirely my fault. She reserved questions about Bank's role as mentor, wondering if when they made such a fuss about a single work she should have insisted I edit it out so things didn't come to such a pass.

17

As for Cap Davisson, he was on the fence until the reviews came out; after that he was head over heels in love. He invited me to dinner at one of the restaurants along the Sixteenth Street Mall downtown. Casing the joint, he asked the waitress to seat us in the far corner, where he proceeded to order drinks, commenting, Don't worry—this is on me. He said he knew I was "just a student" and probably didn't have "a dime to my name." He insisted we sit next to each other instead of across, facing the entrance so we could hear each other talk. The place was called Spit, as in rotisserie; when the waiter came, Cap ordered dinner for the two of us; when I heard the selection I piped, That won't work!—I don't eat meat.

You don't eat meat?! Are you kidding me? Bank was right!—You are an oddball!

I asked the server if there was anything for a weirdo like me, and she volunteered the only thing would be salad. Maybe fries?—I'll see if they can cook them in oil instead of duck fat. Which I went with, salad and fries. I remember thinking, Florrie'd have a fit. Over me making a fuss, having taught us that when you're being treated go with what everyone else is having—By all means don't be difficult! When Cap queried, What in the world would prompt you to such a diet? I said it was a long story, so he dropped it, being averse to long stories I supposed. He dropped the subject, but not the hand on my thigh. It started as a glance to the knee and moved up from there.

You know, I can do things for you. I think you'd fit marvelously with my current stable.

I did my best to sidle away, along the banquette, plush and soft under the recessed light, in the direction to my right, but he kept inching nearer. He was on his third martini before the food arrived, and the more he drank the more he sang the praises of not just my work but me.

You know you're very handsome—his hand was wrapped around my lower back. My instinct was to flee, for several reasons, among which were my relationship status; the age difference; financial chasm; and the science of types.

I stopped wondering at a certain point if we'd get back to discussing the work, whether or not he meant it when he said it was the perfect fit for his gallery, one of the most successful in The City, Bank had made a point of emphasizing. But his mind had run off the rails; his hand too; so I switched to survival mode; watched him attack a cut of meat bleeding out as his hand returned to my thigh; alternately shoving in duck-fat fries. Working on his fourth martini, followed by an after-dinner drink, after the double-chocolate cake and in-house ice cream, made with real vanilla from Madagascar.

He dropped one of several cards in his wallet on the table then signed the bill with a scratch, after which he invited me to his room at the hotel for a nightcap. I begged off, claiming I had to get home, to my partner, arguing he'd be worried, but he kept insisting, No, no! I came all thish way! Jush t' shee yerwork. The leasht think you can do ish join be forra meezhly ol' drank.

I'd be lying if I didn't admit I was riddled with guilt, just contemplating going, but curiosity too, to get a gander at the inside of the historic establishment where Bank reserved a room for him; at how the upper crust lives when they're away from home. Tommy and I talked a dozen times about saving to stay there for a night. After Dan's high jinks in Ojo Caliente—it seems like a double-eternity ago now—in the days when he and so many others were still alive—I learned about what to expect in a case like this. But I wasn't sure in the age of the eighties pandemic—our own pandemic, before the rest of the world got one—if having come "off the market" would wash with Cap. Bottom line, my curiosity didn't allow me to pass on the opportunity to see the place; such a uniquely Western institution, tracking back to the silver-rush days with its historic appointments from what I'd heard, read, and seen on TV; which I now had the chance to eye on the inside.

I agreed to walk the block to Seventeenth; ascend the elevator that still ran in fine fettle, to the eighth floor. It didn't disappoint. I checked the view, followed by the paintings above the bed and on the side walls; the framed photos and intaglio prints; all period. The wallpaper that trailed into the bathroom, which I took the liberty of using; with its gold-handled commode and marble sink; breaking the seal on the soap and drying my hands on towelettes I knew Florrie and Harry hadn't a snowball's chance of touching their hands to. Truth be told, in washing my hands I couldn't help but think of the lady we'd seen on the Mile High Stage, trying to excise a spot. I knew what was and wasn't going to happen once I exited, and I was equally aware that my presence acted as a kind of light, green as a roulette wheel, no matter how I tried to deny it.

When I emerged into the suite I discovered Cap discovered, naked across the bed, arms splayed on a white background, as though fanning wings in deep drifts. I felt as much the worm as I'd considered the famous author, a writer-roadie, whose story I read years before, remembering that one incident in which he allowed himself to be solicited, back to the room of a much older, more portly and more famous author, drunk out of his gourd and wanting above anything to gore the young writer, tracking beats—when I read the book I remember thinking, Well, you rat. Leading him on. With no intention of indulging, and not because you don't "do men." Now here I am, a rodent as well, or more likely a typical human, relying on the sorry defense that he was the one insisted I come.

Anyway, I hit the switch while exiting the loo, at which point he started patting the bed, omitting superfluous lines like, Look! My clothes! They've disappeared! Like an idiot I sat next to him there on the edge, where he kept imploring me to Go 'head. Go 'head. But as I've been intimating I knew it was a no-go, while what ran consciously through my noggin was, That's some kind a body. Even to me, existing in a world of a certain kind of bare life, where naked bodies are my thing. I'd never seen one like it. Is it normal for a man his age? A torso resembling a mountain, like one of the fourteeners out the window? I was far from repulsed because bodies are bodies, in the same way facts are facts and emotions emotions; it's just I'd never seen one like it before, the closest thing being Dan. I'd read somewhere about a philosopher shamed upon leaving the shower to discover his cat sitting on the bed and staring his way; that he was ashamed, and ashamed of being ashamed; which one might surmise to be the case in many if not most cultures, in which bodies in open nudity are considered not available for public consumption, never mind perusal. I thought, I'm the cat, though Cap appeared immune to the feelings of the philosopher. I couldn't help thinking of the many times with Romeo—he of all people came back to me—in which we lamented that people had to wear clothes at all. I mean, a body becomes a body only in culture when it presents itself—there you go people!—and bodies, again, are my thing. Subjects in a way, which was always the case going back to my Romeo days, but even more to Peacoat.

It ran through my mind that if he weren't who he was, with so much standing in a niche of outsize power, never mind means, and not in any world but The City, with so many tony ties—a world I'd never seen—if he were Joe Schmo in an unemployment line I might have offered him a few bucks to sit for me, having never seen a body like that, the corpus of American success.

Try as he might, I couldn't bring myself to play Ken-Dolls, not the way I got them to play when I was a boy, though I suggested he might consider playing Ken-Dolls with himself, which he proceeded to do. It wasn't entirely uninteresting given the mechanics of the thing; given the amount of alcohol; never mind age. I wondered, is this my future? All the while he entertained himself verbally; what he'd do, with, to, on, or in me; next time. A fantasy I let him indulge knowing he'd forget it all as fast as it came, the fantasy that is. When he finished he flopped with a flourish, back to me, an expanse that relaxed as he shrugged asleep, sinking into the sheets.

I'd be remiss not to point out the situation presented options, ones I'd heard of in cases like this since I began keeping company with Tommy and Co.—Polly, Kitty, I hear you—on the subject of easy cash, ready to hand, a slim hundred or two, which Cap carried and I was sure would never miss—I saw the wad when he paid the tip. I was sure Polly would go for it, her and Kitty both—These old farts gotta expect it for the service we provide, Polly argued. I mean—girl-friend! Kitty agreed. I believe Dan mentioned something about it after that night he spent in Polly's embraces in the apartment on Josefina; he found his billfold lighter the next morning, he commented weeks later. You don't need to be a reader of dime-store novels, stories about some moll netted in one tight circumstance or another, to know when opportunity lies naked; when it offers you a lucky hand. What's more, given the way Tommy and I struggled in those days, the things we went without, the fact that Cap represented a Green Mountain—when you consider that, you'll hopefully refrain from judging what ran through my brain. Until I realized I'd have to confront two, tarn-dark eyes once I returned to the trailer; knowing that what pirouetted through my head he'd oppose at every turn; that it'd draw a penalty flag in the ongoing match of our relationship.

I washed my hands of the fantasy; the fillip to our finances; never mind a free meal where I got to pick from the menu what I wanted to eat. Instead I padded out penniless into the dim corridor, pulling the door behind. In leaving I took for granted that the portal to my future in The City, and Cap's gallery especially, was closed from then on, barring me forever.

That my error was saying yes to no.

I kissed my dream goodbye because I couldn't kiss Cap the way he wanted, though I kissed Tommy that way the minute I landed in the door of our trailer. I didn't skip a beat in replaying for him the evening, blow by blow, causing a green light to switch on for Tommy. We engaged in the kind of handsiness I withheld from Cap, while Tommy mused about what people expected from painters like me, people who've seen and done it all, a band of immoralists, a demographic of free-thinkers and -doers as bad as actors.

I groused it was no laughing matter, that too much was at stake; lamented my life was over; that it was a pisser; the jams you find yourself caught in, and not by choice; that the gods of influence come for you, your body; youth; and dignity most of all. There ain't no way he would a ever come for Dan that way, I whined. So near his age! They buy things— dinner!—drinks!—offer you the world; flash titanium after the meal; anything to move you. I complained Bank was no different, though it was a another kind of harassment, one just as bad; similar to prostitution, leading me to ruin. Is that what the Pandemonium ladies had in mind when they assured me I had a bright future? Was that why I needed to get my butt in school? To give it to a stranger? Tommy's sensitive reply as he poured me a drink was, Shut the fuck up. After which he undressed me the way he imagined Cap would, if he could, claiming he'd abuse me and there was nothing I could do. He lay on the bed in the posture I'd related, patting the mattress and bidding, Go for it.

18

THE FOLLOWING DAY Bank phoned to say she wanted to meet, pronto, in my studio at the department, which by the by, she reminded me, needed clearing out. I got there soon as I could, knowing she was not the type to wait, knowing too the boom was about to be dropped. I was sure I was done for, in every sense, like the still-bloody portion of the cow Cap left on his plate. I tried to tell myself it was a big, broad world out there; that there was more than one coast; that a whole other frontier existed, west of the continental divide; that even though I'd have to start over, build a career from scratch, I could find a niche where Bank and Cap's influence didn't reach, atop the North Pole. I could probably pull it off, I reminded myself, eventually, over the course of a lifetime. Worst comes to worst I can stay in the Queen City, sell paintings on street corners, in restaurants or bars, though I'd have to change my game. Completely. Normal up in a world in which pretty sells. Flowers and landscapes; abstracts and sunsets, with lots of pretty colors. Anything that massages expectations.

When I met Bank though, she was smiling from ear to ear. That was a rarity. She commented that Cap Davisson was very impressed. That he liked a challenge, which he said I presented. That he was going to meet us any minute to take another look at the work, canvas by canvas, in the daylight—I heard you two had quite the night.

Quite the—?

No need to go into detail. I'm just glad you did what needed to do done—he's very powerful, you know. He can make or break you. So it's better not to piss him off. And, bottom line, we're all adults; aren't we? We know how the world works; don't we? I'm glad you didn't play the blushing bride!

I was thinking, But I did play the blushing bride! What had he said to the contrary? Bank could see I wanted to protest, but she insisted, Please!—spare me. I don't wanna know what men do together. You know it ain't at my thing.

19

What would it be? And what would be the good of it—if any? Why bother thinking about it? You tell me. But I'm asking you—you brought it up. Is it even worth contemplating, something so ridiculous? And how'd we even get on this? You tell me. If it were worth it, thinking about much less trying, living that way, if it's even possible in this day and age—is it even worth the energy? wonders Skye. Well—. That's a deep subject, muses Tomás. You silly, returns Wren. It goes against everything we believe, insists Charles. Dyed in the wool as we all are at this point. Everyone. In every culture, at this late stage. In its current incarnation, most of all. Everything that tells us grab whatever you can.

Take and take and take some more—

—Well I think it's stupid, the whole subject, complains Ivy.

She has five houses, informs Charles. 'Nuff said. Seven, but who's counting, counters Ivy. Whether she needs them or not, isn't that right, Lucinda? follows Seth. Agreed. Like bathroom tissue during the pandemic, grouses Skye. The way people horded. It's my right! demands Ivy. And you, Seth. I saw what you drove here. It must a been as much as a house, that thing—. We're Americans, judges Seth. Do your own thing and all that—. Hello sixties, my old friend, intones Cinthia. I'm thinking it goes back a lot farther than that, love, muses Debra. Auntie, what we're discussing operates on both those levels, doesn't it? I volunteered. Not just me, me, me, but not group-only either.

To think of the fuss about a shot!

—Masks!

—My rights, my rights!

Well I, for one, get it, opines Ivy. This country was founded on freedom. Choices. The right to die by the millions and take everyone down with you, returns Cinthia. Quite a school for living. How does what y'all're talking about—sorry, baby—even take the group into account? Lucinda peers at Ivy while speaking. That's the whole point, ain't it? wonders my uncle. I'd argue that by group we're not just talking us humans, pipes Wren. Though why stop there? Why not rocks too? Well that ain't gonna fly, all of you, so why are we even discussing it? responds Ivy. The world ain't wired that way, the human world most of all. If they can find a way to horde, they will. But there's a limit—sorry Ivy, adds Wren. We've gone too far—we're eating our own future. You mean *our* future, complains Kenney. Ivy responds, Every generation has its thing, so get used to it—help me, Lucinda. Y'all'll have to figure out a way to deal. You mean to clean up the mess y'all have made; the fact y'all destroyed everything, hogged everything up, and on an unimaginable scale. Don't blame hogs, insists Wren. The tension around the table, a multi-pieced quilt of umbrageous shapes, in multicolored design, lifts some as the group breaks in titters. We can't go back to farm life, which is really the model we're talking about, in't it? challenges Ivy. Apple pie, mom, and not a damn thing to do but rock on the front porch. The same way none of us here are ever going back to god in the conventional sense—. Not after the zealots hijacked him. Him, repeats Debra. No one wants to go back to that. The simplicity that led to the world that created the situation we're talking about—it's impossible, posits Ivy. We've been escaping it as long as humans have been around.

The simple life, and god.

I'll never go back to what they call god, Jake remarks. If it exists it's a billion times more interesting—more intelligent—witty and fun—than the monster religion created. As for the farm—

You mean Kansas before lights and running water, old man?

Serge, don't make fun. Why are you so quiet? Shouldn't you be saying something? You got us onto this.

Can it, Dorothy—

I guess it's how you define farm. It can be a house, any house. An apartment even.

Lucinda pleads, Babe, you've got to admit we've gone too far—you even said it just last week. I never said I wanted to live in a hut. Borrow books on Buddhism and meditate my life away—chant OM all day—oh boy. Just to get back to some fake version of the basics—as though it were possible. We may be forced to it, returns Lucinda. Which is why we have seven properties—I'm talking back-ups. Your back-ups, yours and your generation's, are what's making it hard for us to survive! carps Risk. Don't blame me, contests Ivy. That's the beauty of it. It's there for the taking, for anyone willing to work hard enough to get it. It sounds harsh, returns Wren. I guess what we're talking about is something that can't be named but can be described, from the outside, never reduced to a label, or a known, because knowns become unknowns the minute you know them.

The thing we're discussing isn't a concept, avers Wren. I think of it as a winnowing. Of what matters; what don't. Talk about an idea that could never be popular, responds Donald. In this country most of all. About as popular as y'all's diet. Jake remembers that Toby is outside and excuses himself from the table. After a pause Toby comes charging, leaping in my lap. He faces the giant picture windows, observes a thrasher, stabbing a prickly pear, red as a nipple. Speaking of which, interrupts Lucinda. I just read an article in *The Times* of the fifty most popular recipes, according to their readers, and—sorry you two—what do you think The People want? Tell us something we don't know, replies Wren. Yet another pie-in-the-sky idea, asserts Ivy. Just like that other thing. Sorry for saying. But it ain't ever. gonna. fly. None. of. it.

Say away, mutters Wren. It matters not a thing.

To me either, seconds Jake. You only gotta live with yourself, the confines of your body, your brain. Ain't that what it's about? How to do that. Live with yourself. Bully for you and your hundred properties, Lucinda. No one's talkin' Russia in the thirties, takin' anything away. It was late teens, early twenties, amends Serge. Thanks for that, responds Jake.

We're moving the total opposite way from what y'all are talking about, instructs Ivy. No—it can never work, ever never. People want the good life—fuck it!—the American Dream—. Godless in a different way, returns Risk. Even among believers who think god's blessings come in dollars; stocks; stuffed freezers; IRAs; diverse portfolios; lavish dinners; countless devices—and homes—sorry Ivy.

Well that's where we're at, whether anyone likes it or not. I can't believe we're even having this discussion.

It's an undoing.

I'll drink to that!

20

IN THE SIDE GALLERY where the work hung the night of the opening, it read differently in daylight, the next morning, moving from work to work with Bank and Cap, the light in the space muted by shades, lowered to bar street glances, passersby taking in the work. Though in my mind there wasn't a pornographic stroke to it, one to please lurid eyes— how can disease do that?—it felt that way the minute Cap came in.

Like many who drink to excess he wore a different face in broad day, dead serious, as though he'd just heard of a passing or that he was being sued, so unlike the eager mien I faced the night before. He sported a frown and twenty-four-hour growth, to the point the thought of him when I last eyed him seemed fictional, a dream, the way he'd been in the restaurant, and hotel most of all, when he was so, so perky. When I say he was wearing his serious face I mean math face, as if it jumped from the tape measure he wielded, extending and collapsing it across the canvasses, instructing me to hold one end. I thought, shouldn't he be taking a measure of the room? The work and what it was trying to say? As I say, it was tight in there; I thought it required a few passes to take it all in.

Cap argued insightfully that the size of the space didn't serve the work and even worked against it, that if people were going to appreciate it you'd need room to spread out and lots of it, which Bank whispered he had loads of, adding

106

while gazing straight at me, You should see the size of that place. You have no idea!

After hours of critiquing each image on the mathematics of scale, dissecting the work for its market value and appeal; how "we" might "package" it, in the metaphorical and physical sense, including frames, and including the possibility of no frame at all—"We can hang them naked," Cap mused; how we might couch the artist statement in a fail-safe vocabulary to generate buzz, such that collectors couldn't help salivating; after "repackaging" the show for a "more adult and less puritan"—he might have said "provincial"—audience, by which I think he implied sophisticated and educated, never mind vastly more monied, with different (i.e. better) tastes and different (i.e. less backward) tolerances; different (i.e. calculated) expectations and different (i.e. more elite) sensibilities entirely than the mere locals present at the opening the night before—after that discussion the work was no longer my own. As though it had shrunk, irrespective of the size of the canvases. Cap kept stressing that it was a risk, taking me on; one, however, he was willing to wager, in part because of his— and my—connection to Bank, but also because, he managed to squeeze out, as if beside himself, it wasn't anything he'd ever seen; which, he argued, was Why you guys out here in the boonies are so interesting. You don't know any better. What not to do. You're still on your knees to Art. Too goo-goo eyed to know it's all a pile a crap. A business.

It was a tune he thrummed over lunch among the three of us. The two told me that from now on I'd have to "think market"; that "you only get one debut show"; and that "you don't wanna fuck up your one, big chance."

Jake, it's true, Bank parroted.

While they bantered I was thinking about the women from Pandemonium, a little over an hour's drive away; that alternate reality. I remembered how it was the "mere locals" that inspired me to enroll in school, then grad school—how their faith was absolute. They were there the previous night, eyes wide as moons, taking everything in, eyebrows raised, though peacocks is the better way to describe them, proud as can be, perusing the work of "their little Jake." No matter what they might have thought of what they saw they keep patting me—

—Good job, Jake—

—Show us your hands.

We knew you could do it.

Jake—here you are!—

—You made it! No matter what happens—

—Showing your work at the Harvard of the West!

A school for rich kids, I whispered to Marge. Totally spoiled. I don't know what I'm doing here; in a place for offspring of the wealthy, looking to shack up away from their parents; ski on weekends. Party hearty in Vail, Breckenridge, Aspen, and Snowmass. Play lacrosse. Walk along ivied walls to say they did. Get blotto-drunk, whenever, including after breakfast when they should be in class. Heaping up a mountain a debt, like me.

There's no ivy on this building, Marge returned. Just look! It's brand-spanking new! All concrete an' glass—and modern! Big as a museem, an' you're in it, love.

I wanted to weep, remembering Marge while sitting at lunch, wondering what was to come. My anonymous life back in the trailer, before the bigger trailer Tommy and I moved to, across the road from Derrick, there along Federal with the giant cowboy crumbling before the entrance; passing away.

I couldn't help hugging Marge, who wasn't a hugger—I didn't want to let go, though I didn't know why, apart from what I'd always thought, that she was one of the women in my life who mothered and friended me, making up for Florrie's lack.

Meanwhile Ginny didn't mind a hug no-how, she and Vida both. Can I get one?!

Me too! added Vida.

Of the group there, I would say Ginny understood the work best, better than Bank or Cap, who kept prognosticating and even betting on the press response; the amount we'd have to make to break even; adequate pricing, not too much above or below market tolerance; order of presentation for the biggest bang. Ginny, meanwhile, whispered, Jake, love—the work. It speaks. The body of what you have here—I see a line back to the image you made of Daniel that time, in your trailer, the one we talked about at Christmas. In fact it brings tears to my eyes—Dan is here! With us!—you've done the impossible; returned him to me. And Polly, just there—and look, there's Kitty. Darnell—and Heath. She was having a hard time holding it together as she talked about each image, and at one point she turned and embraced me, shaking noticeably.

I almost can't take it—I mean it's almost too much.

Vida was rubbing her back, moved perhaps more by Ginny than by what was on the wall, even though she hastened to say, Good job, Jake. Good job.

I swore I'd never say it, to Ginny or anyone but to her especially, as one is moved to do in situations like this, in part because it ruins it to voice it, but in part because it's difficult to believe when you're on the receiving end of a comment like that, but I did it anyway. The work's for you, I blurted in her ear. All of it. I dedicate it to you. I had you in mind when I made it, because you of all people understand. I don't care what anyone else thinks—anyone but you.

Scout's honor.

The thing about the remark was it featured the virtue of truth, despite the fact that Tommy was owed something too, literally and spiritually so to speak, which he got in many ways without me quite articulating it verbally, not in the way I did to Ginny. When she backed away Vida stood ready with a hanky. She blew her nose and wiped her lids below the mascara—Did I make a mess? She was stress-laughing, her and Vida both, then me, in my case relieved that at least someone got it.

Fuck the hoopla around it, Ginny declared. Look how many are crowded in this room.

I wondered if the moment would happen again, ever in my life; to be seen like that.

What I wanted to do was clear the space of everyone but the church women—Marge, Lily, Carina, Winnie, Olivia and Suzanne—them and Tommy; tell them, Look what you've done! Can you dissect it the way we used to tear apart books? I won't utter a peep, hard as that may be to believe—go at it. Do your thing. Trash, hate, love, or undo it; be ambivalent; complain; trivialize or monumentalizes it—I would have died to hear them speak without all the noise in the background for just a moment. To get their take, unrelated to any market looming in my face, reducing everything to a singularity; knowing what I knew about the women as readers. Savvy as Serge's parents.

To think that almost none of them is with us as I write.

To think of what I owe.

As things turned out I only had a minute to chat with Carina, to thank her for coming, after she winked across the room, yelled as loudly as she could among the din, Good show, Jake—you rapscallion! I never did get the chance to talk with Winnie—just as I approached her Bank grabbed my arm and commented, I have someone you have to meet. Only brief words were uttered between Lily, Olivia, Suzanne and me, so that in the fevered air I already felt them slipping away; so that in hugging Ginny I embraced them all, bid farewell, unbeknownst to me at the time; bid so-long to my sisters, mothers, teachers, and friends who shaped me disproportionately to the amount of time they inhabited my life. I'd often had it in my mind to motor back up the foothills to the Happy Looker to the Wednesday group, but something always got in my way. And fact was I couldn't find the means of getting there in the months after the show especially, given what I was tasked with, which became clearer as I sat lunch with Bank and Cap, brooding as I recollected the night before.

Whatever the two saw in the paintings I considered a far cry from how Ginny viewed them, Ginny who'd be gone in a handful of years, a victim of "the woman's disease." Different from the "gay disease" that had taken Polly, Kitty, Dan, Derrick, Heath, and everyone in Tommy's and my circle up to that point. Had I had the insight or foresight to glimpse into the future, I would have excused myself, stolen into the men's room, and after crying my eyes out scrambled out the window, leapt in my car and sped away, up the foothills, seeking Ginny in Pandemonium in order to hug her one last time.

Or not. Knowing her she might have scolded me, for running away from the opportunity she wanted for me most, my great, big break. She would have called it irresponsible, horribly. I imagine she would have pushed me away, screamed that I was turning my back on a golden egg, plopped in my lap out of the clear blue, a boon from a world that rarely provided, and that I better goddamn well not fuck it up. Though she would have said it in a nice way. Even when, years after we'd moved to The City and I heard she was terminal, even then I didn't drop everything and fly back, make my way to Pandemonium, where she insisted on dying in the home she and Dan built, despite the fact it had been around well over a century. It came at the end of the semester when my students were the most insane, trying to make up for work they'd put off; painting like maniacs; begging for extra time and credit; anything to compensate for being remiss. Never mind I too had work, for yet another show I also was behind on. When I heard the news I told myself there was no way; to simply drop things and go. All of which I regret. I never paid my last respects, not while Ginny was alive. My only hope is she hears me now, belief or no belief; that she receives it on this or the other side.

Meanwhile lunch with Bank and Cap dragged on. It was my first business gathering, though far from last, over time, and already I thought of it like the pandemic. In fact I don't do business lunches anymore; I refuse. Especially in the City Different. Take the work or don't; it's up to you. That's my thinking. I've no interest in haggling over math most of all; dimensions; height, width, and wall space; square footage; list prices; or any of the demands of the white cube. I've had enough of that, and my feeling is, You don't want it? Don't bother. I don't need the money, and not because I'm rich—Serge, I feel you.

As for that first show in The City, it was a modest success. Not gangbusters and not a bust. At the time I was crushed. I felt I let Cap down; Bank too; and the church women most of all. They'd all taken a gamble, and when it came to the bottom line I didn't come through; didn't produce; which is to say I didn't fatten Cap's wallet. He deadpanned he'd take it out in trade. I must have looked at him like a possum in a beam, dead temporarily, because he hastened to say, extremely generous for him, For the first show—of a complete unknown—coming from the boonies—it wa'n't too bad. The key is what you turn out next—so get to work! He averred that a show was limited in lots of ways. Time- and sales-wise. That all it does is put the market on notice you're there; with the intention of sparking desire. You know all about that, I'm sure. He tweaked my nipple as he outed the remark, and I did my best not to back away.

A few things interested me in the wake of the first show. One was the prices on the list, if I may be that crude. My and Tommy's thought at eyeing them was, Are you kidding?! Something I would have happily sold for a couple hundred bucks, a fortune to us then, was listed for many—many—thousands, more than I feel comfortable revealing; the second was the way Cap reworked my artist statement, which is to say rewrote it; to the point that I was no longer in it, me or anything Ginny discussed when she viewed the canvases, which informed the draft I wrote—the personal, autobiographical elements were completely expunged. He invented a whole other story; a new me; entirely foreign. In that way it—I—became alien to me, as though I became a stranger or facsimile of me. A Jake-bot.

Then there was the percentage the gallery amassed. I would've thought ten percent would a been a lot given the prices, but it turned out to be more than sixty, or was it seventy, given the risk I presented. Not that I would have known what do with all that cash had it come in my possession. It became clear that my share was reduced to nothing when I counted the cost of canvas, pigments, studio rental, framing, taxes—everything but labor—which in the final analysis was nil. Or did I end up paying?

Cap was keen on the bottom line, but it dawned on me, he's making a boatload; so much more than me proportionally; even after overhead—has he ever bought a tube of cobalt? Where does that kind of profit go? It's true he purchased the space in Chelsea, which he moved to in the eighties exodus from Soho—he owned it outright. True too that he supported a bare-bones staff who made a pittance, as I was told by one of the workers themselves, *sotto voce,* who added that she thought Cap was short for Capital, as in the red-meat kind, American style. Given the giant skylights in that space he must not have paid much for lights, i.e. electricity. Granted, taxes in The City were a thing, but wouldn't the commission on a single canvas cover that—even one of mine and not one of the biggies in his "stable"? Instead, I realized, it was Cap's life my work was bankrolling, the floor-thru in Tribeca and the midcentury in the Hamptons, both of which we were invited to over time. They were sumptuously furnished, and during the time I was in Cap's life he frequently decided to "re-envision" the spaces. There was the expense, too, of getting to the tip of the island via helicopter, a monstrous, mechanical dragonfly that alit on a pad beside the beach. Never mind the many taxis to restaurants, on the island and in The City, uptown or down, or anywhere—a native of the place, Cap never learned to drive, and the subway was against his religion. Unlike Tommy and me, who had no choice.

I thought I'd get all the unsold canvases back, that I'd house them in my studio somehow, but he held onto them, warehousing the group in his vault, peddling each until in fact they sold, all of them, though he never mentioned when he "moved" one, as he put it, as though doing so were a bodily function, which left me to think for quite some time, falsely, that the whole collection was a dud. I only discovered their success on what he called Come-to-Jesus Day, not long before the tax deadline.

Last to sell was the one that caused the fuss—Cap crowed he "massaged" it; complained of the way it worked his nerves as he plied a collector for the better part of a year. He remarked, *Damn!* I'm good! You gotta be—to get someone to go for that thing. By which I think he referred to the narrative he invented.

It was one of Cap's richest collectors—he referred to him as one of his Caps—who, I came to understand after meeting him, was another handsy type like Cap himself; someone with nothing to lose and for whom money was no object; who considered donating the work to a museum, the most expensive image of the lot; out of which he'd pull a nifty deduction come tax time; after unloading it. Cap said he kept impressing on him what a great investment it was—It doesn't matter what you actually think of it. I mean, you gotta trust me. He argued I was about to "take off," that I was on the verge of exploding onto the market; that it was just a matter of time. He promised that soon the canvas would more than pay for itself, many times over— and so on. And, in fact, time unveiled that it would have tipped the collector's till handsomely, had he survived. Had he not become handsy with the wrong hombre; resulting in a crime that was *the* story in *The Times*; racy for the readers; laying yet another layer to the narrative of the piece and jerking it into yet another level of notoriety than it might have had otherwise. After the guy was in the ground and his assailant in jail, his collection was auctioned by one of the celebrated houses in The City, with outlets across the globe. They sat on the painting for some time, for the estate, hedging the release date, fretting about the best way to market it for maximal gain; which sale it should go in; which would grow the greatest buzz. I was well into teaching by then, a fallback from my flagging painting career, when they finally put it on the block; my first thought when it sold was, Had you only unloaded it fifteen years ago; I could've passed on teaching; or sailed to tenure, given how drawn administrations are to the scent of notoriety; anyone with a brand; given that institutions of higher learning are first and foremost about endowments; creating star factories. Nothing interests them more than an up-and-coming, which at the time I got the job I wasn't remotely.

By the time the work sold, for thirty times the original list, I was over it, which is good because I never saw a dime. To be honest, as I said, I never really liked the image in the larger size—I preferred and still prefer the smaller version here at home. The other is OK for someone living alone in a mansion with giant walls to fill, of which I've learned there are many more than I could have ever possibly dreamed, coming from Laurentine, or, more apt, sleeping with Molly in my Valiant on the side of the Shagaran. I think my mind would have exploded back then, were someone capable of convincing me of the course my life would take.

Anyway, small things power me more these days, my imagination; if someone's looking for filler for a field of white, I'm not their guy. My gallerist here in the City Different tries to tell me it's the thing, in the homes of Las Campanas, Houston, and the City of Angels, where people are willing to pay the world for monumentality.

I tell her, You're barking up the wrong tree.

21

Jake, I can't believe it. Me either. How many years has it been? marvels Carina. Thirty? Forty? And to think. And to think indeed. That you were right next door. We even waved hi!

How many times? You *sorta* looked fermiliar? Sorta not. Plus you changed your name. I blame it on that. The City changed it for me, explains Jake, still holding Carina's hand. Or Cap did. He didn't think Jake was marketable, not like my birth name. Same with this guy at Tanner. You got gray hair since I saw you—you changed, both a you. I'll always remember y'all's wedding—

—What wedding? queries Vida.

Jake's wedding, love. You were there. You should a seen these two back then, Carina reflects, turning to Serge and me. Do tell! quips Serge. Or not! pleads Jacob. They were babies, both a them. Lost on a sea of adult problems. A killing field is more like it, adds Cinthia. This recent thing was bad, but in a way it was worse back then. T' think a the scale. Let's change el sujeto, pleads Tomás. Jake, next thing I remember is your show. Yet another bittersweet— 'specially for this guy. Jacob gestures toward Tomás. What happened? begs Serge. Oh my god, what didn't? It was your crowning achievement! enthuses Carina. Or nadir, returns Jake. Tell! insists Serge. It felt like I was crowning, birthing something, for sure. Too bad they treated my baby like a monster. Look where it got you though. Look where it got both a us, asserts Tomás. You and me and Lita. Don't forget me, yelps Serge. We wouldn' a met if not for that. And all because a you, reflects Jake, squeezing Carina's hand. You plural. He peers at Vida. The women.

What? worries Vida. What did I—?

You're beautiful, assures Carina. God rest their souls—the women. We're th' only two left, you know. She peers toward Vida.

I remember Ginny and Dan's home in Pandemonium. Such a beauty, that—gingerbread; we had good times there; like in another life. We jus' got back from there, returns Carina. It's lookin' the worse for wear these days. Tell! pipes Serge. Ginny left it to her, Carina explains, glancing toward Vida. I'm sitting across from her; I can't help thinking she's the image of class, with a rugged beauty you rarely see in women, especially these days, and, like, were I were a different person—a different guy—with a different life, I'd look at her and say, I want to be you. The whole package. We go back a couple times a year to check on it, informs Carina.

Where are we going?! frets Vida.

Nowhere, love, remarks Carina. We're staying right here.

I'd give anything to see it again. I wanna see it too, remarks Serge. Inside. He's smiling, always ready for a road trip. When can we go? I took these guys there last year, explains Jacob, indicating Serge and Tomás. And I took this guy here; he indicates Tomás. Just after Dan died; before I left Ojo; after the wedding and before I started school. We stopped to see Ginny, before we moved down.

She told us, informs Carina. She was touched.

Told who?

You an' me, love.

The rite she performed in the ward that time? At the hospital? That was the marriage. The one at City Hall? A formality. Don't say that old man, disagrees Serge. We had a great time. Was I there? wonders Vida. You were, love. At the first one, but not the second. At Ginny's ceremony, the one the state didn't give a hoot about—that was the bomb. I watch as Jake glances at Serge. I wish you could a been there. The other ceremony was for taxes, the wild time after. Wild is the word, old man, agrees Serge. I think you're underestimating. You said you felt different after, you and Tommy both. After the legal marriage. That you finally felt protected. Silence ensues as though there were a pact to pause for a time, leaving a gap in the conversation, both uncomfortable and comforting, for thought or reflection, or because words fail.

I felt bad we fell out of touch, admits Jake. Bound t' happen, soothes Cinthia. It did with us too—you, me, an' Debra. But here we are. We figured after your show you were no longer our own, remarks Carina. Us and the other women. That you weren't our little Jake anymore; whether we liked it or not. That the tide was sweeping you away— we weren't offended. In fact we wanted it.

I think I'll call you that, japes Serge. My little Jake.

Watch it, you—

—Wanted what? confuses Vida.

We're the ones who pushed you, recollects Carina. We wanted him t' do well, she reminds Vida. Didn't we, love? Well I missed you—y'all were mothers. In a good way. Proper laughs around the table, including from me. Friends. Sisters. Compadres. God knows y' needed it, returns Carina. You came to us an orphan. Here we all are! sparks Cinthia. All orphans. Though we come by different paths.

I wonder aloud, How did you and Vida—?

—End up t'gether? Carina reaches across the table but Vida merely stares at the hand. When Ginny passed—the skin above Vida's eyebrows furrows. Is Ginny here? Where?

Apart from the wrinkled forehead, Vida's the picture of vitality, a physical memento of the old days, her body adorned in silver and turquoise—Carina took care to remember the details. The rings that punctuate several fingers; silver bracelet at the wrist, beautifully tooled; squash blossom necklace, trailing from the neck. When she passed, this one here was a comfort. This one here—Carina indicates herself, patting her chest and causing Toby to bark—This one here was a wreck. Not well at all. After Dan passed she moved in with Ginny—again Carina reaches her hand toward Vida, and again she simply stares at it, unsure what to do—much to Hermione's dismay and Lizzie's pleasure— neither of them had a clue about either of their parents, if you can believe it, which inspired Ginny, in her inimical way, to have a heart-to-heart with Mione.

Did it help? wonders Jacob.

Unfortunately no; not with that one. To this day—

She always was a tough nut.

Or just a nut.

She was a believer, no? Her and Steve both, recollects Jake. She blurted a number of unkind things that she refused to take back, explains Carina. Called Ginny a fake and a fraud—a diabolical liar! Ginny of all people. You'd think with all've Hermione's religion she would a had a brush with compassion. Instead it ended things; Ginny died without seeing her.

The beauty of the true religion.

Can I tell my story? begs Vida, petulantly.

By all means, love.

By all means, what?

By all means, tell your story.

Vida looks around. What story? Later Jake will comment in private that her voice is thinner than he remembered, though in my view grit bodied forth still.

What story? Your story, love.

I don' know what you mean.

We're talkin' about when Ginny died, explains Tomás, gazing toward Vida. Cinthia—you would a liked her—Jake used t' say she reminded him a you. Did you forget? We met at the hospital that time? counters Cinthia. That's right! Serge reaches next to him and hands Cinthia his napkin that he's dipped in water, after she dropped a bit of sauce on her blouse; Toby attempts to drink from the glass. I was a wreck after Ginny passed, continues Carina. Have I said that? This one come—*[gesturing toward Vida]*—this one come an' took care a *me*; instead a th' other way around. Did I say that Ginny left her the place in Pandemonium? She didn't leave it to the kids—said she and Dan discussed it—that beautiful gingerbread that I'd only visited now and again. She come to me in Loveland! jumps Vida. That's right, remembers Tomás. I forgot we're both from there. Or near there. I believe y'all are from the same line a work too. Vida, how far we've come.

Come where?

*Any*way—I'm trying to tell the story, dear. The floor's yours, invites Serge, sweeping his arm across the table with a grin. Ginny left *me* the house! That's right, love. She did leave you the house. I was a little overwhelmed, and this one used to invite me over. The house never felt so empty; I mean soulless; like it's really not the structure but—. Even with all that stuff. Did I say how overwhelmed I was? You did, assures Jacob. I observe as Carina peers toward the ceiling, takes in the antler chandelier made of porcelain—Oh how pretty—she wipes below her eye with her index finger. Tell what happened with the house, urges Serge. Yes, that beautiful, old, gingerbread structure—you know how historic the places are there—I mean the whole town's a museum. Ginny and Dan's place was built in 1869, during the height of the silver rush. It'd amassed well over a century a stuff—

—Problems too, I bet, worries Cinthia.

Galore. It was falling apart even when Dan was dying. Repairs on repairs needed—Dan was no Jack of All Trades by a long shot—. —More of the Jack of Hearts, quips Jake. Carina ignores the joke—He was at least able to keep it together when he was alive, I give him that; albeit with glue and spit. After he passed Ginny was too busy. But the biggest question was what to do with all that stuff. I mean—the attic alone! They got the house after moving from the City of Angels, from a couple a sisters, spinsters who died in the place their grandparents built. They were a couple of seamstresses, and there were boxes on boxes of quilts and quilt parts, squares and rosettes, fabric scraps, and needles—stuff they used or hoped to use in panels someday, all filed away, up there. Some were bug-eaten but some in perfect, even mint condition. There was all the fam'ly stuff too—mementos of the City of Angels; head shots; CVs; star photos; promos; some pretty racy letters from a minister Dan was seein' before he and Ginny met; all of which they brought and stored outta sight while raising the girls—I mean, what to do with it all? The girls grew up there, so there was that—stuff of several lifetimes. The things belonging to them was easy to get rid of. The rest though—

Wasn't there a river flowing through the property? remembers Jake.

There was. The headwaters of Clear Creek ran next to it, comin' down the mountain from above Guanella Pass—the house practically sat on toppa it, which was a whole other problem—but never mind. We spent years sorting through it; cataloguing things; only to move out.

I asked her to move in—suggests Vida.

—Actually, Ginny made a point of telling her—Carina glances again at Vida—I want you to find someone when I'm gone.

Why did you move to Eldo?

Because being there was too much. For the both've us. She wasn't working and I'm with a non-profit so I can work anywhere. We ran from all the ghosts. Even when we go back it's hard. The town is still the town, the one timeless place in the world, I swear; practically unchangeable; if that's even possible today. But the house is a shell, like a person after passing, or—. She takes Vida's hand finally. We can't live there and can't bring ourselves t' sell it. Pandemonium escaped the brewerization of Ojo, the casinoficiation of Black Hawk and Central City—I mean, all those places, ruined for a buck. They trashed the state! declares Jake. Turned it into Pottersville. The three a us were driving through—Jake gestures again toward Tomás and Serge. Me and him wanted t' take this guy to Los Dos Mujeres. I remember it! pipes Cinthia. We went there with Debra that time! Gone now, laments Jake. Like much a the town. All a Black Hawk, ruined, bemoans Tomás. Ojo was it in its day, affirms Jacob. I built five homes, just outside, with a guy named Emil. Also gone, all of them. Razed in order to put a zip line, an entertainment complex—five football fields. They covered Clear Creek with concrete, untouched and pristine back in the day, put in a giant pipe, there on the edge of town. Untouched is the thing, declares Carina. Like it was begging for developers.

Too many babies! intones Tomás.

The town and everything around it, invaded these days. There were many reasons why we left, why we find it difficult to go back, though like I says, Pandemonium is one of the few places still intact. They even reopened the Hotel de Paris—it sat moribund the better part of a century. 'Til someone realized it was a goldmine, quips Cinthia. Give the masses what they want, remarks Serge. Fortunately they haven't changed a thing, returns Carina. It's more a museum, untouched like I said. Mis padres love Black Hawk, volunteers Tomás. Ojo Caliente. Central City—they live for it; park in town and catch the trolly that shuttles them and dozens of other seniors to gamble their millions—they sit and hit slots all day. Eat steak for $4.99, all you can eat. Lobster on Tuesday. In a landlocked state, drolls Cinthia. Bless their hearts, deadpans Debra. We fought it for years, apprises Carina. That's what I do for a living—'til we realize it was hopeless. I mean the powers that be—

—The state gambling commission may have had a lawyer or two? quips Cinthia.

Who knew change would come in the form of a legal battalion—

—This guy's sister—Cinthia points toward Jake—and all of us really—eked out a victory or two against them, developers; though the situation was the opposite. The powers that be wanted to thwart them, put their money in virgin land—white suburbs—deny the folks in the city money, which, with not a little effort, we turned around. To the point sometimes we wonder now if we were too successful, if that's even a thing. When the money come to the Forest City, and after such a fuss, no one wanted to be shut out; developers most of all. Our neighborhood went from being sad-frumpy to sad-successful, completely gentrified, laments Debra. To the point we felt we needed to get away too, us and Donald, Wren, get outta town when it becomes too much.

The Battle For Black Hawk, as we called it, explains Carina—an old, silver-rush town like all the towns up there, became contentious once the state passed zoning laws making gambling legit; high-rises too. In a penny-ante town like that of all places; once a swelling in a creek that now rises to meet the sky from the bottom of the valley; eclipsing Central City. The industry sugar-talked people on TV, in ads and infomercials. They turned it into a thing about the survival of the state, schools and essential services, as though it were the only solution. I'm guessing it had to do with dollars, reckons Cinthia. Including your mamma and papa's, Tomaldo. As though the slots were the only option; sitting in a chair and pushing buttons all day in a smoke-filled room.

I bought my first pottery in Black Hawk, declares Jake. It was a potter's town then. Now it's Pottersville.

You asked why we moved here. We had had a minister friend in Eldo that we visited from time to time, a friend a Ginny's. We decided t' set down roots. Not easy in this soil, blurts Jake. Who would ever imagine it'd be right next door! amazes Tomás. And to think we invited you to our party, trying to be neighborly, remembers Carina. To think we hung out at the party, most a the evening, me 'n him, charlando, waitin' 'til you were both free—the place was mobbed. 'Til we got into the dance of Where You From? jumps Tommy. Until Pandemonium came up. The reading group—was that the clincher? wonders Serge. I can't tell if he's bored to death or rivetted by the conversation, neither or both. It was! The moment we both said, as if on cue— Ginny! You said, Jake?! And you said, Carina?!

22

I FEAR THIS WILL FALL in the wrong hands. People who won't get it, who can't, including meine kinder und enkelkinder und ihre kinder usw. My kids and grandkids and their kids etc. But how do you ever know where a thing will fall, if it's a seed to land on good soil, the right hands, after floating over time. Will it find a place? Take root with the right reader? I mean you had to be there, in a place night and day different than this country so how could people have a clue, I think the expression goes. Some times you gotta let sleeping dogs lie and this might be one. My kids use to ask me when they see me and Maria crying, when we talk our language, what was it like daddy? in the Old Country. Which I can never respond. It's about more than what happened to Vati and Zimmi, though that's plenny. To a ten year old learning about life, adult life especially, right there in the room. Its already enough but there were lots a other things I still have a hard time thinking never mind talking about, which is why Maria used to talk to me in a language the children didn't understand and never will. In unsere sprache, our dialect, the unique language of Frühling that I can't bring myself to write. Not even people in the mother country get it.

Like I say it was swampland. Everything we had we put there, timbers combined with mud and straw and effort, so we didn't freeze; that's how much they wanted to escape the Junkers, who knew how to exploit people. They come to Frühling and turned a waste land into the bread basket of Europe at the request of the Habsburgs, which they called the jewel of the east. The eastern miracle. No wonder no one wanted to rock the boat, allow in a ripple a change, including who sleeps with who behind close doors. Whatever they did was working, working for centuries, so why change?

Once Nikolaus and me knew what was what we remained tight lipped, can you blame us? I think we felt uncomfortable in the same bed after that, even though we were sleeping on the same mattress for almost a decade. I wondered, are we supposed to do it too, put this in that? I didn't want to, and when I finally ask, Niko says are you verrückt? Crazy? To mein and his relief. It wasn't until I come here I was able to ask why do I care. Me and Niko ate like princes, had four parents instead of two so twice, though the others didn't know, not for a while. If Nikolaus wasn't direct bruder blut or brother blood he was my brother still, and a cousin, because Trina my other mother was my aunt. Vati's sister. Mutti's spezielle freundin, one she lay with at night the way I did with Nikolaus, though different. Mutti filled my brain with pictures of Zimmi and Vati in the barn after the kirchweih, liebe machen, but she never mentioned her and Trina, two Katherinas, which was common in Frühling for girls. To be named Katherina. It seemed like all the women folk were Katherinas, though they went by their other names mostly.

Zimmi nailed Vati oder machte liebe. I dance with the idea still, after all these years. I danced with it in the fields in my teens while slicing wheat, corn, grapes and tobacco, but especially after the growing season when I had too much time. Me and Niko schlepped alongside Vati and Mutti, Zimmi and Trina, as though the six of us were lashed like cows. The routine was unchanging every day, every day except sontag, sunday. Wake before dawn. Slop the animals. Drag to the fields. Sweat. Drag home. Eat abendessen. Sleep.

Unlike most people we were tagelöhner, day laborers, and not bauern, landowners. Vati blamed his great-grandad for that, for being Frühling's first lehrer or teacher. He gave birth to the school in Frühling, but what good did it do? Vati use to complain, pounding his fist. If he didn't have kids it would a been one thing, but if you come to a dorf where working the land is the only thing, then you die there, without land, what good is it, for your kinder? So you can read. Where's that get you? What are your kids gonna do without hectares like the other people? Half or quarter hectares. Eighths even. Vati's namesake, Stefan, might a enjoyed reading, unlike most people in Frühling, and maybe he could run a school, but he doomed the rest of us to poverty greater than the other kleinbauern because how many teachers does a dorf need? A dorf like Frühling, with nothing but peasants—alle diese kleinbauern, Mutti use to spit. She liked to call them peasants I think because they had more than us, and we were bigger fodder for overseers who could boss, move us around, more easier than peasants.

I attended the school my great-great-granddad built, I couldn't write this if I didn't. Though I could go only in the winter when the field work ended, me and Niko both. Like Vati I could read. Mutti's family the Kleins come from Temeschwar already knowing how. First chance they get to own land that didn't got to be tilled, they snatched it. The same roadhouse where Zimmi and Vati got up to their high jinks, causing all the ruckus and nervous laughter, it's hard to say who the joke was on. What did Opa Andres think? He owned the place and sat in the band belting his clarinet. Did he have thoughts about what was right in front of him while blowing his instrument, along with the rest of the band? Did Oma Susanna have thoughts about Mutti, her only daughter, living the way she did? She's the only person come over we didn't rearrange for, who sat by who. For everyone else we traded places, putting on a show, including before Opa, so she had to know. Is it possible she didn't care?

23

Granted Opa was katolisch and she wasn't. What does it say about her people, who are my people? When I get to thinking that I'm from a family on Mutti's side with a history in Temeschwar going back a dozen centuries, long before the Swabians came, and that Oma didn't mind, what does it say? Did she reveal anything to Opa Andres? We use to play musical chairs when she come with him, but not when she come alone. I think Mutti might have been her favorite, the last born of a generation before they changed the law about people like Opa and Oma marrying in the first place. They were funny about things like that, back then, about who could marry who, what religion with what, like it mattered. I'm surprised I remember it now because I haven't thought about it, though if I'm honest there was no difference between Vati and Mutti and my other aunts and uncles around Frühling, and maybe they even got on better, despite or because of the difference in religion.

Vati's great-grandad and namesake, again my great-great-grandad Stefan, was in the first wave of people to make the trip along the Donau or Danube, before Frühling existed or had a name, but he wasn't the last. A decade later his brother come, and a decade after that the youngest brother traced their steps and stayed. The last one got right to making babies, in large part because he could. Frühling was settled and livable by then because the first ones did all the work, and also the Ottoman raids stopped so no one had to leave while the soldaten cleaned things up. The youngest brother had a dozen kinder, I mean imagine that. Each of them had a dozen and so on down the line, so that most people in Frühling with our name come from Onkel Franz, the baby. Though great-great grandad enjoyed reading his baby brother couldn't, but he had the last laugh, because what did people worship in Frühling more than kinder? Not how many books you read, sicher. Kids were your money; your afterlife. I had more schooling than my cousins, but thanks to Vati and Mutti my onkels got bragging rights where numbers matter, like they had pockets bulging with cash and liked to show them, die kinder, off at die kirche on Sunday and holidays. People never said, but I could tell they felt sorry for me because I had no brothers or sisters, which is when it struck home that Nikolaus only felt like one but never could be, though like I say he felt like the real thing and for that reason the two hundred some families in Frühling busting with offspring made us feel left out.

There were things that made us more different still. Although Mutti didn't go into detail, she swore I was made by Vati and only Vati, right around the time Nikolaus was fathered by Zimmi. Months later we entered the world only a few days apart and one of the first things Mutti caught eye of is that she fed me the same way a cow feeds her calf. Soon after I was born she got to thinking, which is a dangerous thing with her. That she and Frida, the kuhe or cow, were mothers the same way. That the cow's tits were no different than hers except in shape. It was then Mutti begin shying away from meat, starting with beef. Come the kirchweih that year and the usual slaughter she held Vati's hand when he went to do the deed to send Frida to the other world. Her calf was right there, moon faced and baying, old enough to manage on her own but Mutti couldn't bear the idea of depriving her her mutti, as though it were me having to get by without her. So Frida chewed her cud along with Effichen her offspring, which killed our chance of eating rindfleisch or beef at home, followed by schweinfleisch or pork, our two main options in Frühling, and ultimately any other kind of fleisch including hühnerfleisch or chicken, and all because Frida had tits like Mutti.

Mutti insisted. On never cooking animal fleisch in our home again, reducing the rest of us to taking advantage where we could, and Trina stimmte Mutti zu. She agreed. Like with most of what she said, like it was a conspiracy, forcing the male folk in our house to grab portions at baptisms weddings and funerals, man handling the buffet. Vati called it Mutti's Folly, a conspiracy of women, even child abuse to raise a son without meat yet here I am. I'm not a woman in case you haven't noticed so how would I know what Mutti saw in Frida, who continued year after year to offer us yogurt and cheese, and eier from the chickens because she refused to take their lives too after awhile. Mutti didn't mind depriving them of other things like time and energy—she made them work. We gotta do it, why can't they? To live is to work she said more times than I can count. I'm the one gotta feed them, all of us. They can give back.

A logic that must seem extreme from the floor to the ceiling. There was no one in Frühling with her scruples, though the message echoed with some, almost always other girls to the point there was talk of another epidemic, like the cholera or diphtheria. Instead it was a dietary disease threatening to infect the town, until people give it up one by one, everyone but us.

Despite das alles we still ate like kings. Better than we eat in this country. Straight from the cow and hens. Freshest eier with yolks the color of gold and not puddle water, nothing like the pale things here. If I were honest I'd say we eat better than most given Mutti's ability at the stove, the ceramic beast that sits across where you come in from the frost. She could make it whistle and pop, her and Mutti Trina. We ate different, but a lot. What I wouldn't give for her knödli und kraut this minute. Donuts made not with schmalz but oil. They were lighter—it only took more time than rendering schmaltz. Pilzterrine und tomatensalat mit käse und brot. Mushroom terrine and tomato salad with cheese and bread. I didn't just survive Mutti's Folly I miss it I admit. Maria tries, but I think we left Frühling too soon. I left with her family to Reschitz when I was a teen and not that long after, less than a decade, we were on a steamer here. To this country. In Maria's defense you would a missed out on cooking too if you were there. After twelve hours on the shop floor who has energy, and plus, Oma Fisch had everything ready when we got home. I felt a little guilty eating all that fleisch once I left Frühling, not being used to it, after having it only at baptisms and weddings. There I was eating it every day, too much to take. If Maria didn't have the time to learn from her mutti she tries to make up for it in Waldstadt, the Forest City, a place where women mostly tidy house and ready meals for the man.

24

The image that caused the to-do? The representation, expression, quotation, essai, or epitaph? Like I say it fetched thirty times what the old guy paid. Too bad he had no family to benefit, though he had an unrelated beneficiary, the name of which I never learned, given how the industry mums around sales like that. In fact once the painting, made increasingly famous, as though it alone defined what I did, who I was, what I aspired to—as a result of the manipulations of the market, the auction house, but also the torrents of abuse heaped on it by the zealots in congress, it waxed in price. The zealots called themselves the moral majority, especially the most vociferous among them, a senator from my home state by the name of William Bradford, a preacher from an eastern suburb on the outskirts of the Forest City. He railed in speeches against not just the painting but me, given I landed a grant from the government to pursue a new body of work that I was in the process of peddling to the very museum Molly and I used to visit, after I ditched school. He hammered away at the idea that a degenerate, a pervert like me, could lay hands on a penny of taxpayer dollars, such that I was required by the increasingly skittish committee either to switch my project or return the money.

Once the painting passed to private hands it took on a life of its own, though like I say I have no idea where it ended up; I know I shouldn't care, especially considering my feelings about the work, but I admit I can't help indulging my curiosity. It and I are estranged like Frankenstein and his monster, but I'm interested in tracking it. Which is impossible because like Peacoat, Ginny, and others it faded from my life, at least physically. I fantasize some priest coveted it, that he purchased it in secret precisely because of its "blasphemous themes," to quote Bradford and the bigots. Why else hide it, unless because of Bradford's tirades on the senate floor, about public funds wasted on trash—he spared no invectives, labeling the work and me dangerous, a threat to society, the way bigots do, strum an ominous note of fear and impending doom—Armageddon rising—because of a painting. Which only helped skyrocket the auction price. Did the unnamed buyer(s) have Bradford to thank for driving the bids so astronomically above book, creating a frenzy—I mean nothing causes a person to salivate for a thing like a prohibition, which Bradford was happy to provide. As the only member of that august body that was single, OK him and a senator from one of the Carolinas, he seemed to harangue an awful lot about what kind of couple should occupy a bed or mingle among sheets.

The market seemed to have a mind of its own; like it didn't give a fig for what Bradford thought, him or his god. At times it seemed the opposite was true; that it was playing off events like that, ones Bradford created. I imagine the painting was nabbed despite or maybe because of his tirades, designed to botch the sale, but especially some subsequent, future sale, one in which the final figure would multiply the value more still, during the incubation time in which the painting, with Tommy and me sprawled across it, limbs and torsos twined, our skins diverging; poxed and spotted—I imagine it, which is to say we, Tommy and I, sat in a closet, waiting for the fuss to die down. Or did that hypothetical Father, with his private quarters and private tastes, hang it in some locked room to which he alone holds the key, where he can ponder it, a viewership of one? Because, quibbling about scale aside, the thing was made to communicate—I'm speaking to you, Reverend Pastor. Oil baron. Floor trader. Eye doctor. CFO. Tribal chief. Sheik. TV producer. Celebrity actress. Quarterback. Hoopster. Broadway hitmaker. Dentist. News editor. Oligarch. Patriarch. Bishop. Madame President. Senator. Reverend Billy.

Bottom line, it sold. To someone. And for a weighty price that must have stood in stark contrast to the buyer given the emaciated figures inhabiting it. AIDS bodies. Which, far from sympathize with, Bradford condemned. He frothed, God's wrath is upon you! All you sinners! A scourge, bringing a plague upon this country. The miscreants are getting what they deserved, he pontificated in one of his floor speeches. Let that be a lesson—to people like me presumably. The fact the work was meant to be empathic, sympathetic—whatever the word is—never seemed to register. For he'd come under scrutiny of his own, in the courts and in the press, when two of the women in his former congregation accused him of an unsavory impropriety, accusations that not just he but other zealots neatly quashed. It came down to he-said-they-said; the death they alleged he caused occurred sometime before the charges were brought, causing the authorities to wonder why they sat on them so long; on a dead body; that the women harbored an unholy vendetta against the reverent, demon inspired; end of discussion.

The invectives mattered little to Tommy or me, protected as we were in our urban cocoon that quite frankly looked down on ranters like Bradford, coming from the boonies as he did, same as me; where people, never mind the market, focused on matters other than zealots could devise, especially one from a town bordering Laurentine. When Bradford brandished a reproduction of the painting in the chamber, people focused less on its immoral content than the immoral price it went for the night before, without a penny going to Tommy and me. It did nada for us, and did I mention my career was in a slump? Cap had sat me down quite some time before for The Conversation, in which he made it clear I might want to look for "other venues" to show in, given "the reality of the situation." I chalked it up to the number of times I refused him, on the Island in particular where he made advances toward not just me but Tommy too, and sometimes the two of us together. After some reflection I couldn't help but think that it had as much to do with the fact I'd lost the apple of youth, physically and professionally, given the age and sex of most of the artists Cap took in. I was middle aged and midcareer, the most perilous time in an artist's life, post-splash and pre-retrospective.

Save for the rare exception, no gallery wants you.

When the work went for what it did, several years after The Conversation, he was heavy with excitement, the first to phone before the hammer hit, while the price was hovering in helium and lilting higher. He was harboring on the auction floor—I could hear him panting as the bids came in. Ha, ha! he gushed. I handpicked him! I handpicked Jake! I *knew* he'd come home to me one day!—I could practically feel him salivating—Come home to me, baby! he moaned as the gavel came down at last.

You know you belong to me.

25

BUT I'D ALREADY GONE with another gallery by then, many times smaller than Cap's and many times less visible. Things were just starting to come together after a decade-long dry spell. Thank god I'd landed the teaching job or I would have made good on Tommy's mother's suspicions of a gringo-mooch and son-wrecker, in a city where two paychecks aren't enough to go on, especially given how Tommy'd been seduced by its blandishments.

Whatever windfall I reaped while at Cap Davisson Gallery early on, it went straight to loans, including the mortgage on our Kensington flat, halfway in the middle of the ocean it was so far out. The Pandemonium women warned me it could take the better part of a lifetime to polish off the loans, but I dispatched them in my twenties. Unfortunately, however, just surviving in The City incurs debt, and by that I mean the basics. We perennially withdrew from one ATM or another, just to make ends meet, almost every day. Machines dotted every corner, bank branches, bodegas, convenience stores, and restaurant lobbies, urging you to spend, then spend some more. It was interesting, the disconnect between the image of myself in the glass as the machine shot cash, compared to the picture Bradford painted in the senate hall. Until he didn't. Sadly, he contracted a rare form of cancer, as his obit noted, one that covered much of his body with lesions. The zealots were distraught in the extreme, to have lost, they said, one of the most upstanding members ever to grace that hallowed chamber.

In the middle of the hubbub both in the senate and on the auction floor, Geist Junior, of all people, phoned, inducing an even greater shock. It'd been decades since Romeo and I spoke, after which he called out of the blue, remarking in that inimitable FM voice of his, Yer old man died. Buckled. Crashed to the floor. Y'know, it caused one hell of a fuss. Shut down the entire goddam place, for the better part of an hour.

It was quite the fuss I gathered, considering Harry'd been slogging at Geist & Son for over half a century. His passing caused no small stir; among the old guard especially; women and men who'd kissed their youth goodbye there; some their virginity; lost a body part or two, eaten by the punch-presses—Finger-Eaters they called them. If Harry escaped the loss of a digit, something much more profound had been amputated over the years.

His hearing for one, almost entirely. Because he refused to wear protection you fairly had to shout to communicate, that or write it down. Only in his last few years at Geist had there been any concern, never mind effort, coming from Uncle Sam most of all, about prophylactic measures against the roar of the presses, punches hurtling along tracks, the flywheels groaning—it was never on the radar of the Front Office when I was there. Over the course of his tenure he lost touch in his fingertips, burned thousands or millions of times by the dies. His front teeth had gone AWOL, not to mention a row on the side, along with the dreams of his youth; hopes of a brighter day; belief in a god of goodness; good government; the love of a wife; faith in his son and daughters; the white world of privilege; the good old days— all wrecked like a vehicle abandoned in a ditch. He worked through his life the way he plodded through a shift; until he didn't. Dropped before the almighty press as the flywheels rumbled, shaking the floor beneath, not unlike a nation shaken to its foundations by a swindler, sworn to mendacity and his own self-interest; occasioning a seismic undoing, signaling a tragic turn to an experiment in living, flawed as it was.

Romeo added it was a while before anyone noticed the monster advancing on autopilot. It wasn't until Shirley, stationed at the press beside Harry's, stepped back to light a cigarette; catching out of the corner of her eye that something was off—the die continuing its journey, up and down, without a driver. She hit the emergency button, ran to a machine operating with the force of a meteor or an escapee from prison. She claimed later when asked why she allowed him to lie there so long, that she had a hunch something wasn't right but at first paid no mind. Then on figuring out the deal she gave a shout. After which first hers, then Harry's, then a handful, and ultimately all the other presses joined in a hymn of silence.

Someone breached the door of the Front Office to inform Geist senior, who charged junior with looking into the fuss. After calling an ambulance, the thought alone of which was enough to induce Harry to revivify and run off, that or pour a drink—the horror! Doctors! Which he'd never visited once in his life. Neither doctor nor dentist, audiologist nor dermatologist—he always claimed they'd be the ones to kill you—if he said it once he said it a thousand times. If it weren't for Florrie putting her foot down it's likely my sisters and I would have never seen the inside of a waiting room because physicians were out to get you, of that he was sure. You were better off avoiding them altogether because you went to a hospital for one purpose and one purpose only, and that was to die. Like the idea was written in his DNA; the single thing he adhered to like religion.

26

Soon as he knew, Romeo began the process of tracking me. His secretary called someone who called someone who called someone until he succeeded in ringing. Like I say it'd been years. The five kids, which I didn't know he had, were out of college, he bragged—soon the youngest would be married and out of the house. So if you ever want to visit. . . . he suggested. I'll have the place to myself. In fact we had an uncharacteristically warm chat, during which Romeo revealed he was divorced. He insisted I not be a stranger, next time I come to town—Or maybe I'll come down there and invade your place, he warned. After which I phoned Florrie, whom I hadn't spoken to since the letter I wrote in the trailer in Ojo—what had it been? Twenty? Twenty-five years?

What am I gonna do? she wailed. What's to become a me? Who's gonna take care a me? Why did he go and do this to me, of all people? And me such a faithful wife. She could have filled a cistern with her tears, large enough to irrigate my fruit trees here in Eldorado.

As soon as I hung up I phoned Wren, who pleaded that I get there soon—I mean pronto. Jake, she moaned. If ever I needed you. She's not even talkin' t' me, I countered. It ain't about you, Wren insisted. She ain't spoken to me a lot longer than she ain't spoken t' you. With Harry out of the way, she'll act chummy now—mark my words. But I can't handle her alone.

You got Donald, I reasoned.

Jake! Drop what you're doing and come! Now!

It was an inopportune time but I did as I was told. If there was any constant in life, my life, the entire arc of it, it was Wren, and now she was phoning in the favor. But in returning to the Forest City I was approaching a place I no longer belonged, at least in my mind, even though it belonged to me in some way I couldn't undo whether I liked it or not. And no matter. What I learned in the Queen City was that in the bureaucracy of death there's no room for feelings. Beefs or grudges. Chips or cracks in relations. Simmering piques. That or reflections on what might have been. There are only official hoops to dive through, given the way a death is above all an administrative affair, settling bureaucratic conundrums about what to do with the body, which came into the world X number of years ago and is now leaving X number of years later, leaving X number of people, but mostly X number of tasks to tend to, occasioning X dollars to spend—and quickly.

There was all that, all the questions about what to do with Harry, how he was to be disposed of, because a body can only put off the stench for only so long, akin to the stench of remembrance; and also because the church had given up its scruples about cremation, the way it gave up the prohibition of eating meat on Friday; creating options, at a time when options aren't always helpful. Given his Gaelic roots, there was the question of ritual, including feeding a crowd no one had seen in ages and Harry could give a fig for, much less know it was going on. There was no time to contemplate the decay of a thousand connections not made over a thousand opportunities. The way life starts promisingly and ends so heartlessly, as the singer says, even if in Harry's case there was a footnote to the story, about which more later.

With Harry planted in the ground finally; without a living, breathing body to contradict her; Florrie began the process of his sanctification; sailing right past the beatification. God help anyone who dared utter a word about her beloved, departed all too soon, in the very pink of life; leaving her bereft. She said there was no more tragic loss than that of a loving wife robbed of her husband, especially one in which there had been so many, many happy years together, many blessed decades in such a happy, happy marriage, and with so many more happy, happy years ahead. All stolen. Cutting her to the bone. When Diana rolled her eyes at yet another encomium about a relationship that no other human could ever hope to rival save that of the Blessed Mother's herself, sexless as that union was—when Diana dared to insinuate that it was Florrie who put Harry in an early grave, complaining like a fishwife about him for so many years the way she did, never giving the poor guy a break, driving him to drink—It definitely wasn't Geist Manufacturing, I can tell you that, she assured everyone. If anything, that place was his only refuge! When Diana landed that punch at the bereaved widow, still in the nightie she wore after the funeral, she approached her daughter feebly, looked her in the eye and slapped her hard enough to knock her to the floor. Which put everyone on notice—Tommy, Wren, Donald, Will, Uzuri, and me—it served notice that Florrie and the memory of her dear spouse was henceforth off limits officially.

That was one thing. The other was that each and every one of us, except for Donald, Tomás, Will, and Uzuri—meaning Diana, Wren and me—who for all those years did nothing but take, take, take, we were told, were from that moment on expected to give, finally, as it should be, given all Florrie did for us; in the form of a monthly check, no matter how we chose to work it; in order to provide for Florrie; her livelihood, mortgage, vehicle, hair appointments, and any other necessary expenses—we needed to pony up and for the duration, so long as she yet may live. It was on us, which as things turned out meant Wren and me, because Diana plum refused.

I ain't no meal ticket! You an' Harry should a planned for this. Don't expect nuttin' from me!

After all she'd been living a life a poverty in a community in the south, where they pared their needs to bare necessity— If you and Harry weren't so irresponsible, she complained. But all that's on you.

In fact Harry had planned, we learned years later, though Florrie calculated it wasn't enough, not to sustain her in a way that would maintain a lifestyle befitting her, leaving Wren and me with a choice once Diana bowed out, ignorant as we were of the nest egg Harry'd been sitting on. Wren reasoned the options were, A, let her starve; or B, find a way. To sustain her—there's no wheedling out of it, Jake. So far as I can see. Though I know we both want to. On the scale of family pariahhood, she and I ranked high, and I may have even outdid Wren because she at least produced a child, the entire purpose of living as far as Florrie was concerned; never mind the circumstances. Also she was now raising another as her own. Which by the by caused no small to-do among people that no longer communicated with Wren. We heard from a woman at the funeral that Florrie commented to her at one point, I told you! The guy's no good! See what he done! Went an' knocked up *another* girl, *another* one he wa'n't even married to. It didn't matter that Wren adopted her, unofficially at first and then officially.

Florrie was down to Wren and me, or we were down to her, never mind our history. It wasn't until decades later we learned Harry's nest egg was enough to keep Florrie happily for life, had she managed it. By the time it became clear she wasn't the best at planning, at stretching money, she'd already drained the entire amount, in a matter of a couple years, living high off the deceased Harry like a fly; renovating; spending on whatever she wanted; like a Laurentinian Cleopatra or Nefertiti. Like she hit the jackpot. Acquiring a mink stole, a new car, a pearl necklace, among other things; a cruise around the Hawaiian Islands. All while continuing to cash Wren's and my checks, which after a couple years she intimated were no longer enough to make ends meet—Not even my most basic needs, she pleaded.

I never asked for this—this cross! she railed on weekly phone conversations. To end up a poor widow, all alone! To think that one day I'd find myself having to write checks!—me! of all people!

Wren made weekend trips to Laurentine, taking time from an unforgiving schedule that didn't understand the concept of a day or even hours off, for parental day care, carving out time on weekends to check on her birth mother. Initially she brought Uzuri, who quickly complained that White Granny scared her. So Wren left her with Donald, who said in her defense, What in the world would she have to do with, let alone owe, that woman?

Once when Will was in town she dragged him too, the sight of which made Florrie cry. I don't get it! she wailed. You were such a fine young lady when I met you that time on Liberty. With such a *pretty* face. Why would you wanna go and do a thing like that. Which made Will cry on the drive home—that was a rarity. The idea of an old lady on her mother's side who'd occupied a null set to him his entire life—And now she comes along—out of the clear blue! Thinks she has the right to say *a thing* about my life!

To be honest I wonder what they might have said, transition aside; liberation. Will and Florrie being perfect strangers; more strangers-on-the-street than stranger-relations; in that their entire history was one of estrangement;

intentionally on Florrie's part. How do you surmount a wall like that? An abiding, lifelong disaffirmation the nature of which was so pointed, so focused, and so dismissive. Never mind the working-out that Will and Wren were dealing with themselves at the time, also estranged in a way; Wren, and in a sense both of them, grieving; in different ways and not about Harry.

One thing I knew was a no-go was any reckoning with decades lost. I figured Florrie missed that sermon at daily Mass, which after Harry's passing she took to attending, sometimes twice a day. Which made sense I guess because god was her man now, given Harry'd gone and abandoned her. As though he'd never been her man in the first place, even as he was paradoxically the best a woman could ever hope to have. It didn't occur to her to lift a corner of the blanket on the past, what it meant to ditch a daughter; take refuge behind her husband; avoid breaking rank long enough to check in, at any time; wonder how Wren was doing, not just on her wedding night, once it finally happened, but the delivery, and after; including the many stages in a child's life, which is to say a mother's. Not only was that never broached, the past and so much more, but the present too. Who Wren was; her husband and family; how they lived; what brought them together in the first place; what it was like then, the blush of youthful affection; what they lived for; how they handled the challenges that society was known to present; where they hoped to go. Florrie inquired about none of it, including the doubling of Wren's offspring; what might have precipitated it and why they chose to stay together; whether it was a personal failing of one or both their parts; a flaw in society; or no flaw at all; a mere fact of life; possibly a guy thing, no different from Jake or Tommy; or something else entirely; a person thing; nature being on us all; a simple case of mutual liberation; as bare bones as that. Was it a reaction to the way life boxes you in, inducing you to rebel? Or was it something else, occulted or obvious? Some umbrageous chip, or embracing life while you can. Selfishness or kindness. A gift. Recognition of bare matter. There were no questions about that or anything, what it was like to be moving up in the world after so many years in the trenches, literally saving the Forest City in a sense, her and Donald both, in different ways, along with a cadre of like-mindeds, monitoring the pulse of the city; its rhythms, demographic shifts; depopulation and povertization; followed by gentrification. What life was like as the head of a philanthropic; or for Donald with his burgeoning career at the national paper; the sole thrust of their careers being to right the failings of American-style democracy in some small way, which is to say American-style greed; hierarchy; developers dishing red-meat capitalism as Serge calls it; as blind to justice as you can get, and Donald as its scribe or griot, tracking, commenting on a world of changes occurring faster than the couple could hope to comprehend, storying it all in the pages of not just the local but the Nation's Newspaper, the Paper of Record, now gone digital, changes traveling around the world, as fast as light. How life was going in Midge's old home, the one Harry used to say needed to have a bomb dropped on it, along with the neighborhood, and the entire city, in order to start from scratch, as though that were ever possible—truth be told the place was looking a lot more desirable, more marketable than Laurentine these days with its fallen gutters, browning lawns, matchbox homes, and graying residents; especially among the youth of the city. To everyone but Will, who, like his uncle decades before, wanted out. At least part of the year.

27

NONE OF THAT WAS DISCUSSED or even entertained during Wren's visits to Florrie's, who for all intents and purposes was a stranger, some old lady she never knew. A charity case. In fact with Florrie there was no need for discussion because if someone needed an ear it was her—I never wanted to end up like Ruby, and now look! she wailed.

I know all this from phone conversations with Wren, but truth be told she didn't need to say because some things you know in your gut; that the sun will ascend tomorrow; that it's often obscured by clouds. Which didn't stop Wren from spelling things out, at times ranting on her freeway drives from Laurentine along windy Route 2, then Liberty, or MLK Boulevard.

The woman's a total narcissist! Do I even exist to her?

Did you ever?

No I didn't and I do not! You either, Jake.

For me it didn't matter because I didn't have to see her, so I had it easy. All I had to do was write a check and drop it in the slot, month after month; pay dues in the form of a call on Sunday evenings mostly. I could set the phone down and waltz around our Brooklyn apartment, cooking, cleaning the bathroom, even vacuuming, trying to get things done while she held forth—unlike Wren who had to sit there and appear engaged. For me, it was a matter of returning to the handset when I heard across the room, Hellllll-ooo-ooo! Are you there? Jake?! After all, she only wanted to know I was on the other end, listening and not speaking.

Even before the break between us I sensed I didn't exist to her, as Wren said, other than as a cut-out marked "Son," whatever that meant. Diana used to complain I got special treatment because I was male, but I never saw it. What's more, upon discovering she had a certain kind of son she split, the way I lit out on her, decades ago. I still can't excise the image Diana painted when Wren and I were old enough to understand, about visits we used to make to our great-grandpa Jakob, my namesake's, home. Wren and I were too young to remember, unlike Diana. Apparently we were fidgety; busting our leggings; cowed into submission; read the riot act in the car as we pulled up the drive—we had the daylights scared out of us, as Diana noted in a voice cold as math, all so we would make a good impression on Great-Gramps and Gramma Maria. A couple not long for this world, Harry used to say; a couple with a nice big house. Diana remarked she actually felt sorry for us, as if it were possible; for Wren for sure but even me; catching the fear in our eyes, glued to the spot. We were arranged like cushions across the back of the davenport, facing relatives from The Old Country, whatever that meant, ancients who spoke with an accent, whatever that was. She said Gramma Maria even used to comment, Florence, why are they so still? Shouldn't they be tearing up the place? Breaking things? Making a mess?—They're babies for pity sake! To which Florrie replied, Not my kids.

Not like that.

So the disconnect began early I reckon, before I realized, starting with her denial of not just a boy's but a girl's energy, both part animal. It mushroomed from there, the disconnect, over decades, to the point I grew dead to the subject of Florrie. And yet I mailed the checks, though after a while I addressed them to Wren, who combined the amounts in one figure. To make matters worse for Wren, I often had no words during her drives home. All I could muster was, You know you don't have to.

You're not a mom, she countered. If you were you wouldn' say that.

Isn't a sense of motherhood the bone Florrie lacked? I protested. Our whole life—I said that.

Granted, it's flawed. But—. She tried.

Funny hearing that from you—

—It's only three or four hours a week. I ought to be able to cope.

But are you?

So long's I can complain to you. I have a daughter, Jake— she said that. Two. I mean one—I still forget. Though I try not to—which only goes to underscore my point. I hope they, Will, will forgive me someday.

After which, what was there to say?

In a whole other universe which unfolded, parallel to the one we live in, stretching out and expanding over time, with Harry gone in the irrevocable way that death deals, that one-way street you never get to joyride down the wrong way—with him gone I was able to finally get to know him. It was an intimate process, with several hurdles to overcome— granted. I mean, how do you cozy up to a racist? A sexist? An antisemite? And a homophobe? How do you find your way over or around those hurdles? But it's correct to say I came to view him differently, minus the synthetic glow in which Florrie cast him. He remains all those things, in all their unglory. And yet I came to view him differently, warts and all, slurs and slights. Wren and I both began that journey, albeit with bumps along the way, so that now, years hence, I believe we've come to view him in a new light, though I'll leave it to Wren to explain for herself how she feels, which reason suggests would be different from me, twins or no twins.

Two events sparked the process in my case, events that loomed only after he passed. One occurred on a visit to the Forest City with Tommy. We were walking around the newly re-filled, which is to say newly re-laked or re-lagooned reservoir along Liberty, or what was called Liberty in my day, before it became Martin Luther King Boulevard. Wren fought to have it restored; debris cleared; so that now people dot the edge, cool their legs on a summer day as if posing for a pointillist mural. Tommy and I took a seat on a bench, newly installed, waterside, and who comes along but the devil himself. I nearly fell off my seat, not just eyeing Harry but watching him approach and assume a spot, there at the other end. I wondered, Do I know you? It was one of those out-of-body moments you don't know whether to believe or dismiss. But it was the physical, corporeal, embodied Harry, the real thing and not some haint.

Tommy and I stood up.

What in the world?

Huh?

I repeated myself.

Wha' d' y' mean, What'm I doin' here? I live here, don' I? Not here azackly, in Laurentine. Here in a way—I use t' spend a lotta time here when I's a kid. Me an' your mother both.

But you—

—Name's Harry, by th' way.

Tomás. Mucho gusto.

Huh?

Pleased to meet you.

Sorry it's taken s' long—

—Dad!—

It never dawned on me that running into us was a mistake, encountering Tommy and me, that it wasn't us he came to see, except by some cosmic blip, unknown to him and us both. It wasn't until after we'd been talking for some time, awkwardly as one might expect, that I realized he'd probably happened by, on that particular turf, pointedly looking for someone else, as the case turned out to be, who by then had changed quite a bit, but who still came out on his own, bird-glass in hand. That is, when Will was in town.

When it finally dawned on me I commented, You know they live just up the hill. You've been there enough times.

Huh?

I repeated myself a little louder.

Lemme do it my way.

You don't think he'll be freaked to have a strange man come up to him, just like that? Someone he never met and has zero memory of?

I got no idea. God knows I freaked out—is that what they say?—a couple other young guys, though not 'tentionally. I guess the picture I got from Diana is a little old.

You want me to go get him? He's at home—

Jake! Promise you won't, that you ain't gonna tell—How are yous boys by th' way? Yous OK? Need anything? I saved a li'l after all these years. You ever need sumpin'—

We spoiled things for him, cover most of all, and I felt bad, knowing how I'd probably react despite Harry's wishes. Until he gave both me and Tommy a peck on the cheek when we parted, then a kiss on the lips, plus a handshake that held ten twenties, bills that flew higgledy-piggledy when our hands unclasped.

Grab 'em, Jake! Tommy and I were scrambling and darting, doing our best to capture the notes fluttering like melancholy butterflies, twirling and swooping—we netted them back.

When we finally grabbed the last one I tried to return them, but Harry refused, and in fact I still have them, to remind me in empirical terms the event occurred, that it wasn't a fantasy or wishful thinking—it was no small sum for him and Florrie both, I was sure. Anyway Tommy and I kept mum as we vowed, though I was sure I wouldn't, remain mum until he was in the ground, the timing of which in retrospect is curious, even particular, given he was dead only half a year later; as if he possessed a foresight about what was to pass. It haunts me, whether he got the chance to talk to Will directly—god knows they haven't said a thing. Neither has Wren or Donald. And yet again, Will's a funny one, holding their cards to their chest—I can never get a bead on them. They were never one for sharing, especially with an uncle they have so little connection to in the scheme of things, including when we co-occupied The City, given they were uptown and we were cross-river—to anyone from there it feels like different worlds. Of course I spilled the beans to Wren in time, what went down, who for sure would have told me back then if Will and Harry met. Wouldn't she?

After time and Harry went the way of all others, enough to begin reworking the math about him, put two and two together in a novel way—after that I began rethinking not just him but me, as he'd obviously done some time before. What was it? Age? Intuition? Fear? Worse? Or better? What prompted a rethinking of what it meant to be both father and grandfather? He seemed a shadow of himself, life's damaged goods, with his bad hearing and missing teeth. He'd made only one concession in his campaign never to consult a doctor, and that was to see an optometrist, though the glasses he wore, no doubt the freebies that came with the factory plan, sat askew on his nose, slant across the face, to the point I wanted to straighten them for him.

I remember thinking, This is who conceived me. Fed me when I couldn't feed myself.

28

As the philosopher says on the subject of gifts, it was thing unplanned, unknown, and unwished for at the time, on all our parts, I reckon; an event evading the economy of trade, exchange, much less capital. He hadn't come to see us, nor we him, and most of all none of us understood in the moment what it was; not until years later; on both my and Tommy's parts; perhaps Harry's too; beyond the grave.

29

WHEN I WAS IN PRIMARY school my father walked me in the morning and fetched me in the afternoon, until I put a stop to it. When I was old enough. For the other kids it was their moms who dropped them off, though by luck or design my father did with me. I don't know how I could've done it if Wren took me because it would've blown my cover, revealed something I didn't want out there, namely that my mother was white.

I mean the kids already had their suspicions. They used to ask, What are you? Why you so light? To which—try answering. At that age. I didn't want my mom taking me no-how, and my father intuited it, or so I like to think.

He took me to sleepovers, parties, bowling, skating, and anywhere else I needed to go, thanks to his unstructured work hours and the fact that my mom's job was demanding in a different way. It wasn't until middle school the shit hit the fan, when they started student-parent conferences in earnest.

I wanted to die.

I pleaded with Wren, You don't need to come! It's enough if daddy's there—you only need one parent, I'm sure. It can even be Grandpa Lloyd or Grandma Delma! But lucky me; she insists on coming. Like I say that's when the shit hit the fan, when I was outed, turned into a freak among my peers. The shit hit the fan; the names started in earnest. Suspicion morphed into knowing that couldn't be undone.

My girl Tariqua stuck by because she had a white dad. But the others.

By the time I got to Morningside I was done with black and white. Blaque Life tried to recruit me, said I had to join; watch who I hung with; something they didn't need to elaborate on because I knew what they meant. But I was done with the rules of association. I hung with the Jewish girls, Spanish, and Indian, who didn't have a problem with what I was and who in a way I resembled. I was always around white people as a kid because of my mom, but it wasn't until I was a senior in college that I had my first white friend, the real deal. It took that long. I'm talking about a friend-friend, the kind you tell things. It wasn't 'til Kristian came along that I started to think things more complicated than I'd allowed. Not too long after I met Serge, who, let's face it, is a weirdo. Does he have a clue about the rules of association? Rules, period? He's all, I'll decide what makes sense. How is a person like that possible? Either his parents did something right or something terribly wrong because he's strange that way.

With Uzuri the story's more complicated. She's younger for one. And because of her mom and where she come from she doesn't question herself the way I do. Maybe because she came into a situation at such a young age, there in The City, before her mom passed, that she was able to see things differently than I was able, at least 'til I was grown. We couldn't be more different, but we get it, each other. I think blood helps. I worked hard in therapy, trying to convince myself that the reason my father had her wasn't because he missed the old me, or that I was a half-breed. I need to get over the idea, that there's such thing as half-anything, except in the mind of bigots. Where else would I have gotten the idea, given how they never stop harping? Every time you open a paper or turn on a TV.

Anyway I worried my father was jonesing for the real thing; that he missed with me; that he had regrets; that my half-sister was a way of righting a tilting ship. When I finally confronted him, after years of talking about it with my shrink, his reaction was like, Oh! Really? You serious? Then: No way. It was simpler than that, he said. Tamarra wanted a kid and I gave her one. He didn't go into the ins and outs—he had the nerve to say it wasn't any of my business. But he was emphatic in saying I was the girl of his dreams, then apologized for putting it that way. He said that Uzuri was different, a gift to him too, but Tamarra mostly, who wanted a child but not a husband; that she was now a gift to the family, a family of four, with a son and daughter.

30

When I met the guy I wasn't lookin 4 nothin cept a good time, a wild ride and a course someone with a good one, we were all on the hunt for that then. The dick a death 😛. I definally wasn't lookin for no gringo para nada, I was happy so I didn need it. Someone who spoke my language if ya know what I mean 😛 and expecially not some egg head. But like I says here come this paddy outta the blue on the side of the lake and I din't know what come over me but I says 2 myself go 4 it. It wasn't my first time with no anglo nohow but the first time I can say I like it. For lotsa reasons. Maybe cuz he seem so broken, like I thought this guy needs help. He seem like some wounded duck an I guess I felt sorry 4 him. & he was a wild 1. I didn't know he was on the run from his life from god knows what or where, who ever talks about that or anything at a time like that? including asking a guy's name. Who talks period? I still don't get it, why I went 4 him, like I gone loco. I mean he's different, almost 2 different for me, más diferente than I know what to do with most a time, I mean a handful.

Like I says I don't know nada. Why I show up at his trailer that time and then when I met his twin & her family. So I skipped out. Like I couldn't do it. You know, It. Everything. Like seein his twin & her spouse, them & la niña, was demasiádo, too much. He prolly thought it was the meat thing but that's his prollem. He's hung up about it, feels guilty like he took it away from me. Like

159

I don't have la inteligencia to pick 4 myself but it weren't that. I liked el cabrón, fuck him. I did fuck him. Don't ask why. Like I entered the twilight zone all these years livin with a gringo and after so many before him, not to brag but 1000s and all unlike the gringo or he was like none a them. He was practically una monja or una religiosa. Like ascético. And seein his twin hitched so tight I was affected profundamente, I just wasn't ready 4 none a that, I mean we made un pacto, my sissies & me. I knew it was all or nothin that's just how I roll. Don't think it was anything 2 do with mis padres or la tradición as it is with so many en el barrio it was none a that. That or god god forbid. What did any of that do 4 me? I mean I still haven't had La Conversación with mis padres an prolly never will.

31

ALTHOUGH MI MADRE was religious we never went to la iglesia as much as his family, not til Gabriela got older. I went to una escuela publica, public school not católica like him so I didn't have no BS like that. Also Lita and Pop back off from la iglesia in Las Nieves, though for the longest time I didn't know why. My father never would allow me 2 b an altar boy when I was growing up, & sometime I wondered why he is so against it. Only thing I know is that 1 by 1 the families in Las Nieves start 2 distance themself from the church. Some become methodist, some luthern, some aleluya types, total holy rollers. When I ask Lita one day if something happen, why papi was so against me being an altar boy, she barks, hijo no hagas tantas preguntas! Don't ask so many questions. That was always what she said when it had to do with the church. Including why it become empty over night, why people change religion, what happen when the penitantes met in the chapel on the hill.

One thing that never change for Lita was her religión. Her novenas, rosary every day, raising the May altar. She make Pop pray b4 each meal until I was grown. We prepared the farolitos every nochebuena, putting them out like the rest of el pueblo in anticipation of la navidad, and we even made a trip to the outside of the church to see the livin manger. At la pascua we did the stations behind the guy draggin the cross. But we never enter the church, not until the pastor pops a clot and some other guy takes over.

We were religious in a different way than mi niño. Like avoiding la iglesia was more than just a thing, it was more private than the gringos who are in it mostly for show no judgement. Like Lita thought different about la religión, la que es algo más que un simple edificio. More than a building or a lot a ranting about what everyone else should do.

4 me the idea of a man in the sky who knows all your thoughts and gives a crap about everything, including who wins el partido de futbol, who's side he's rooting, someone who causes a flood when he gets mad 2 get U back it never made no sense. I mean it makes not just the gringos pero todo el mundo totalmente loco that thinking. Pero no es lógico. And plus who wants 2 ever be en el cielo with a guy like that, some old geezer with a grudge against just about everybody? A god whose always mad as a hornet and lookin to rain down fire. El dios de abuelita, he's differen. I mean take Jake's madre. She din't talk 2 her son 4 decades when she find out. Like her frumpy god mater more than el amor de una madre. Like a group of bad hombres or viejos maricones infelices, unhappy queers en Roma matter more than her own. Unlike abuelita who knows whats up and whats down. El bien y el mal.

So I got hitched 2 a gringo of all things b4 what we did was even legal, on sissy's account, and after she spent so much time trying 2 split us up. Maybe she saw the writing on the wall like el padre de Jake, like Polly realize it wasn't in the cards for her, I mean her an me. I think she wanted me en secreto, and she couldn't think a me old and wrinkly and still chasin cock without her there to hear about it. Maybe she din't trust me or she got to thinkin that her & me was a dead end street sooner or later and here was this guy who actually got a thing 4 me. She push, push Jake an me 2 say the words, different from another promise Manuel and I made long before Jake and me met. So I got what I wanted, namely steady cock though I didn't know I wanted what came with it, dick a death or no dick a death. I can't believe I'm saying this and don't tell noone but it's about more than that. Sissy would b really pissed 2 hear me say it.

I got un artista un lector loco y La Ciudad. Cuatrocientos pies cuadrados, y el mundo. Four hundred square feet and the world in The City. So did Lita, that was divertido. If I did anything 2 thank her 4 what she did 4 me an Jake it was that, I give her La Gran Ciudad, the Big City, which is the world really, I'm tellin U, or una versión pequeña her an me taking the gringo world by storm me an Lita, ownin the bitch as the kids say, everything it has 2 offer, which doesn't belong 2 the gringos even though they think it does, all the land, water an air, which they stole, all of it, along with motherhood, fatherhood, dios y la virgen, historia y cultura, arte, la política, la tele y las películas, movies, they think they own it all. Todas las cocinas, la gastronomía de las culturas del mundo, around the world, which they suck in like a black hole.

Lita and me took it back.

32

Hace quinientos años, 500 yrs ago, mis padres brought the world with them when they settled in La Tierra Montañosa de las Nieves de Nuevo Mexico en el Nuevo Mundo. It was a lot more than the Anglos brought 2 these shores. They come from Irlanda y Inglaterra but mis padres straggle in from el mundo entero, España seguro, pero Africa también, Arabia, all the way to India and China, but mostly from Russia across the land bridge 1000s of years ago, headed south and becoming indígenas, mestizos, and more categorías than I can count. We carry the world in our blood so in fucking me Jake he's been fucking el mundo the world. El diós sabe what I been fucking in him, what his blood brought with him aquí en Eldorado.

Me and Skye of all people. Who would a guessed we both come from Santa Ágata, though my people got out long b4 her, mixed with los Mexicanos and now here we both are back together, livin in Eldorado in eye shot of the Sangre de Cristos, in this place that everyone thinks is gringo heaven.

Anyway 2 Lita La Ciudad was just another version a Las Nieves only más grande so she an me felt right at home. Unlike Jake who finds La Ciudad way too much. Until he meets Sergio. Then he starts to like it a more. What happen only dios knows. Think I care? We all have our secretos I mean if Las Nieves taught me anything its that you can live in a pueblito in bumfuck America where you think everyone know your business and you still don't know crap, in a town of a hundred people. Incluyendo why they stop attending la iglesia. Not until you're gown and figure it on own your own. What I know is Jake brings it home when I want it the rest is his thing, though sometime I wonder. La Ciudad, though. Era una prostituta, un puto that never stops giving. The hard part is sayin no an lets face it you gotta grab la oportunidad when it come your way. Never mine the timing.

La Ciudad give me el arte most of all, la comida, arquitectura, moda you name it. Joyería. Lots a jewelry. It was Lita who says to me when she first arrive, after she flies for the first time in her life, Mijito, she says, Own esta mierda. Own this shit she says. It's yours. All of it. Don't let nobody tell you nothin else. Which she didn't have to say out loud because I already knew, but I got it. Unlike Jake who feels like the outsider en La Ciudad and everywhere, including aquí en Eldorado. Like places are 4 everyone but him. No matter he took it by storm at first. ¿Qué le pasa a este tipo? Lita use 2 say. What's wrong with this guy? I mean he's like the rest a the anglos. And he don't wanna partake. She wasn just talkin about the meat thing at the restaurantes we enjoyed her and me. I apologize to Jake 4 it, para la festival de la carne, but 2 be honest Lita saw things different than Jake, coming from Las Nieves. So I was in the middle between those two though I don't want 2 make more of it than it was. Lita warmed up 2 niño once she get 2 know him an I'd even say the two liked each other an got each other except 4 the meat thing which made no sense 2 her nohow. 2 the point I use to think that all the wild ordering of todo eso on her part use to be a kind of preaching, like she was into another kind a religión but if there's one thing Jake can't take it's religion a no kind. Includin meat religion so it was a waste of time on her part, if that was really her thing. I use 2 say Lita! No necesita comer carne siempre!

I mean they never ate that way in Las Nieves. Like I says she mighta a been tryin 2 make a point, or like she doesn like the no meat thing so much as he dislike the no meat religion on niño's part which is what it was 2 her. After all those years we've been together with Jake doing most of the cooking I gotten used 2 it that's all I gotta say. Though I resent Jake making me think about it because I was happy not 2. I use 2 pat his thigh when he realize there wasn nada on the menu 4 him but what I wanted 2 do I admit was hit him for taking away the fun of not thinking. Until at 1 point I says 2 Lita Lita tal vez necesitemos un descanso de todo esto. Maybe we need a break. I let on that it had 2 do with the money which in a way it did. I din't wanna tell her though how I really feel or she'll think I've gone soft, 2 the white side. She says look where u work an look how yer dressed u must make more money than el dios! But after a point I just couldn't do it no more 2 my niño.

So Lita does the next best thing she takes Jake's hand to teach him how 2 cook her food pero con las diferencias. It was interesting to watch her in our piso in Brooklyn. How to make her favorite things sin carne without meat I mean your kidding me. She keeps askin, Es pollo OK? Pescado? Mariscos? And each time Jake says no no an no like he's a robot. No seas estúpido! Lita says when she realizes he feels bad. Es lo que es it is what it is. So she makes a list to get at the Safeway on Atlantic for the basics and Sahadi 4 chili & spices, the Asian store 4 bean curd. After all them meals Lita has a formula in her head a way 2 make do. Decades later what she showed him is what we eat and when Sergio come into the picture he has 2 adjust after all the cabbage an potatoes he knows, carrots and beets, so he 2 was Litafied I mean she still lives with us cada día in what we eat every day. Like she's cookin meatless for us. 2 the point that I'll kill anyone who tells Jake this but I don't miss carne and am even OK without it. Its possible the idea of it even turns mi estómago ahora. I eat it when we go 2 other people's homes in Eldo because so many people say they feel sorry 4 me and U gotta go with that where U can get pity. But I don enjoy it like I used 2. It even sits uneasy with me 2 the point I don't sleep after and I wonder why did I even do it cuz now I got the acid. I been eatin sin carne 4 so long an I aint getting any thinner.

No one our age is interested in copyin Jake. Debra and Cinthia come to it on their own ages ago. Carina too don't forget. OK Wren them two decided early on an Wren decide 4 Will who never had a bite his whole life. Everyone else we know outside a the family so 2 speak they tolerate the food here but they ain interested. I forget about Serge. How in the world he make that transition over there in meatland I got no idea an maybe thats one reason he an mi niño hit it off. Like I says people feel sorry 4 me so when the 2 a them go on their trips they have me over and say I don know how U do it tu pobrito U poor thing 2 never get meat at home. They slap down a Roman orgy with a mountain a flesh of all the usual kinds. I don't wanna be rude so I says thanks a 1,000,000 because I got a image 2 live up 2 but I slip in also that I like Jake's cookin. I accept the pity along with a glass a vino tinto, which we also stopped imbibing Jake and me, doing my best to make it through the ordeal until I get home when sure enough the acid starts big time. Sometime people say to me right in front of Jake less go for lunch we can eat meat youn me. Even Lita wasn't that cold though she did love the carne, I think because she has it so rarely and can eat it any time she visited La Ciudad, unlike in Las Nieves. It's just it takes her a while to figure out what she's dealing with with Jake. After she figure it out she just gets on with it.

33

WE'LL DO IT DIFFERENTLY today, I remarked, after Kenney and I talked about it. You'll disrobe for us. He goes, You want me to do what? You heard me. I'm sure you don't want to see this—he motions toward his midsection. You see us, week after week, says Kenney. Now it's our turn. Ohhhh boy. I don' knoooow. What do you mean you don't know, repeats Kenney. You don't have a choice, not if you want us back. Jake blushes, looks distraught. I've never done it before. Then you're overdue, I remarked. D'you need help? I reached my arm forward and Jake takes a step back, almost tumbling on the modeling platform.

It's been awhile . . . in front of other people. Take your time, I assured him. To be honest I wasn't sure about the whole thing myself, and I think Kenney wasn't either. But it had been ages of working with him, and something seemed out of whack. He saw us, but—it wasn't equal. How many times had he painted me and Kenney, in one iconic pose or another, including what was down there? Though the paintings were small, you could still see me, showing out. How many times, if ever, had he thought about clothes, the meaning of them, why I wear what I wear, to cover up an imbalance? Had none of his models ever addressed it before? As though the fee were a firewall against questions.

Slowly he begins to unbutton his shirt, then stops. As though something's wrong. I look at him and he renews the effort until he's arrived at the last buttonhole, after which he removes it. He unbuckles the belt holding up the jeans, unzips, then lets them drop to the concrete. He struggles to raise the tee over his head as Kenney and me peer on—Let us know if you need help, Kenney comments.

I can do it. Just gimme a minute.

He takes stock of what he's revealed, says he needs to get some cream. For what? I wonder. Age spots? I was thinking more of dry skin, he replies.

After his tee clears his head he glances at his stomach, which protrudes in a way he must have seen in the mirror for some time, a thing he has known for a while. So different than decades ago, he mumbles. With Peacoat. What's happened to me?

Who's Peacoat, Kenney queries.

Someone I knew.

He takes note of the fact he has breasts.

Keep goin', padre, Kenney coaxes. We wanna see it all. Jake's standing in his briefs and stockings. His legs look like two straws plucked from a bale, too weak to hold the pear of his torso. His skin wrinkles and sags, from age but dryness too in these parts, as though he needs to wallow in a tub of lotion. Where his tee was he notices a farmer's tan, and a second, paler one at the wrists. The muscles of his upper arm droop. Hair covers the tops of the shoulders and sides of the back when he reaches behind.

Why are you stopping? I wonder aloud. Kenney and I stand apart, observing.

Risk, gimme a moment.

Again he pauses then lets out a long, slow breath, and resumes. He removes the socks followed finally by the briefs. As they clear the ankles he has to steady himself against the wall to avoid falling. He glances down, aware that his penis has shriveled, which I suspect is the opposite of what used to occur in days gone by when he used to disrobe. At the moment it seems it's trying to hide.

Silence fills the room as Kenney and I circulate, taking in Jake's body as he stands there, hands at his sides, shoulders slumped, as though he were being scolded or corrected, atoning for something, a lifetime of something, the way he's been observing Kenney and me time after time, unclothed. Tears flood, blur his vision, so he wipes them—Jake, honey, I say. Why all this? Do you see us crying? Have you ever? More tears fall, silently, though he protests he doesn't know why.

Do you feel threatened?

Do you think we're being malicious?

Why should you?

Why should I? And yet.

And yet—what?

I've been asking people to do it my entire career.

 So what is it?

I started by asking Peacoat, and briefly Romeo before him. Then Dan and Emil, in the trailer in Ojo.

Was there ever a time it didn't feel right?

Every time.

Then why'd you do it?

It's a lot more than "just because," he muses, air-quoting. More than a kinky curiosity—I didn't need it for that. More too than dumb tradition, the fact painters and sculptors have been doing it for thousands of years.

Then why? Kenney prods.

I don't know. Voyeurism maybe—I don't deny it—it's not the same as kinky curiosity, though I guess it can be. Doesn't every art exist for voyeurs? Isn't every person who reads the papers one? Readers of novels, the gossip pages? Watchers of nightly news? Everything on line—could there be a more voyeuristic realm? Jake looks small, like he's being pinched by demons and is trying to protect himself. Maybe I'm making excuses, trying to justify what I do. Maybe I'm trying to find something, that I'm paying you to help me find it, though I don't know what I'm looking for. Something beyond clothes, which is to say culture. Something other, past what people put on. But is it even possible? Does it exist, a something-beyond? Or does it stop at what we see, what we feel? Is there anything real?

Can't get much realer than this, I replied, gesturing toward him.

More reality than I can handle, really—I mean, look at me.

How does it happen, with all the mirrors in the world?

I have no idea. It takes over, like a thief. I guess you look backward, imagine things haven't changed, that they're just the way they used to be; you try and live there.

Week after week you ask us to do the same, so we can't forgot any of this—Kenney touches his chest. Clothing, how it lies, but also tells a truth.

I didn't—at last—I hope I haven't.

Now you know.

Shall we hang out this way a while?

Do we have to?

I still don't understand why you feel so weird. A body's a body? Isn't that your mantra? How you lured us? Sweet-talked us?

Why should it be any harder for me than you?

You tell us.

It was clear Jake was uncomfortable, shivering even; that a single time wouldn't do for him what had taken multiple session for Kenney and me, made us comfortable under the gaze of another, that abyssal force, Jake's or anyone's eye, first a stranger and now less so, prodded—still—by the need for cash. I didn't want to tell him how the experience had changed me, in part because like him I couldn't articulate it. I only know I'm not the same person disrobing in front of him as I was months or was it years ago when we started this project. To expose yourself to another, and not for sex. To work through the shame and embarrassment that goes with it, at least initially, and for what? Something common as air.

Cover up old man—do you mind me quoting Serge?

Go for it.

So . . . . How do you want us today? queries Kenney after a pause. We should get started; I got my gyno today so I'll need to leave early. No worries, Jacob replies, surveying colors. I don't know why but I'm exhausted. I don't think I could last the whole time if I wanted, he adds. Funny, ain't it? I really don't get it. Kenney gathers the hair on his chin as he's wont to do, brushes the fuzz on his chest and stomach, while I lengthen my spine up and back, leaning my breasts forward.

34

I'D LIKE TO UNREMEMBER most of it. Could there be anything more tiresome than a career, despite the rewards? More taxing? The expense of spirit, the distillation of a self in a performance, in accordance with others' measures, other than your own; the reviews; feedback; the injunction to calibrate your behavior; looping toward what? By what or whose standard; put in a position by whom; to judge whom; and how? By a careerist? A climber? A power-hungry maniac? One with a syrupy smile or sulking scowl, acerbic or sweet, grasping underlings in their mitts like the Cyclops, to be consumed at their leisure. All for a buck. The things you tolerate; and have to; a long, extended undoing; reward for which is the boot someday, a not-so-polite ushering out the door, and after you've gone and taken the job to heart. Been transformed. Given it your all. To think of the lengths people go to to burnish their star; reputation; buff and brighten it; their standing; hoisting it toward heaven like an ensign; as though it afforded protection from what comes after. As though what happened to everyone else won't happen to you someday. The clamor of status. Stockpiling money. Real estate. To think of what people will do; put up with; stoop to; entangle themselves in; tolerate—at least most people, though maybe not Risk and Kenney. Serge. OK Will, you too—young people, who never got the boomer memo, how to play Barbies nicely with The Establishment. Exposing themselves to hazard, debasement, only to rise higher. Walk

173

a little taller; but by what metric; and among whom? If I only had it to do over; take a leaf from Serge's book—

—Or would I?

Especially after having been raised in that mindset, after having gone and drunk the Kool-Aid. The way time is a prison you can never escape. I'm not putting anything on the church women—I made my own bed. Their line was, Educate! Never: Court fame! Kiss ass! Make money! Lower yourself! Much less whore yourself. Metaphorically, literally, or any other way. There was no wink-wink about having to do "whatever it takes." I pursued it the only way I knew how.

I kept going, like an addict; like I misread the brief. It didn't help that I met people who entertained ideas for me, my life; how it could go; ideas I never would've dreamt on my own. The one thing I brought to the mix was an aversion to ending up an octo- or nonagenarian in Florrie's position—reduced to a yoke on someone's neck. But even if you set out to construct a life different from your parents, to the point of turning a side hustle in order to avoid it, there are other options, and consequences for what you pick. Forcing you to hold a part of yourself in reserve, hopefully, something to fall back on in the event you put your eggs in one, i.e. the wrong basket.

35

In all honestly I had no idea anyone stepped on the stage when Serge tiptoed in. True, at the college where I taught, I was on the committee that hired him, and either he'd been coached or possessed a gift because in an environment like academia where custom and tradition are royalty, the way they've been doing things since time began, he stood out, ingratiating himself with the younger, but more important the older set, who don't take kindly to novelty. He seemed to have a gift for figuring them, figuring old farts; like me today. The chair made a point of saying after Serge's campus visit, the kind of situation where you encounter a person very differently from the animal you met on paper, in the CV—the chair made a point of outing in earshot of everyone, his voice wavering, That Sergei—I must *say*—was I wrong about him! He's *maaar*velous!

It wasn't until he and I appeared early to a meeting, sitting across the room before the others straggled in, that I remember eyeing him for the first time, when the idea popped into my head, I gotta paint him. I knew. It took a while and several more meetings to pluck the nerve to leave a note in his box, in a sealed envelope for sure, that I asked if he'd like to come for a studio visit.

To my surprise he showed. It was one of those muggy, mizzly mornings you wake up to in The City that feel like the inside of a banya in Belorus; just add smog and sirens. He made his way from the subway to the former factory in

Queens, not far from where the tracks rise to the El from under the East River. When he arrived he was surprised by the space, especially for the price, which, coming from Laurentine, I was incapable of not divulging. The downside of landing a place like it, I lamented, was the wait, on a list as long as my arm. He was crestfallen to hear it took years, ten or more these days, a thing common in a city where people are expert at gaming the system. I explained I got lucky, in on the ground floor figuratively, the moment the factory closed its doors and The City publicized it in the paper. Never mind that many of the applicants used the space as a residence, explicitly against the rules; never mind that it was a stretch to use the word Art to describe what came out of most of the studios, given what I've seen or gotten a gander at through open doors or on the freight elevator, propped against or chucked in the dumpsters below. In fact only a small percentage of tenants in the building actually showed in a gallery or museum, I reckoned. And most never showed their faces; their doors remaining shut; such that I often thought I was the only one there. But here's to subsidies! I enthused. Golden when they work.

When he showed up I was more than a little nonplussed; on tenterhooks is a better way of putting it. I knew what I wanted, but I was no longer the type to go bulldozing the question, especially with a stranger, the way I'd done with Peacoat, Tommy, Dan, and Emil; before I started paying. With Serge I remember thinking I've lost it—I must really be ancient. Lucky for me, in retrospect, was the humidity, truly stifling; the drizzly morning in mid-May; the sky a pewter dome. All the windows were pitched, leaving a fuzzy view of the skyline of the island, not unfamiliar to what we look at here in Eldorado during a prescribed burn, gazing toward the Jemez.

36

Do you mind? Serge queries.

Mind what?

I'm sweating after the walk here.

He proceeds to remove his shirt and undershirt, until he's standing naked to the waist, his skin pale, warm, and transparent, almost glowing in the artificial light, veins bluing under the skin. Two nipples dotted an imaginary line across a field of not white so much as pale latte. I thought, this is where millenniums at northern latitudes land you. A lightening. More than my own complexion, which wasn't much darker but is a good deal paler than Tommy's. I was pleased to look, I admit, having been so long since a stranger disrobed before me, albeit partially, without me paying a fee. But I was also fearful. I wanted to say, How 'bout if one of us quits the department, which you just joined, and we start again; press replay? Instead I squeaked out something like, You sure you're OK with this?

What d'you mean? Well, we're in the same—you're untenured. Aha! Oh! I see! If you're uncomfortable. *I'm* not uncomfortable, I pleaded. I'm only worried about you. We're adults, aren't we? quizzes Serge. Want me to put it in writing? "I, Sergei, came to Jacob's studio on my own account and removed my shirt without coercion—."

No need to make fun.

I guess I don't know what you're on about.

Ignore me. I wish I had half your—

—My what?

I dunno—I think I'm losing it. Becoming cautious. Which I swore I'd never do. I'll call you Methuselah in that case—what are you, forty? queries Serge. Add a decade, I blurted. OK, so you *are* ancient. I should put my shirt back on, dirty ol' man. It's up to you, I countered seriously. You look—. —Yeah, yeah, old man. I asked you here, I ventured. Yes? I asked you here. . . Truth be told—. What is it, old man? To pose for me—there I said it. Aha! OK! No problem. On one condition—. Which is? You pose for me.

Where?

Here—where else? Could it be any better? Miles from that place, our own little world.

I mean it was a little off-putting, his familiarity. I wondered what the machinery behind it was, what produced it, parents or culture or both—I knew some things from the Curriculum Vitae, a reduction of a fully-fleshed, abyssal entity to mere words on paper; flat; 2D; including schooling and work. But a world was always occluded on a document like that. I only knew the prejudice of my upbringing, that "those people," "over there," "in that country" were godless, at least according to Florrie, who declared a thousand times that nothing good could come from that place. Is that why I was drawn to him? Considering the source of Florrie's comments, the Cold War context; that I was interested in a person as godless as Tommy and me? What would I have done had he turned out to be Orthodox? A believer? Why was he so at ease and me a bundle of nerves? I couldn't help thinking of the line from the movie about the Ziegfeld performer, who is told by—is it her mother? aunt? neighbor?—that the guy she likes is just a little too familiar, among strangers; that a stranger ought to act just a little—strange.

We'll work on that, I replied. The idea of me posing. Honestly I've never done it—not since grad school when I posed for a friend, Vittoria. Fully clothed. She said I was terrible at it. Way too fidgety. I guess I'm used to people posing for me, I pleaded. You'll pose old-timer, Serge asserted. He was removing his pants and socks. Where you want me? Which was a good question—where did I? I knew as sure as he was standing there, naked to the very skin after only ten minutes in the door, ushering in the event a world, choking me up—I knew what I wanted. But—let's see . . . where do I want you? What do you want me to do, Jacob? I guess I want you to be dead. Dead, dead, dead. Like painting nowadays; moribund. DOA. Isn't that what they say?

Twisted bastard.

Sorry.

I like it.

So I want you—

To be stiff.

Yes.

No problem.

The platform was large enough for five, so Serge was able to dead-out without a problem; to unfurl on the surface. He fetched a folding chair, the only place to sit in the space other than the platform, and positioned it at an angle, then draped across it, his head tilted from the back, chin against his chest in a gesture almost too tender to tolerate. As though people are the most approachable—observable, inviting, and loveable—when they're that way.

I went with it; started sketching; and in the process felt a spark, though I didn't know what it was or why it happened; the opposite of the image or gesture Serge presented. I flipped the timer and he became death in earnest, breaking pose rarely except to confirm, I'm dead. Dead, dead, dead. Then he cracked up, returning to position after a time, as though he were practiced at that sort of thing, enacting *nature morte*—or was it myself I saw?

Flopped on the chair, against webbing stretched over an aluminum frame, the same kind Harry used to fill while the radio blared on a summer day; downing beers atop a carpet of green; shirt removed; the announcer calling strikes. He was regularly naked from the waist up, though I'd forgotten 'til now; having a thing for it as he did; like Serge apparently; as though they hailed from a similar place. Serge slumped, I imagined, like Harry after passing on the factory floor, like he often did in the early days, after the ninth inning; like a push puppet or thumb toy for children that flops on your hand. If I only had it in me at Serge's or any age, to remove my shirt as a matter of course, in public, eyes closed and body vulnerable, without requiring a cocktail, the way I did in order to remove my shirt on a dance floor. To be seen without apprehension, exposed to the abyssal nature of a gaze, scrutiny beyond one's control, rendering a body passive; and known. Though Tommy and I were together for decades by then I couldn't remember the last time I eyed him that way, or felt he noticed me, the way I was observing Serge: the dint of familiarity. As if we arrived at a point of too much knowing in the biblical sense, a familiarity hedging on encyclopedic, which paradoxically has the effect of shrinking desire rather than inflating it. Knowing every nook and cranny of a landscape, growing fleshier by the day, an intimacy hedging toward estrangement. The good book makes it out to be a good thing, knowing a body that way, but I often thought what we needed to do, Tommy and me, is figure out a way to unknow. The way Serge was unknown to me, foreign as the Muscovite streets he hailed from; Mother Russia; which I knew only in books.

The novelty seemed to work on Serge as well, though neither of us noticed out loud. I was thinking of all those episodes of *Jim Doney's Adventure Road*, all those trips behind the Iron Curtain, to the Soviet Union, that Wren and I watched with Harry. Visits to banyas and saunas, thermal springs and spas, men on benches, chests bare; they were all here now in the person of Serge.

The bell dinged. When he sat up, stretching his limbs, exposing his armpits, swiveling his head from side to side, flexing his wrists and ankles, he stared me in the eye.

I like this.

—.

You're twisted, old man. Were you always like this?

Were you?

I was flustered and didn't know what to say—I was sure I was envisioning my undoing—so I blathered something like, I don't know what in the world you mean.

Why do you act so unpracticed, he replies. As though I'm stupid enough to fall for it? As though we're not adults, or we're in need of pretense? Is it common in this country? Ruining a good thing with words like that?

37

THE BELL DINGED and the pose resumed. We worked quietly, to whatever degree that's possible in a city that never rests, for a second, a terrain that hasn't known quiet since before the Dutch, when Natives thrived. The City, like the country, occupying Native land, no matter what the bigots say; not unlike Eldorado. Land taken that survives in foreign hands. The pleasure of being seen, the thrill of it—noticed, eyed, watched, absorbed, studied even—but most of all seen, at a relatively young age, bracing the dynamics, for three-plus hours except for chit-chat during breaks.

While he was dressing I showed him the drawing.

OK.

Wha'd you mean?

Wha'd you mean what do I mean? I don't need to see.

But—OK?

Wha' d'you want me to say? My god it's great! You're amazing! His face reddens. I can't believe you did that! And in such little time! You're something, Jacob!—Is that what you want? Saliva shot as he spoke. Do you think I'm so stupid I don't know your work? That I haven't seen it in books? Galleries?—Museums? Do you really need me to tell you it's good?

Now I reddened, ashamed; and ashamed of being ashamed.

I'll return in a week. Then you'll peel one for me. Show me what you got.

After which I emailed to say what a pleasure it was to meet him properly, that I looked forward to our next session, to which he replied, Dirty old man.

No matter. Because there he was the following week, on an even muggier, more sweltering day, air thick, as is the case when the days are tending toward summer. He arrived with a plan for how I was to plant myself, in a gesture stiff and artificial, not at all natural, and I said so.

Who asked you?

I mean—

—Just do it.

I wanted to protest that I'd drawn the bum card in the posing lottery, that all he had to do was flop in a chair, while I was left standing, unclothed and stiff, my balance thrown.

Dem's da breaks old man. Is that how you say it? Shut up an' hol' still.

Which I attempted to do while pondering yet again what it meant to be unclothed with another—the layered quality of it, beyond the layers. It was one thing with Romeo, at six- or seventeen; yet another with Peacoat; Dan; Emil; and Tommy especially. I was young and didn't think, not much, or of much else, especially the way culture writes itself on you, in a language you're born into—I was young and had no hope of understanding what it meant, irrespective of the fact it was the hippy days, that momentary glitch. I had no hope of understanding how vehemently puritan America was and is. I was clueless to just how rabidly the country as a whole regards the body, queer bodies most of all, but of every orientation; ones that don't reveal themselves specifically in the confines of a bed-room; on a mattress; in the missionary position. I mean the hatred is hyperbolic, toward bodies like Will's in particular, Risk and Kenney, because they reveal the lie about bodies as givens; genders;

and binaries in general, on a mission to preserve dualities, which is to say privilege. I was fortunate or misfortunate enough to be tipped off to the ire early on, what diverging implied, how it can leave you washed on a beach. And now here comes Serge, giving the finger to it all, in a way that can only come from a person not from here, which is to say Puritania.

I was waiting for the bell to ding; feeling my joints seize, numbing, growing stiff, here and there; begging in my head, Can I stretch now, given what was jigging in my arms; trembling from the cockamamie position I was in. I did everything I could to keep from breaking, Is it time? That's gotta be—isn't it? Are you sure you set the timer?

I focused on ambient noise; a siren doppeling past; a roadster peeling rubber; the El; ejaculations from the street here and there; all streaming through the glass. There was the unmistakable smell, one I don't know how to describe except to say that if someone dropped me from a plane, from anywhere, landed me in the middle of The City with a blindfold, I'd know exactly where I was. In Gotham for sure. Streets washed in rainwater and piss; trash liquids and engine oil. Pan-fry. Burning tires. And factory smoke.

I guess I forgot to set the thing.

See how you are.

It's good for you, old man. I just made the next round easier.

I was thinking, "Old man." Me of all people. I was sure it'd never happen to me, the turn of years; the march of the sun. Thanks a lot. I was also thinking old man, OK—but we ain't unsimilar—I mean just look. But I couldn't bring myself to out it; say the obvious; or anything. Best I could manage was, Do you get a kick outta this?

Do you?

No, do you?

Why ask? If it makes you uncomfortable—

—Who said that?

Do I look uncomfortable?

I don' know what you mean, old man. When he said it I got the first hint of an accent. I mean it threw me, to think you can come to this country as an adult, not just from a non-English-speaking country but the former USSR, with its many animosities to things American, over many decades, as much animus as Florrie showed toward them, I'm guessing, then waltz in like you were native. Like he was a spy, trained by the KGB or FSB, a product of a system superior to our own despite the yawning differences in GDP—to think an average guy coming out of what Florrie always deemed a failed, godless society, that he could be so comfortable. His English was scary-good, better than many natives, if not most; only rarely revealing a miss, and when I least expected. In fact there were times I wanted to say, Admit it! You were born here! Your parents brought you as a kid—they raised you in Coney Island, didn't they? You attended grade school there, not far from where Tommy and I live—then moved back; after perestroika. Glasnost, or whatever. Only to return. At times I wondered if he were parading as an immigrant, fabricating a past, an impressive CV; doing a great job of pulling the wool over people's eyes, mine most of all; over the school's, which had a thing for migrants, including or especially from Serge's home. But there it was, a slip-up, lapse, a teeny-tiny failure from someone who seemed not to know failure; inducing me to breathe a sigh of relief, to wonder if it weren't exhausting; having to police everything that comes from your mouth, including that it's waht not vaht in a rapid-fire string of words.

38

ALL YOU DO IS SLIDE from your mother; or you're tugged, pushed, cut, or yanked; the product of not just some fleeting pleasure but thousands, millions, or even billions of years of DNA-building; constructing bodies; mutating too; but also minds, desires, personalities, and profiles. It isn't destiny, but it bends you, either to conform or correct, and there's the rub. Culture plays the game of amending nature, bare bodies, whipping them into shape, until such time as someone has the temerity to say, Who said? And why should I care? As though matter makes mistakes.

Thank god for a series of queries over the years about bodies, going back centuries, because one thing you never hear about in civilization's celebration of itself, or religion, is the countless bodies broken, littering the paths of history, because of antique beliefs that many refuse to let die. In the transition to now-me there were several disaffirmations from that entire, ugly, even murderous cadre, created by religion primarily but with a leg-up from secular culture, that incestuous pair, to which I had to yell stop. I mean I couldn't exist in this world otherwise, a place that challenges my right to be; at the most basal level.

I was luckier than most—sort of. Once the cat was out of the bag, once I came clean, Wren and Donald did the right thing, or tried. The recurring muffling of pronouns aside, adorning them across a range like some millinery product, topping one gender or another—that was one thing; a work in progress still. But letting go of the image they entertained of me, before I was even born, lingers to this day, which one might argue is a given of parenting, knowing a thing before you even saw its face; as in in-the-womb.

No, Wren, and no, Donald, you did not have a girl.

That aside, they've tried in their way—I give them that. And if I grew up in a bigoted, naysaying, cross-burning, bible-thumping state, a land of no, similar to my uncle, albeit much improved, I admit—as that goes I'm not alone.

I also knew after leaving the state I had to go for it, once I got to Morningside, though I was unsure of how to go about it. At least in the Empire State there were maps so to speak, never mind spiritual kin, and if the school wasn't mandated by government statutes they made the maps available to anyone who persisted. Doctors could be as blotto as the ones back home, or worse, but if you did your homework, asked around, you could end up with a few signposts, never mind friends; like Kristian; him and me; such that after a while I realized I wasn't alone after all, not in a city that big, and not on campus in particular; maybe there most of all. In fact the admin was so freaked about the possibility of one of us sailing out a window that they bent over backwards, especially in this hyper-litigious country, but also in an era in which every student seems to arrive at orientation with a diagnosis in hand.

They were watchful, and helpful ultimately.

I found my way, with all the fluttering and purfling of order that coming-out of any kind implies, not with the admin, who always want to make a beeline to your folks, but with my roommates, who did the work of family; making adjustments in their own, inexperienced way; not as consciously faltering as my parents. Which is funny. They talk a lot about parents' rights these days, but they never stop to consider those of the child; whether parents are not in fact the problem; thwarting, spoiling, babying, and traumatizing; damaging their offspring ultimately. As though parents are always right; as though the Roman idea of homo sacer, the notion that a parent brought a child into the world and had to right to fuck them up, either by killing their body or destroying their soul, their right to determine their own sex or gender—it's an idea that survives today.

In fact in many if not most cases like mine, parents are the problem. The destroyers—though like I say I got lucky to one degree or another. Of course they rose to the occasion once I tipped them off, my father when he was in town and my mother over the phone—I didn't want her to see me until the thing emerged. They rose to the occasion at the moment of telling most of all, after which the work for us began; the task of letting go; grieving, and embracing most of all.

I live.

I leave it to them to work the details out among themselves.

39

THE DUDE WASN'T MY TYPE, I mean he could a been my father. Definitely not someone I would ever look for, one of a dozen old farts in the department, a group that hangs around forever and never leaves. They never think of throwing in the rag I think the expression is. Like they have no life outside, which to me is a joke, because for me work is a side hustle to living; or should be; what you do for rent. I wanted to ask my colleagues still working in their seventies, eighties, and even nineties, WTF? Don't you have a life? Where I'm from people can't wait to retire, and for any having second thoughts there's the government to help you out, to push, birth you into bare life; that and old age. In this country they stick with a job like a bad haircut, I think the expression is.

A lot of them are fakes. Full a themself; their own importance; why else would they stay? Like the place will collapse without them. Most haven't been to a show or opening in decades. When I first started I used to say to my colleagues something about this or that gallery show, and they would stare back blank face. Like to say, Gallery . . . gallery. I think I heard a that. Long time ago. Mostly they want to spend their time in their second home on the island, and that takes dough. They haven't made or painted, sculpted, woven, or thrown in ages. I wonder what it's like to have a teacher old as Stahlin.

As for Jakob, I don't know how we ever started talking, he must a come up to me because I avoided that group. He asks me straight out, Wanna come to my studio? Very original, no? Not the usual line about etchings. I know what he meant and I think I took a step back, like really? REALLY? Anyway I was dumb enough to go. First thing he says when I get there is, You can put your clothes there.

So I did.

First thought shoots through my mind is, I can get this dude fired.

Second thought is, He's weird. Too stupid to be guarded. Not normal in a land of fake-os. He comes right out with it, no pussy-footing.

So I peel it and after he gets me how he wants he immediately starts talking, going on about this and that, asking about life where I'm from, what is it like in the old days, before glasnost; of all things. The more he's talking the more I'm thinking who in this country even heard about glasnost or is dumb enough to want to talk about it? A part a me didn't know how to respond because I wasn't used to it. Do I want to feed this guy's stereotypes?—and trust me that's all they got here is that, about my country. He's going on about some show he used to watch as a kid. He even says, get this, he'd like to visit my country someday. I'm like, dude you're nuts. You have no idea. While he's talking a part of me keeps saying he's off his rocker, wanting to go to a place I couldn't wait to leave. Talk about a nerd. I mean he flat out says, I can't wait. Wanna go together? You can show me around.

Show him around . . . a country half the size of the globe.

After that we'll go to Disneyland, I say.

I mean I was all like, whoa nelly, show him around. How do I advise him he better get a Ph.D. in the culture first, because it's that complicated. I mean that's how clueless people are here. "Wanting to go" is putting the cart before the mule. I mean, I just met the guy. I'm lying buck naked and he's already talking about going on trips, like does he got a screw loose? Next thing I know he's gonna ask my father for my hand. He even tells me he's been trying to learn a little of my mother tongue, online, for some time, and I'm like OK whatever. Just so you know, for someone not born there it's impossible, especially someone your age; like solving Fermat's Formula before it was hacked by the guy in New Jersey. He tells me that by coincidence he spent the previous summer re-reading (!) novels from the nineteenth century in my country, and the century before that, and I'm like, Why the hell would you do that? No one but my parents and other old fogies do it, not anymore, OK except Alexei, but he's weird too. Everyone else my age is too busy going to Red Square McDonald's or playing Orlyonok to read that crap, not unless we're forced in school, and even there there are a million ways to get out of having to read a page. What kind of kook reads a book twelve hundred pages about some war no one cares about—just for fun?

I was like, dude, you really are strange. But while I'm thinking all that in my head, my body is registering something else, which got me mad.

He tells me, I was so happy when I heard they hired you. I was really looking forward to talking about the novels with you, with anyone really. He rattles off a list of names, going back to the Decembrists, and I'm like, the Decembrists! Why not let's talk about dinosaurs while you're at it? Because dude they're like the same era. I didn't want to tell him I didn't know shit about them, that I only know the word and that they were ancient, like nobody talks about them except nerds. He has the nerve to tell me, Sounds like the education system in your country has gone to the dogs like the one here, and I'm like, How the fuck would you know?

Anyway after he finishes the sketch I stretch and tell him, Now you take your clothes off and I'll draw you.

And the dude does it.

At first he's like, You don't want to see this mess, motioning toward himself.

I'm like, old man, I'll decide. I did it, so get going.

And the guy does. He unjeans himself. Unteeshirts. I'm thinking to myself, this is awkward, not because I was never buck naked with an older man; have you ever heard of a banya? It's mostly old wrinkly dudes who smoked and drank too much in their day; we do it all the time. Peel a tomato in front of each other and not just dudes.

Jacob was undressed lickety splits, and I'm like he's had practice. Strange for an Amerkan, which is when I realize maybe he has possibilities. He's naked and I'm naked and I get him in position and he starts to show he's into it and is stupid enough to apologize. I tell him he's a perv. A dirty old man, but my body is saying check it out.

He's like, What are you thinking, and I'm like, Dude, I'm married.

You mean to a woman?

What do you think?

He replies, It is what it is, the way everyone does here.

Then he has the balls to say, I'm married too. To a man. He blurts it out like that, like only an Amerkan would.

And I'm like, So you're a double perv. Unfaithful.

I'm thinking there are things he doesn't need to know. After I'm done drawing we both put our clothes on and are ready to go out, and the guy actually says he wants to give me a kiss. Like he didn't hear about my wife. I had my backpack on and I was about to go out the door when he stops and comes out with it. I scream, Child abuse, child abuse!—What the fuck are you doing? And first thing he does is apologize again, like we're in kindergarten. At the same time I'm stiffened by the idea but determined not to say. Wait 'til the chair hears, I deadpan—is that a word?

He says, Well I caught a vibe. . . . Men kiss all over the world, like it's no big thing. He says he saw it on that show when he was a kid.

Which might a been true, but slow down roadrunner. I mean I haven't been in this country long, so show respect. I might have liked him more if he had just gone for it, planted one on without asking; before I had the time to think about it. I wanted to say, Do you need permission for everything? If I didn't want it I would've just slapped the shit out of you, and you'd deserve it. That or report you. But I kept my mouth shut, except to say, Dude, I'm straight—I said that.

He looks at me funny and then goes, Ohhh kaaaaay. Is what it is.

I almost felt bad for him, except, I mean, I just met the guy, and he's telling me he's married to a dude while showing me and god and any fly on the wall what's up. After we get ourselves buttoned for what lies beyond the door I think, ain't this a pisser; the whole goddamn thing. I mean ain't it just my luck.

I think he left that day worried what I'd say in the department, if I'd tell, and I left too, no matter what he might a thought, with a pinched heart.

But there we were a week later, naked again and waving banners for Mother Russia, perhaps our department chair, that troglodyte; and all our sexagenarian, septuagenarian, octogenarian and nonagenarian colleagues. For Amerka too, my adopted country; and home now at the point of writing. We waved flags for the country. The poor in El Salvador. All your huddled and tired masses yearning to be free. Father Church. The discerning Amerkan viewer. The joys of social media. Jerry Falwell. Ice cream socials. Frida Kahlo and Diego Rivera. The astronauts on the Space Station. Those slogging for world peace, including diplomats, NGOs and their silent partners. Animals traumatized by industrial farming. Global warming about to destroy us all. We were checking each other out across the room, him with his man's body.

The following week I ordered him to help me move the mirror he had leaning against the wall, mural size, doubling us like everything in the space. We set it toward the east to catch the light. I set us on the platform and arranged us slant, so that he was spooning me. While we lay I drafted what was in the glass, running my pencil on the surface of Jake's skin, there on the pad, glancing back again at the mirror. The light was spectacular, which is amazing when you think it raced ninety-three million miles to illuminate us, him and me, through the gray-city air, past the smog billowing from trucks and taxis, factories, cars, and jet planes, landing on our bodies. I thought I might cry the way it was lighting Jacob's flesh.

Usually never one to shut up he hardly said a peeps. When my sketch was done I remarked, Back off, Bozo. Don't get no ideas. You're married and so am I, to a woman; which I was, technically. I'm thinking, Nothing's gonna happen, so get over it.

40

THAT WENT ON for some time. I think I could've even got away with it had I not been stupid enough to say, Why not come to my flat? So dude calls his husband and says he'll be late and we head to Brighton Beach. There was not much in the fridge but cheese and a couple wrinkly tomatoes; dry crackers; but he's like not interested. Take your clothes off—he says it like that, soon as we're in the door. I wanna draw you on the sofa. He was going on about some tacky table—he taught me that word, tacky. Tacky this and tacky that—including tacky lamp, tacky picture, tacky TV, tacky apartment. I wanted to say I got it from dumpster on the corner, or was it the tree lawn, before pick-up, but I said here and there instead. It was the one time he drew me he wasn't naked too, which is a good thing because out of the blue I hear Alexei's key. I exploded like a Russian rocket toward the bathroom, just in time to grab my clothes and slam the door, giving the old man time to close his sketch book and shove it in his knapsack, based on my reaction alone; like for once he was at least smart enough to read the room.

Anyway Alexei comes in and I hear him and Jacob beyond the door; exchanging small talk; as though the situation were as normal as an Amerkan stuffing a burger in his face. I was standing, listening, hearing how two people get by who never met; like I was god or something. How they talk across a divide, especially given Alexei's English, his personality too, in a country that treats every interaction like a social in a candy shop, sweet and smiley. Fortunately I told Alexei enough about Jacob that he wasn't flying entirely blind, including more than I need to say, though I never mention Alexei to Jacob before then, which is what I was most afraid of; interested in too. What way it would go. What Mister Big Talk would say; or more likely ask.

Alexei should've been at work, and it was just my luck that he comes back early, and wouldn't you know he goes introducing himself as my partner; I mean I want to kill the guy. First thing out of Jacob's mouth is, Must be cozy with the three of you in a one-bedroom. I mean leave it to Jacob to do the math regarding square footage, bed counts, the amount of people that can comfortably fit. But do you think Alexei's dumb enough to say, Three people? What do you mean, Three people? There's just the two of us here! Instead he replies, Professor—may I call you Jacob?—like any good Russian.

Call me Jake, the other says.

Oh, we're Jake now, I say to myself.

Well Jake, it's a tight fit, believe me. With the three of us. I guess!

The other—Alexei doesn't even know the gender— They'll be home later.

It's no small irony that at the time a female friend was visiting who could have played the wife in a pinch, if I was able to warn her—she wasn't supposed to be home yet, and fortunately wasn't; instead she was checking out the city and was always late to return. But knowing what I know about everyone from home she could've done it as easy as Alexei because that's Russians for you. She could have become my wife on a dime, I think the expression is, without help from me or Alexei who would have instantly switched from bed partner to couch-surfer. There was no need for Jacob to know any of that, especially that Alexei and I sleep pressed together naked every night, as we did for years before coming here.

When I finally come out of the bathroom, we played roommates, partners of a different kind, and even if I say it about myself I think we could have won an Oskar; we were that good. But, although they're a bunch of play actors themselves, Amerkans couldn't tell a good from a bad actor if their life depended on it, which is the paradox of all paradoxes. I mean every Amerkan is an actor, smiling all the time no matter how they feel, putting on a show even if they're dying inside. Jacob plays that game too, don't get me wrong, but then he comes out with a zinger that lets you know he's not totally lost. Also he doesn't suffer fools. So, more than anyone I met til that point, he had me on my toes, minding my P's and Q's I think the expression is, like I finally met my match in this country. I mean he had me going—is that it? Especially because for all our time together one of the few things I wasn't open with Alexei about is the fact that Jacob had tenure and I was hanging by a thread, and for me there was no way I was going back where I come from. I was the one to get a real job and not some under the table thing that paid shit, which is what Alexei was doing. Including working the ads. Amerkan dudes were willing to pay a fortune for him. I only had a temporary work permit, and I relied on a fake marriage and the school to print a ticket for both me and Alexei to stay.

I was in a bind. Thanks god Alexei was a champion that day. Jacob commented how glad he was not to be assaulted by meat at someone else's home, though neither Alexei nor me remarked we couldn't afford it if we wanted. We didn't say there were times we dined from the corner bin. Also I didn't want to get Jacob going by telling him I wouldn't buy meat if I could. My thought was baby steps, Jakey; baby steps. We're gonna do this my way or not at all; given how free your tongue is; the way you're like a labrador puppy. Like I say I was in a spot with Jacob and Alexei both, and neither of them had to really know about the situation shaping with the other, against my will. I'm not sure I knew myself where things were going; I mean I was flying by the seat of my shorts.

41

Only thing I knew for sure is Alexei and I were still together, by which I mean together-together; we came to this country, or ran here, flew like two doves in the crosshairs of hunting rifles, because the situation in our country was changing for people like us, and fast. That made us not just an endangered species but endangered period, which is a crime after The Openness when it seemed like things were on the mends. My parents couldn't believe it in 1989, what was happening, compared to how things were their whole lives, and also given what they were always pushing for, working for Remembrance. We pivoted to the West finally, after centuries pinging and ponging back and forth, west and east, the post-glasnost, western turn making it possible for Alexei and me to exist at all in the open, making it possible too for people of my parents' age to begin documenting The Terror while people were still alive to tell their stories. But sure enough, just after opening, the door begins to close again because the thing apparatchiks hate more than anything, apparatchiks anywhere in the world, is change, especially when it comes for them. Their privilege. I mean the dead like change little by little, so little that nothing alters and things remain the same. Dead. Worst of all was they resurrected the church; once they did that it's goodbye freedom for me and Alexei. We started to feel uncomfortable, and even our parents were like, If you guys can't cover it better you should go to Germany; maybe

Sweden. Norway. Anywhere they don't care about people like you. It was my idea to go to Canada, thinking they're basically Amerkans, though without the gun; where you don't need to lock your doors. But Alexei says, Why not go to the belly of the beast, the great Satan, hater of socialism to the point of insanity.

I said, Sounds good.

I was smitten with Alexei, is that how you say it? Smitten with him? In love is more like it. And he was smitten with me. I was practically a baby when we met, and he was older, though not half as ancient as Jacob. Alexei must have been in his thirties at the time. The love of my life. For a long time, especially at first. But after we came to this country things begin to shift. Right off the bat he goes, I hate it here; it's a country of phonies. All they care about is money; things; like that's gonna solve anything. He said he missed our country, with all the problems, that he was never going to learn to like it here; even in Brighton Beach where we could eat our food and speak our language, kind of. He went on to the point that I found myself defending the place, not to mention to my family back home who made comments like, How many people get shot on your street today? Has your head fallen off from the stupidity? How is it in the land where gold grows on trees? Then they would laugh.

Starting the day the two met, Alexei seemed to want to take out his feelings about the place on Jacob.

I hear you're a reader.

Now and then.

Alexei proceeds to go into full nerd patrol about The Tradition, not just the obvious ones like Lev and Fyodor, Ivan and Alexander, the latter being one of the Decembrists, who unlike the others escaped being shipped to the camps. It was less of a conversation about Herzen and Chernyshevsky than an examination to see if the Great Jacob, such as I built him up, could pass the test, because he didn't believe any random Amerkan knew squat about our country, including literature.

It's one of the greatest traditions the world has ever seen, if not *the* greatest! Alexei insisted in that accent of his.

No argument, says Jake.

No really—I mean it! There is nothing that compares in Amerkan literature to a Dostoevsky or a Tolstoy.

We're talking apples and oranges, aren't we? says Jacob, stupid enough to argue. They all use the same devices, don't they? To say complex things?

Does that even exist in this country, complexity? challenges Alexei. I mean, you can't get any more complex than Raskolnikov.

Again, no argument. Though Ishmael is complex. And Gatsby, deceptively.

Pfft! Ishmael! Gatsby! You can't even compare!

I was sure Alexei had no knowledge of either but I kept my mouth shut. The two carried on the better part of the evening, with Alexei insisting repeatedly that no literary tradition was more layered and nuanced, complex and complicated, more *musically* sophisticated than the Russian—It has to do with the language! he insisted—though he didn't use those words exactly, and Jake wasn't really arguing, no matter how much Alexei wanted to get him to try; Jake readily granting the point that it was deep and storied tradition, never mind history; that he wished he could read it in the original; while Alexei basically refused to hear it, convinced as he was that Jacob was humoring him, refusing to engage, saying what he wanted to hear while adhering to the secret view that no literature compared to the one of this country.

I yelled at Alexei after Jakob left, saying he was a bully, that he didn't know when to stop.

Amerkans are Amerkans, returns Alexei. They all think they're better.

42

I GOT A SINKING FEELING, because I became Alexei's main connection to this country. I was starting to know more people at the time I met Jacob, while Alexei knew a series of older men who never asked questions; who were singularly focused; so that Alexei grew disillusioned. He became jealous of people I talked about.

I couldn't take it. I felt like I was back in the situation we left, always under surveillance. Not very long after the afternoon Jacob visited, Alexei and I stopped sleeping together, though we were naked around each other as we'd always been. He started sleeping on the sofa and I kept to the bed, and more and more I could tell he resented my experience here, at first a little and then a lot. It wasn't like everything was easy for me either. Like Alexei, I longed for our country, our language and food, our humor most of all, which is nothing like the scrubbed and sanitary, puritan version you find here. Hallmark humor. I always thought growing up if I moved here it'd be easy because after watching so many Amerkan movies and going to so many Amerkan shops around Moskva, buying so many Amerkan brands, that it would feel like home, but fat chance. Instead I was depressed like Alexei. At the ugliness of the place for one, beyond believe, a horrible landscape, driving from the airport in New Jersey down the freeway. It was crowded too; people were rude and unhelpful. I didn't expect everyone to speak my language, but I thought they'd at least be more patient while we got used to English. We didn't want to live in Brighton Beach because we wanted to get to know the place, improve our speech, but after a year we said fuck it and made the change. It isn't our language technically, though because Alexei's mother is Ukrainian he could at least get by; for me it was at least Russian. Ish.

43

AFTER MARIA'S ELTERN PASSED in Reschitz and at such an early age, we decided to go for good, after our familien had been in those parts for generations. Companies posted signs everywhere at the time, at the train stations in Frühling and Reschitz, on the rathaus wall, the Post, even die Kirche, about a better life in Amerika, the place where gold grows on trees, we were told, including in the Forest City where we heard anyone who wanted a job could walk right in and get one, unlike Reschitz where things were bleak, with so many farmers fleeing the land because of the drought, crop failure, epidemics in people and pigs. So we saved over many years until we had enough.

I thought after the train ride to Bremen, which lasted days, tending our three little ones—I thought the minute we boarded the ship, also called the Bremen, that in leaving I was leaving behind 12 hr days and the shop floor, forever. Goodbye old world, old problems, old struggles, from death til you drop, scheisse überall, the smell of shit everywhere, mud on everything, your pant legs and the hems of ladies' dresses, including at the kirchweih. Scheisse scheisse und mehr scheisse. Sweat. Early mornings and late nights, dark to dark. Cholera, diphtheria, and infant death. Fire that destroyed half of Frühling not long after I was born, killing three of my cousins and their vater who couldn't bear the loss. So he killed himself. Did I say frequent drought?

Hello new world. Land der möglichkeit or possibility, without problems, where no one works hard and money rolls in. Heil saubere welt hello clean world where you get up after the sun and go to bed when you want.

Little did I know on the plank as we were leaving Bremen that we were in for worse. Maria tries in the kitchen, I give her that. If she can't cook a pilzterrine or mushroom terrine like Mutti's her tomatensalat und brot come close, even if the bread is bought. I know it's hard for her, trying to survive in a world where food is bought and rarely grown; some gray, bland thing from cans mostly; only one kind of green they call iceberg, something that would a made Mutti laugh until she peed, Mutti who almost never cracked a smile. The sickly one or two kinds a potatoes you get and one kind a carrot, orange; as though carrots are supposed to be one color. If Mutti could only hear me after all my whining, what I wouldn't give for anything from her garden, her and Trina's both. We were different and even unknown to ourselves when we arrived here; people called us krauts then nazis. Never mind we never stepped a foot in deutschland or had anything to do with it, me or generations of my family, for almost two hundred years. Never mind we don't even speak the language they do there; we speak a mix of dialects that come from all over the south of the country and parts a France that people put in a bowl and made tossed salad with.

To think a the way things turned out, how our world fell apart, the bottom dropping from my life after Vati and Mutti sat me down for the second time, was I even sixteen? Seventeen? When they told me, they told me when I was only sechzehn oder siebzehn I think, 16 or 17, that I needed to *geh*, go, get out of Frühling. For good. And never come back. They arranged it all with the Fisches, people who heard about jobs in Reschitz, the mushrooming manufacturing town, which would get my back up off the ground, out of the endless loop our line was stuck in like mud, everywhere you step in Frühling, even in der Kirche; for generations as though the whole place was cursed and trying to rise because of my great-grandfather who came as a lehrer or teacher and never thought to invest in land. Unlike uncle Franz who'd been warned.

We want you to geh; it sounded like gay. Schnell!

Zimmi had already gone by then, leaving a hole in our lives, and Trina was on some kind of verge with Mutti now that she was seen the way she was, by people who didn't know better.

Geh! Scram! Beat it!

Mutti's hands were trembling as she spoke, her eyes dead serious.

But I wanna stay with you! Whose gonna take care a you when you're old? I'm all you got!

No you're not. We're better without you. Vati had tears in his eyes.

But I wanna stay.

Well we don't want you to—you're in our way. Mutti's hands wouldn't stop shaking, a thing I never saw before, but she absolutely refused to shed a tear like Vati. Her control was as fierce as der teufel, swearing he'd get back at gott.

Dein vater und ich, we want you outta here. So go, she said.

I abered or butted them a million times, but, but, but, said they weren't serious, that they were joking, or hiding something, but then Vati performed the most manly act I'd ever seen in my life. He threatened to throw me out, Vati, of all people, the most mild-mannered person on die Erde on earth, in some ways he was half the man Mutti was. Get out before I throw you out! he yells.

I stood in silence, studying their faces, blank as a side of a barn that the possessed climb without a ladder. They were unwavering like TV actors, something they would never know or imagine. The thing I didn't know bei der zeit or at the time was that it'd be the last time I saw them.

They formed a wall I couldn't scale, so I left. Me, Maria and the Fisches made our way to Reschitz and a new life, with nothing but the clothes on our backs and a rucksack on our shoulders filled with questions, including how Mutti and Vati could be so mean. Such bad parents, and me so young.

I carry the rucksack still, every minute of every day.

When I first arrived in Reschitz I thought me and Maria would be there for life, that I'd get a job and a house and Mari and I would marry finally and settle down and raise a family, not far from Mutti und Vati. Maria and I could take the train back to Frühling so they could see the grandkids, little people who were raised in the hope of a better day. But as things turned out it was impossible to get a footing even in Reschitz, where jobs were suppose to be as plentiful as the soot you inhale with every breath, but with all the refugees from the farms any job you got came after a lot of waiting, and it was a lot more deadly.

When we finally did get married after several years Mari got pregnant right away and couldn't work. My pay was nichts and we couldn't make ends meet, not on our own, especially after Mari's Vati passed, mutilated by a machine on the factory floor. You could argue Mari's Mutti died too, there on the floor with him, because she began to go downhill, the only adult looking after all us. Until me, Mari, and her siblings found ourselves around her grave too, next to Peter's in the giant cemetery on the hill, looking down on the factories.

I mean Reschitz was something, the kind a place you had to be there. Factories peering in the windows of your apartment, peeping toms spying on your every move, with the cemetery monitoring them like an angry god. The sun was the absentee landlord of the town, hiding behind clouds and grit from all the stacks, burning your eyes and crusting on the corners of your mouth in that "Hungarian miracle" they called it, dumped in a valley of the Carpathians, a bowl that trapped pollution like a bottle holds arsenic.

44

Word come that Mutti and Vati left Frühling and were living in Winterfeld, just a few miles down the road. I heard they were living among die Tiere or animals in a barn adjoining the house of a farmer. When I tried to find them my plan was to insist on bringing them back to Reschitz where they could live their days as großeltern or grandparents and not as day laborers, in Winterfeld where work was more of a prison sentence. I stopped at die kirche or church in Frühling where we sat Sundays and feast days, a second home we came and went from more times than I can remember; that humble beauty the color of crockery with its bell tower replaced after the fire, standing over the town. When I approached Pastor Feri, whose hands, grown twisted, shook water over me and Niko when we were a day old, all he would say is they come back to stand as godparents for a sucio kid, a bastard boy, but then disappeared; as though they fell off the planet. I couldn't help thinking that getting rid of me didn't stop them from taking on a godchild, one without a father in the eyes of the church; in that part of the world a godchild is as good as the real thing; like blood or better because godparents were committed and never sent the child away. I didn't say to Fr. Feri that they took on someone else's infant after dumping their own blood, but I felt it. I also didn't say that if they took on a sucio boy Feri knew damn well where they were because he had to find them in the first place. So I gave up

210

on Feri. I decided to look myself, walking from Frühling to Winterfeld, surveying the fields and fieldhands along the way, gathering fear and determination as I went, hoping to spot them. I spent many a Sunday on the eisenbahn straight to Winterfeld, searching around the towns near Frühling, including Tivoli and Weinbergen, Schwulhimmel and Vogelein, looking, on the idea that a body can't disappear or run forever. I figured I knew Mutti and Vati better than they knew themselves. I was sure they would give in, forced by need or a broken heart, that they would cry uncle as they say here and come out from the fields when they spotted me hunting high and low.

45

It was on one of those journeys when Mari stayed in Reschitz that something Vati said come back to me. He said Geh ins Amerika; deine Mutti, your mummy, has a will of eisenbahnschienen stiff as train tracks. So go.

After trying to locate two foxes who were evading me, we decided to go after all, finally, Mari und ich; though not til years passed, trying to find our way in Reschitz, ten years to be exact; a decade of looking, until I declared they won; the woman and man who conceived and birthed; fed and raised me; verschwunden or disappeared from my life after I tried every road, path, field, and farmhouse. It struck me then that me and Mari were orphans in the truest sense, alone on our own, no longer leashed to the Banat, us und unsere kinder, five motherless childs.

We decided to go.

Not knowing still today what happened to them. Where they ended up. When they passed, if they passed. How they passed if they did. In comfort or on a pile of scheisse. Who went first. Who was alone after der tod of the other. How much they missed me. If they missed me, or if they were glad they tricked me. How long the loneliness lasted for the one who remained. If it was drawn out or short? I told Feri on another visit, You know where they are. How are you so sicher, so sure? Because you know everything! You spent your life writing it all down in the books just there, there on the shelf, leather and worn because they were pawed so many times. Births marriages and deaths. Nothing happens here or fifty miles around without you knowing or recording it, every little thing. Who had her first period; who fucked who; whether they were single or married; who is happily and who unhappily joined; whose having an affair—you know it all!

I'm sworn to secrecy.

Ja, ja. Aber Vater es ist meine Mutti und mein Vati—but it's my parents.

They always will be.

Back and forth we went, arguing, playing cat and rat, until it dawned on me I would really never know. Including whether and where they were alive, though the answers were in Feri's books, I was sure, the ones he never showed, a record of what's what in Frühling; following from the Father before him and the one that would replace him some day; like it was a secret society, a cult, a guardianship of knowledge. If Mutti und Vati were alive today they'd be a hundred and twenty-something, and you can add another twenty or thirty years for Feri, in a village where people have something to celebrate if they make it to fifty. Sixty. One or two even stuck it out to seventy. Here in America I'm older than all them I'm sure. And I hate Feri still. That hasn't changed though more and more I think I gotta work on it. On his silence, which may or may not have saved Mutti und Vati from worrying. I think he knew I'd show up and he could pass the knowledge to them, what I'm doing, how it was going, what my plans were. Until I stopped.

46

For all I know it was Feri who put them up to getting rid of me, after Zimmi was getötet. Killed. To save me and them. I mean, why did he always ask my parents to slink in the church with the mother and baby, the father nowhere to be seen; to perform the rites, swelling the numbers of their god-kinder to three dozen or thereabout; as though he knew that they were his people, incapable of judgment. Because like I say godparents are the real thing except for blood. Three dozen bastard children and me a bastard in my own rite. Feri picked them, two people he knew were experts in secrets, in knowledge like in the books, unlike Zimmi who didn't know how to keep a thing to himself.

I'm only beginning to hate Feri less in letzter zeit or lately, after decades of wanting to expose him and the thousands of secrets he kept, written in latein or Latin in the ledgers, along with his embellishments and notes. Secrets that duty required him to pass on to the authorities in some cases, officials who seemed to care to a strange degree, church and state in a kind of incestuous marriage, pursuing the kinky pleasure of surveilling private lives, the bodies of women most of all. In fact both church and state were inordinately interested in the actions of female bodies while the men got away with murder.

47

WHAT'S BEEN CHIPPING AWAY at my feelings toward Feri lately is the realization that he probably took more secrets to the grave than gott possesses, ones he never recorded, allowing people to make it to the other side before the church or state could get them, like the situation in my home growing up. Safe below, in their forever homes, where no one could unbury the past the way I'm doing now. Where no one could put them through hell for being human. Breaking rules that should never have been set in the first place; like it was anyone's business; the way they expect people to bottle things, including their human or better part in this exuberant life; I mean fuck the bastards who are always on you for the most basic things. The many ways it's possible to harm a body, physical or otherwise.

As for mutti und vati, for most of my life in Amerika, long after it was practical to ask questions, I was haunted. Are they still with us? Do they have a roof over them or are they sleeping in a ditch? An open field. Are they eating? How and what are they eating, especially Mutti with her scruple? Do they have a zigeunerin to call, a gypsy women, when they're sick? Vati always said a gypsy was the only one to call, never a doctor, who you know will kill you. I dream about them still, the three of us happy, at home in Frühling with Zimmi und Trina, Mutti, Vati, und Niko, before the donut talk when Mutti und Vati und ich were the happiest family in der Erde, the

215

three of us feeding our faces with donuts that Mutti made that morning.

Then I wake up to too much presence, the kind that mauls you, day after day, makes you wonder how long a life lasts and when it will be over.

48

ONE THING I LEARNED early is Zimmi had a eye that wandered. I used to hear Vati plead after he returned, after the rest of us were supposed to be asleep. Vati used to say, Why are Mutti and Trina happy, and me too, the way things are. But not you?

Because I got to, he says.

But why?

I don't know.

He was in the habit of going out nights, meeting men at Opa Andres's roadhouse and disappearing in the fields around Frühling, a town that by that time had six or seven hundred kleinbauern, as Mutti used to say, filthy peasants, and Zimmi with his wandering eye. I wouldn't have thought anything of him being gone if it wasn't for Vati's pleas, which got louder over time to the point they got to waking Mutti and she shushed them, after waking us all up, all four of us. There were noises we heard from Mutti and Trina's bed and Vati and Zimmi's too, but the noises when Zimmi came home late were not the same. In that way his roaming was revealed, leaving me to realize there might be more men in Frühling like Zimmi und Vati than I knew, to the point I started wondering maybe it's not only my family; and that it might be in the villages nearby. Men looking for a moment's pleasure, some forbidden fruit; to ease the dullness des nackten lebens. Mutti's donuts did that for me, eased the dullness. For Mutti and Trina it was each other. Zimmi needed more.

Were there other families in Frühling like ours? They must have covered it up as good as us because you never heard nichts. The only thing I knew or thought from Vati's reaction was that Zimmi didn't come up empty handed when he was on the prowl. Until he did.

A peasant found the body in the morning in a field next to the cemetery west of town, opposite Winterfeld and toward Reschitz. He was naked. His private parts were sliced away like a chicken head, his eyes, tongue and nose gouged out. He was stabbed dozens of times, making him unrecognizable. The only way we knew it was him for sure is because he was the only one in town not to come home the night before. Thing was, when Vati ran and told Feri first thing in the morning, that Zimmi didn't return, Feri ask him and not Trina to identify the body. That sat funny with the kleinbauern as they crowded the carcass. Why wasn't Frau Zimmer called? someone whispered. She's his weib after all. Which became a thing.

Why wasn't *Frau Zimmer* called?

Why wasn't Frau Zimmer *called*?

Why wasn't Frau Zimmer called?

Why was it Vati instead, who in the moment wasn't able to put on his usual face, and who could blame him after keeping things bottled for so many years, especially after Zimmi started catting around. He couldn't contain himself. The reverend rested his hand on his back while the kleinbauern gawked, stone faced as cattle, as the morning light glared. They looked at each other the more Vati carried on, gushing tears, then one by one they backed away. I felt his grief and their contempt in my balls, a feeling as gross to contemplate as Zimmi's corpse. Then the kleinbauern's silence turned from Zimmi and Vati to me, Mutti, Trina, and Niko. We felt it. From everyone on the street. From my cousins first of all, Franz's kinder and his kinders' kinder, then the others, everyone but Niko who was in the same boat. People crossed to the other side of the strasse when Mutti und Vati and me were on our way to church. Trina become afraid to leave the house, as though she were the one to blame. It was a while before she could show her face in the church without people sucking their teeth, as though what passed was rooted in some kind of lack on her part.

49

Morte violenta necatus. That's what Vater Ferenc Farkas
noted in the *Matricula Defunctorum Eclesiae*, in his own
unique way, unlike his windy manner in person. When Vati
insisted that he view the register, claiming Feri owed it, as
a friend, Feri relented on his prohibition, the only time I
know. In the same way a child out of wedlock was simply
sucia or sucio, spurio or spuria, Zimmi was reduced to
Death by Violent Means. It was only then that I began to
feel different toward him. Weißt du, what was his crime
after all? Loving Vati. Maybe another kleinbauer, or a
hundred, until he latched the wrong one. One thing I can
say is he always come home sooner or later, until he didn't.
If I could go back as the old man I am now and console
Vati I'd say that to him. He came home to you; sooner or
later. Though I'm not sure it would have made a difference,
hearing it, especially then. If Zimmi's ramblings caused
herzenkummer for Vati, trauma, they also unveiled a truth
about Frühling that nobody wanted walking around freely,
judging by how the town reacted—at least initially. Until
it had time to think about it. What mattered most, having
never had the opportunity before. As though initially it
was worse than the plague or drought, the fire that wiped
out half the town. There wasn't a whisper, at least at first,
along the lines of I'm sorry for your loss; and after all the
years you shared together; unbeknown to us. We share
your pain, your einsamkeit or loneliness. Instead any pool

of compassion in those early days dried like chicken bones in the fields of August. Like me the town grasped things lately; what it must have been like; for Vati and Mutti both, how it must have felt. No wonder they wanted me out given the situation at the time.

I'm only sorry I didn't bring them too.

50

Polly and Kitty were mi familia real. Al menos at least until they passed. On the outside I was mad Sissy tried 2 break up Jake and me, tried 2 keep us from tying a knot, and on the inside I was mad at her 4 getting sick. After all the years we were family. It wasn't easy hiding from my blood family when you think I saw them daily at the lot. I acted the dutiful son and went along those times mi madre use 2 pray.

Dios, familia, uno mismo. God, family, self was her motto.

Which is funny when you think about it. Mi madre wore the pants, she's the 1 come from money. She never let my father forget, ese maldito pueblito that goddamn village he came from she used 2 say, which was her way of taking a swipe at Lita and Pop too, who she thought of as campesinos and who she complained spoiled mi padre rotten, made him useless in the world outside Las Nieves. It was another way of saying he couldn't do anything without her.

As 4 papi he used 2 complain that Lita, his own mother, liked me better. Whether that's true you'd have 2 ask her because she's the only 1 who can say, though good luck getting her to admit it. What I can say is from all the times mis padres used 2 take me there 4 summer me and her enjoyed something especial. She got me. In ways my parents dit'n. It's true we were different from each other in that she prayed and I never saw no reason. Come 2 think of it I loved

Lita despite her religion or maybe because've it, not just because it mattered 2 her but it was different. It also dit'n hurt to have someone that's a friend 2 el hombre upstairs just in case. It's possible she's the only person I knew that took it serious, whose religion had an effect or left una marca. It's possible now that I think about it that that was just Lita, that she was one of those people you're lucky to know who would've been that way religion or no religion. Like someone else I know. It gave her comfort, which I guess is the true santa fe, one not connected to a building in Las Nieves that emptied out one day after something happened, the thing nobody talked about and my father refuse 2 explain. He only said he didn't want me 2 be an altar boy.

So I prayed with Lita in front of la Virgen when I stayed with them. The wrinkles on her face deepened in the warmth of the velas. I said the words but I was concentrating on the smell of the wax, the glow dancing on the white walls, the fragrance of the flowers in the glass by the statue, between las velas or candles. My favorite time was when the peonies were in bloom. Big as platos some of them, they perfumed the air la Virgen breathed. Lita was so used 2 the smell she didn't notice, but coming from Loveland where that smell was never not in the air I couldn't help but notice. I used 2 get drunk on pink. Peonies and lilacs, rosas—seguro—pero white ones 2 sometime. La baya de saúco. Elderberry. She would stick anything en el florero, ruibarbo, current and cactus flowers, anything she could find in bloom 2 please Our Lady.

If I never felt the spirit move me the way it did her I liked the ritual I admit, the light flickering on her face, the tiny room that was dedicated just to pleasing the virgin, an addition Pop gave her when going to la iglesia was no longer possible. It was bigger than a closet and had a tiny altar with the statue on it and a kneeler in front. Lita didn't let just anyone in there because it was small but more important it was just 4 her. Except when my brothers come 2 stay and we had 2 sleep on the floor. Though he wasn't barred like others Pop stayed out 4 the most part, I guess because he figured Lita was taking care a things upstairs. Por otro lado or on the other hand it might have 2 do with the incident at the church because after that Pop cut ties with religion in a way Lita never did. She insisted it was her religion and it didn't belong to no priest. A sinner like her.

51

I ALWAYS WONDERED if the reason religion never stick with me the way a yucca never takes, not when you dig it up and try to replant it, was because it never rooted with los otros hombres en mi familia también, the other men in the family. There was a time I used 2 even wonder if religion wasn't a thing 4 las mujeres because they were the ones who were into it. Al menos en mi familia. Of course it was more complicated because the women were no dummies and often smarter than the men; it's just they seemed to work around la desconexión better and insisted on owning la santa fe for themself, not giving it over 2 men. It could be they were the ones saving la fe from the men despite themselves, who thought they were in charge.

In my mind at least back when I was un joven or young, Lita used to seem like a priestess, chanting her prayers 2 su dios, un poco complicado, a complicated god. Swathed in layers de la historia y cultura, so that it was difficult 4 me as a kid 2 separate la parte humana de la parte divina. By the time I was a teenager I came to think the two were 1 and the same but I didn't have la corazón or heart 2 ever say that 2 Lita's face.

I would love to be able 2 be comforted the way Lita was, though not my mother who goes to mass every day like Jake's madre. She didn't talk to her son 4 decades after he writes 2 say he's in love, and as 4 me I've always known better than to try talking 2 Gabriela about life with mi gringo. I may try and tell her someday just to stop her once & 4 all going on about my roommate. I guess I wish I told her years b4 and got it out of the way, but what matters is I know she'd react like Jake's mom if it were in the open like un demonio on the loose. If she realized it was real and not una fase like she told me it was when I told her and papi originally; the time they kicked me out a the business. Because the thing was said. Like saying is worse than the thing. I couldn't bare the idea of her responding the way Florrie did, saying she'd pray me out of it until the day she died. That she made a vow when I was baptized 2 raise me in the church & god dammit she's gonna do it; that there was no way of staying in the church no how the way I am, and especially me and mi niño together. Neither of my parents can accept it, not the way Lita or Wren did right off the bat, not just because they knew all along and were waiting 4 us 2 grow the balls to tell but because they didn't give a fuck. If Lita had 2 take a moment 2 adjust her TV it was like a whiptail's breath in the run a things, given that Jake and I are together decades.

52

Es un hecho or fact that its complicado, Jake and me. I'd like to say what helped most is we did it without the church and especially church people breathing down our neck, los intolerantes, but what do you call Ginny? It's just that she and that bunch were different, so we were free. Free like with him and Serge whatever it is. Living unknowing is a thing like the big bang, same way Jake lives with me. I mean, who knows anything, except es lo que es, is what it is. In the early days when we lived in the Mile High City and our pasts come up to us on the street to haunt us, just about any time we went on a walk or were seen together, it was hard to hide from such a vocal past, strolling our way constantly, pestering not just me but Jake with preguntas, too many questions. We made a habit a that from the get go and here we are decades later, avoiding questions that don't need to be asked, and here we are, still together and living in Eldorado. We get on with it, with living. We haven't gone anywhere. Unlike my parents who try 2 nail each other down, who saw who what they saw what was said who looked at who. They sit in their loungers and watch TV when they're not gambling, not talking except through the crack of some invisible wall, spreading dirt on this and that one.

I wanna say, Mami! Who gives a fuck?

But with her there is no separation between public and private, who gets to know what about who.

It's not just them who care but the people they vote for.

53

IF YOU GIVE A GROUP of students an assignment, someone inevitably raises their hand to ask, What do we need to do to get an A? Not, What's the exercise about? What muscle are we working? but: What are the rules exactly? A, B, C, and D—to get the best grade? They're thinking enrichment of a certain kind, a step up the ladder, and not about the fumbling, failing, and fucking up that learning requires.

With most adults it's the same. To know the rules, to get in with—not the teach but the man in the sky. To avoid perdition; getting an F in life; or worse, a D. The rules never query the heart of the thing, what makes living living. And it's not just christians, muslims, and jews who fall prey to that thinking. Buddhists do it too, the doxa du jour among so many Americans who reject the judeo-christian-islamo creed, especially but not only them, of whom I've met a few—even they go on about their Practice, as though that's what it's about, actions and not a state of mind. To the point I've dined with a few in my time and been flummoxed to find them sitting there, ordering a burger, the ground portion of an animal force-raised and force-slaughtered in the most brutal way.

If I have one thing to thank Wren for, it's that she saved me from any of that, something that doesn't remotely register with the majority of people, not just in this country but around the world. It's true I was born into it, into a politics of eating, so I'm not claiming to be better. In fact I whined about it as a kid, that I couldn't have a burger like normal people, and all because of Wren.

There are scruples and scruples I suppose. By the time I was old enough to make my own decisions, without Wren breathing down my neck, the idea of a fish filet or a chicken tender, eating the flesh of another, had become appalling. It's probably even accurate to say, I admit, that by the time I reached Morningside Heights I thought I was better, though that didn't last long, in large part because of Serge. He was a veg and I vegan. I used to chide him, that he was propping up a brutal industry, dairy and eggs, even when they call it humane.

He goes, Have you ever had a companion animal?

And I go, Sorta. When I was young. Her name was Molly.

What did she eat?

Don't ask—it's the stuff of family lore.

Have you ever taken a pill?

Dumb question.

Where do you think it comes from? Not just pills but procedures, all the medical miracles—derived from hundreds of thousands and maybe millions of tortured animals.

Well, it's relative.

How? The cars we drive, planes we fly in, homes we heat and cool, burning up the planet—for who? Animals smashed on the road or driven to extinction by development—

—Stop!

Which dislodged my thinking I admit, and not just about crowing rights. It dislodged my thinking about Serge too, not to mention Wren. Without her uttering a word and by dint of modeling she testified to the horrors of the dinner plate, how to carve your own space in the world, brace and inure yourself for what's to come, every time you eat outside your home, that you might find something akin to infant on the menu, braised or fried, breaded or baked, where everyone but her not only partook, chowed down, but gazed at with delight; all while gazing at her in disbelief; as though she were the flake, the barbarian, that or a rabbit; as if it were the height of culture to eat newborn, a delicacy, a requirement for belonging to our race.

The veneer of civility at a party as a stack of brisket is served, slipped quietly on a table or presented with fanfare—a conquering—or goring. A death drop. Like a potluck where the dishes appear kindly; green, delicate, and inviting; until you ask, Is there meat in this? Only to discover bacon's been added as a culinary flourish, unconscious or robotic; obligatory even; because everyone knows that everyone loves bacon. Don't they? That it's universal. Isn't it? The veneer of civility masking an underworld, mothers deprived of their young, mechanically, straightjacketed in pens, hemmed by bars making them unable to turn, for the duration of their short, brutal lives; the elision of which results not in heartbreak but a macho-amazon smugness called civility; conquering nature and the human soul.

The unknowing, willful and calculated; the veneer; soul of civility, in just about every culture; every group. Believer and atheist, educated and illiterate, rich and poor, male and female, cis and trans, black and white, straight and gay, liberal and conservative, foreign and domestic, lover and stranger, hero and criminal, poet and cowhand, painter and piemaker—they all converge in a hatred of animals, which is to say a hatred of bodies; those feral things. Cousin to my own.

54

Alexei changed, grew suspicious, made comments like, Who knew you'd be a sellout? That deep down you're an Amerkan; the real thing. To the point we hardly talked, though we were stuck in that small apartment. When I invited Jacob over Alexei could be rude, borderlining on hostile. Jacob was dumb enough to bring up what was going on in Ukraine, and Alexei goes, What would you know about that? What would any Amerkan? Then he starts to school the guy, as though he was asking. Who are the people involved? What's the history in the region over the last thousand years? He goes on about his double nationality; that he understands the situation from the inside; from both sides; in ways that even Russians don't. That The Great Mother Russia is nothing more than an offshoot of Ukraine, after the Vikings came, and not the other way around; no matter what lies the Russians tell. That Kiev preceded Moskva and Petrograd for sure, by hundreds of years, and that starting with the tsars, as late as the sixteenth century, the Russians had one goal and one goal only, and that was to get others to believe a lie; lasting centuries. The lie that Ukraine belonged to them, that they were first. Not just Crimea—a party the Russians came late to; centuries after the Mongols, Ottomans, Tatars, and Cossacks, who were all there before the Russian; though they act like it's theirs. Never mind the western region near Donetsk, Luhansk, Kharkiv, and Kherson, where ethnic Russians poured in; invaded because of jobs; to a region where Stahlin set his camps, filled with Romanian Germans mostly—Old Whiskers had a population ready and willing to man them.

I couldn't help thinking that in stressing the Russian fantasy of owning Ukraine he was taking a dig at me; I mean he was one too, at least by half. He starts going on about how the Cossack in him has half a mind to return and take up arms; against a Russian tyrant; a fantasy that hasn't quit; from the tsars to the Bolsheviks; all the way to the little, tiny gnome in power today; that Russians are incapable of respecting borders, even though they already own half the world by sheer size alone; that they only respect a strongman, dictator or terrorist, to which I replied, Alyosha! Stop!—

—You can call me Oleksii.

Why are you doing this?

I didn't understand. I was like, Why are you taking it out on me! I have nothing to do—. It felt like the world disintegrating. That I was being besieged like Ukraine. I thought about kicking him out, after more than a decade; to think it could end that way. Because of an invasion thousands of miles away, motivated by a madman, as most invasions are. Or was it something else? Alexei was a popular commentator in our country, not unfamiliar on TV, before we came here. He gave it up for me, the two of us, and I felt I owed him. Like an idiot I asked him after Jake left if he were ever going to get a job—a real one that did him justice. There are plenty of Russian papers, I argued. You can't always be pulling tricks. And he goes, No way am I gonna start from scratch. For some penny paper here.

My argument was the sooner he started the faster he'd be in. But he didn't want it. He said everything they said in our country about this place was dead-on; that he no longer wanted to stay. He told me he'd been teaching Russian to kids of Jewish immigrants, for people who wanted their darlings to know it but didn't care to speak it themselves. The only problem was Alexei hated kids; from any background. So in addition to his weekend gigs he made money learning basic grammar to tots.

When I think back on the year before he abandoned our Amerikan dream I wish I did more. I just didn't know what to do; like I was watching a car wreck unfold in slow motion. I wish I let him know many things—why didn't I say them? Why couldn't I? He was the last who spoke my mother tongue from birth, a music I get only here and there these days, so poetic as Alyosha used to say, ten times more musical than English and a thousand times deeper; which anyone can see just reading the paper; talking to family; cashing out at the market. I'm alone now, a stranger in a strange land speaking a strange tongue, where no one, even Jacob, can say my name. I use the words "mother," "love," and "friend" in English, but they're empty; void of all the feelings I get when I say them in Russian. The way they move you, sometimes to tears. Sometimes I can't even write them down less I lose it. I'm afraid little by little I'm becoming a foreigner to myself, that I'm being remade. It matters, the few words Jacob learned, the few lines, but we can't have anything like a conversation and never will. So I cling to my country any way I can, the world I knew before things changed, including Alexei.

I wondered how he could go back. They blame us! he used to complain. Of all people! he used to shout it when he finally started warming up to Jacob. They brought in religious bigots from this country—the gnome, Vladdie, invited them—and what brainy idea do the Amerkan bigots come up with? That it's us to blame for Russia's problems— the collapse of the family. Of all things! As though modern Russia ever cared about that. As though slaughtering thirty million in The Terror had nothing to do with it; as though Soviet life itself wasn't the problem, turning not just neighbor against neighbor but kids against parents; spouses against spouses. The terror families were subject to. But apparently it's none of that that's to blame; the Revolution most of all; designed to break up families in order to make everyone dependent on the tyrant. On Old Whiskers. After glasnost a new tyrant turned to bigots in this country to help find someone to blame for Russia's problems, and lo and behold—Seryozha, Jake—you and me—we're it.

Knowing all that he returned anyway, on the grayest day I experienced in my life; as though preparing him for the grayness of Moscva, saying again before he boarded that he couldn't take it anymore; that it was a matter of two evils, and that at least he knew the devil there; intimately. Not to mention he could work again; speak his mother tongue, crack irreverent jokes, and be understood. He could sit in his apartment and read books, start a new life.

One without me, I thought.

During the few times he phoned after that, he was a zombie. We spoke about the weather, which always made me cry, right there on the phone. I wanted to shout, Alyosha! Talk to me! What's happening!? What are you doing? Who are you fucking? Are you happy? Ask me that question! Ask me anything! But it was weather talk, I assume because he was paranoid about the police, especially given the war, the one you weren't even allowed to call a war. I continue to read they're arresting people for talking on the phone about it, in private conversations. Alexei knew the deal. He told me he'd met a woman and was thinking of getting married, which I knew was bullshit; which nearly made me laugh out loud. Him of all people. But that's what he came to, to telling lies; afraid of saying what was what. He stopped texting and emailing too, the way I did with my parents, because the FSB is on people. Vladdie is on people.

That time he burst in on Jake and me he got a glimpse at my future life, one he's not around to see. The light between us will never go out, because he was my first true love. When the communication stopped altogether, I knew something was wrong, though it took forever to learn the story. That gangs of thugs inspired by the zealots in this country were roaming the streets, looking for enemies of Mother Russia; that Alexei was in a park one night, doing what he did, and was lured; that just when the other guy gets his thing out thugs jumped him from the bushes—an elderly woman watched it from not far off. They kicked and beat him with billie clubs until he was on the ground—there must have been a dozen of them. They yanked his pants down and stomped his privates. They kept kicking him with their boots, punching him with their fists, kicking and punching, pulling his hands away and going for his face, knocking his teeth out with their clubs, swelling his eyes, lips, and cheeks. They turned him on his side, shoved a club up his anus and urinated on him; then left him to die.

For the love of Mother Russia and the bigots in this country.

55

AT NINETY I'M TRYING to make sense of what happened to Niko. Was it eight years ago? That everyone in Frühling between the ages of seventeen and fifty were herded at the end of rifles; forced into cattle cars; carted to camps in the Soviet Union thousands of miles away. The great Koba turned the government into his lapdog, also at the end of a gun; he leashed it and trained it on people like Niko, Mutti, Vati, and me, on all the kleinbauern because of the language we spoke and where we came from, hundreds a years ago. The soviets owned the government after 1944, the one that took the Banat after the great war, WWI, the way a spider snags a fly. They couldn't bear the idea, them and Wilson both, of the Banat existing as a country in itself. Niko's age spared him, but he wrote that it could have been him, that he knew the men with rifles, men from Frühling and nearby towns who often came for the Tuesdy market; a thing created over a century ago by order of the Imperator himself. Niko recognized them. All the arguments in the world wouldn't stop them from squeezing his flesh and blood, and mine if I were there, into the cars. Enkelkinder und urenkel, grandchildren and great-grandchildren, nephews and nieces.

The regime was under the thumb of a madman who had a thing against kleinbauern, much more insane than Mutti; more deadly—he called them kulaks—the bourgeois, capable of insurrection. He had a thing against

Germans generally after the führer invaded, after he'd gone and betrayed their secret pact. Tired of killing in his own country, he went shopping for others to murder, so he picked my people, even though we had nothing to do with that mess in the Old Country, in deutschland. In the end the firing squad would a been better, because of the many hundreds of Frühlingers who were rounded up, forced on trains, labeled enemies of the commie state. Only thirty of the many hundreds that were put in camps, in the Ruskie part of Ukraine, returned. The rest were worked or starved to death. Niko nearly passed from kummer und traurigkeit, grief and sadness, when he discovered that none of his sons or daughters, or their children, were with the survivors. He nearly starved, from that and what was happening around him. The homes of the people were also taken by force, land and animals, tools and equipment. I wondered, how he can stay, with almost no one left, because the men with the rifles weren't picky.

Not much after that they rounded up another bunch of Donauschwaben or Danube Swabians and shoved them in wagens, unable to move, eat or geh auf die toilette. Some froze. Niko watched as they were sent to reservations in the east and their homes occupied by people apparently as hard up as the Swabians. That was the last I heard from him. My reply was, *Komm! hier! Nach Amerika. Du und Catharina!* Aber ich denke his heart was still there.

Die wahrheit or truth is I had mixed feelings about him coming to the Forest City, where everyone like me is pegged a stoolie for the führer, a toady, for an insane fanatiker, a bigot. Never mind I never stepped foot in that country or Niko either, because like I say our people left centuries ago. None of us had a thing to do with the stinking nazis, I mean think about Mutti and Vati. They could have never survived the land of the führer, being mixed in many ways;

setting me, my identity; allegiances too. Think of Oma Susanna. How would that have worked? Such that I'm glad we left there hunderte years ago. In the Banat, the only place in Europa where people like her and her family weren't deported, she wasn't alone; until after the war when anyone speaking unsere sprache or language, no matter the religion, was shipped to the camps. I remember the friedhof or cemetery there, which I'm sure is the same today—a place where the new townspeople refuse to be buried—there are crosses and stars on the same stone, though time must have worn them away by now. I wonder if one belongs to Mutti und Vati.

Considering the people I met hier who are straight from the führer's land, who never made the detour the way my people did, we don't speak the same language. Not in any way we understand except for a few words, though I do better when it's written. I speak an old, dead dialect, like a fly in amber. It's true I learned the official one in school, the one I'm trying my best at here, but the one I spoke at home was unknown in deutschland, and unwritten in the Banat. The one I learned is as familiar as Mutti's milk, one die deutschen don't grasp a word of.

What good would it a done for mein bruder Niko to come here given what Maria and I go through? People spit at her and me. Die kinder throw stones. Adults greet me with heil instead of hi, as though I didn't have a soul. The government sent the only friend I had from the Banat to a camp in Texas, just like the Japanese. Half of the camp was Japanese and the other half German, but people only cry about the Japanese because the Germans deserved it. They go on and on about the Bund here, as though that had a thing to do with me, or ninety-eight percent of the other Germans, who are directly from there. The Bund, the Bund! they proclaim, soon's they hear your accent. As if just being

German is a crime. Sometimes I cry. But what good does it do but get Mari upset? We avoid speaking on the street in the Forest City, in unsere muttersprache or mother tongue, in case someone hears us and does or says god knows what.

Like the Indians who they pushed to a reservation with no good soil for tilling, they did the same to my people. The Habsburgs promised us the world in perpetuity, put out the red carpet for the kleinbauern to leave their Swabian homes and start a new life near Temeschwar. We turned a waste land into a bread basket, then we were turned on, by the American president most of all. Then another American president, along with a British PM, came up with the idea of deporting all the ethnic Germans outside of deutschland back to "their home country," all twelve or fourteen million of us, depriving us of everything we'd known for centuries, forcing us to live in the very lagers just emptied by the amerikaner und britens.

Thank god Mutti and Vati weren't around to see it.

56

I DIDN'T WANT TO BE another old fart graying the department, teaching into my seventies or older, picking up a paycheck on the way to the Hamptons. So I resigned. We packed the apartment in Brooklyn and studio in Queens and again I went west, though I didn't go alone that time. It took us a year. When we settled finally the news arrived that Florrie passed. It was strange because I'd spoken to her only a couple days before and she seemed her usual self. What made it a surprise was that we wagered she'd outlast us all, longer than the piñon trees in these parts, out of spite as much as anything, that and grit—hadn't she made the point a thousand times, crowed about her doctors marveling at how spry she was for a woman of ninety? Said they said she could pass for forty, and that she could easily make it past the century mark.

Before the end Wren tallied what we shelled out over the years and the figure came to several hundred thousand each, well over a million combined, over decades, enough to buy Will a mansion in the Forest City several times larger than that crackerbox he owns; all spent in order to maintain Florrie's membership in the hundred-or-bust club. She forgot to thank us as a rule, because she knew she deserved it, and so did we. When she phoned it was to report the medical establishment's elation over her health; bragged she was a medical marvel; fit as a fiddle; an extraordinary specimen for her age; enjoying a tenure on the planet that vied with the gray brigade in my department. They must have been born about the same year, though unlike my colleagues Florrie gave up on the idea of working decades back; or she was forced out; we were never really sure. Plus she didn't need to worry. Diana cashed in a boatload of stocks she bought before entering the community in the south, vowing to let them sit there, earning away without touching them. By the time she left they'd appreciated enough for her to purchase a grand, old, two-story in Collinwood, not far from where Peacoat and I used to skulk around the railyard on a snowy day. It was there she brought Florrie to live after liquidating the house in Laurentine.

We wondered if the move would dampen Florrie's enthusiasm for longevity, cause her to stumble toward her goal. It wasn't just she'd been uprooted from the house she and Harry built; that homerun of a dwelling the two chose in order to raise the perfect family; a place she ended having to take a second mortgage on after Harry passed in order to cover her ambitions. To which she added a screened-in porch; a fully finished basement; bringing it up to the level of the other homes on the block; all inhabited by Joneses. She hounded Harry umpteen times to improve the place, and after he passed she seized her chance, consuming the nest egg he'd sat on and running up a mountain of debt; took out a sumptuous mortgage on a property Harry had just paid off.

In a sense the house was sold from under her, the purchase price shy of breaking even; a shortfall made up by the selling off of Florrie's possessions, which Diana saw to after taking over her finances; declaring in the event that Flo should never have been allowed to have control in the first place. Diana said it worked well because she had no interest in looking at all that junk in *her* house, things which after her years of elected poverty she considered superfluous and evil.

They own you, she pontificated, echoing the view of her community, not quite Franciscan or mendicant in the antique sense. They were semi-religious, not overly influenced by olden creeds but not untethered either; from teachings dating back to the twelfth and thirteenth centuries.

Maybe someone Florrie's age and background might not see it that way, Wren hazarded.

That's because she's been hoodwinked! By capitalism! Corporatism too, returned Diana. The mania for things. I mean, people are clueless about the grip they have, Florrie most of all—she's a slave to ownership!

She's a product of her age; her culture.

That's the prollem, Diana argued. You gotta be dragged out of it, kicking and screaming.

When I passed the story on to Tommy, straight from Wren, his response was, Henny, things *are* my god. The more the better! Can a girl ever have enough?

Meanwhile Wren became more than a touch concerned. Some things are sentimental, she reasoned. And like I say, she's old. Too much to change at this point, don't you think, and—you know people. It's harder the older they get.

She has more'n enough. She's still got the goddamn rosary tree from Gramma Ruby, two in fact, and two night stands! How many rosaries does a person need? How many night stands? Isn't one enough? Does she really need twenty rosaries—or is it thirty?—those ugly things. I mean does anyone say the rosary anymore? It's so medieval! If she insists on it still, one is all she needs.

They're hers, bottom line. They were her mother's.

Which she bought her herself—Gramma Ruby used to complain she was drowning in rosary beads. She's got more than I want in my house—in fact if it weren't for her this place'd be a lot different—her stuff is everywhere!

Diana—could it be more spare? There's no place to sit!

There's not even a sofa.

There's two've us. And two chairs.

But what if mom wants to lie out, like on a couch—what would she do? And what about when company comes?

She's got a bed. And a bedroom. There's plenny a room in there t' lie or sit—and plus no one comes to see her.

I remember during my days in Laurentine when Florrie used to send me on one of her charity missions, in which it was my duty to perform a Corporal Work of Mercy— beyond simply praying for a person, which would be a Spiritual Work of Mercy—I remember when I was set to shaving off time in purgatory, at the age of eleven, that I was charged with keeping several of the elderly folk in Laurentine company on a Saturday or Sunday afternoon, anything but allow time to play, read, or draw, which would have led to sin, as idleness does. Anyway I remember entering homes where people were down to bare bones, the mean basics. I wondered how they ended up that way, worse than us even; what the machinery was that manufactured so much loss? Was it the crush of poverty, or did they choose that life on purpose? One so spare. I couldn't imagine they opted for it consciously given there didn't seem enough to get by, including plates and cups in some cases, never mind anything in the fridge.

In retrospect I wonder if they didn't have a Diana too, some offspring who saw their parent barking at the door we must all pass through someday; if they were focused on what was behind it and thought, Better get it going now. De-acquisition. While they're still around to help, save me from getting stuck with the job; of liquidating all this crap. Why wait 'til after to get this mountain of junk outta here, which'll just have to be chucked anyway; sold or tossed.

Accordingly, each time Wren visited she noticed another item missing, including the chair she sat on the previous week. When she confronted Diana, asked what gives, her sister flew off the handle.

She didn't need it! She can sit on the bed if she needs a place to sit.

But what about me?

You can sit there too, there on the end! By her side. There's plenny a room!

Wren took upon herself the task of rechairing the space, the chamber Florrie had been relegated to by god or fate, acting in concert with Diana—beginning with a chair for setting.

The following week she found the thing removed, so the next week she brought another, and another the week after that, purchased at a second-hand store or picked from the curb before collection day, anything she could find for herself and Florrie too, in case she got the notion to sit a spell.

After months and hundreds of dollars at that game, Wren threw in the towel, confronting Diana—I mean, what is wrong with you?

First of all, it's my house. I get to decide what's in it. Second, she doesn't need a goddam chair!

But she wants one.

Let's ask. . . . Florence, you don't want a chair in there, do you?

Florrie: Weeeell . . . .

Diana: See.

Wren: But you didn't ask her—you told!

Diana: Mom! Do you need a chair?!

Florrie: What? Me?

Diana: I told you.

Wren threw her hands in frustration, not just at Diana but Florrie too, then phoned on the ride after—Those two! They're twisted! The two together. To be honest, it feels like abuse.

I asked if we needed to intervene, and Wren replied, I'm not sure. It seems off, but every time I ask Florrie, she replies, Oh . . . don't worry . . . about me . . . . I wouldn't be here if god didn't want me here—she says it every time. But when I see her slumped on the side of the bed, forever in her nighty, hair undone—a mess really—not primped or dressed, the way she always was, I gotta wonder. Her face is gaunt—it's clear she's losing weight. Whenever I point it out she always replies, Are you kiddin'? Me?? Gaunt? I been trying all my life to get this weight off!

What can you say to that?

When Florrie finally passed, EMS carried her as though carting a dried insect carcass. There was nothing in their way to fall or trip over, to the point a woman wondered, Are y'all movin'? Did y' just put the place up for sale?

Wren was crying and Diana responded, Why ask a thing like that? What business is it of yours?

I was jus' noticin' s' all—there's nothin' here!

Long story, Wren remarked, blowing her nose.

Florrie had no pulse, was already gone, but the ambulance delivered her to the hospital all the same. It was there a doctor noticed her weight.

Did anyone feed her?

Diana: *What* is that supposed to mean?

Doctor: This woman is egregiously underweight; in fact I have little doubt she's malnourished.

Diana: I take total offense at that—you know, that's an actionable statement. I'm the one fed her, me alone, but she always said she didn't have no appetite. We ate the same, and you can see I'm healthy.

Doctor: I'm talking about something on a whole other level. There's something wrong here.

The two went back and forth, Diana taking umbrage at the doctor's tone, the inference, according to Wren. If she didn't want to eat what was I supposed to do, force her?

Doctor: If you were her main caregiver you should have brought her in. Was she depressed?

Wren: She was.

Diana: She was not—don't listen to her! She wasn't depressed a day in her life! In fact she was annoyingly upbeat.

Wren: She used to tell me she wished she never sold her home, that she wished she were still back there.

Diana: Seriously, my sister's blotto. Or drunk. She doesn't know what she's saying. Flo thanked me every day for taking her in. She used to say, *What in the world* would I a done; without *you*?

Wren: She used to complain to me that life wasn't the same. That she no longer wanted to live to a hundred—I should have done something, because I realize now it was a cry for help.

Doctor: Sometimes people make up their minds. If she said that there wasn't much you could've done.

Diana: See!

Wren (*tearing up again*): Making up your mind and crying for help are separate things. This will haunt me.

Diana: Well. My conscience is perfectly clear. I put a roof over her head. Gave her a bed. Food if she wanted. It would a been abuse if I forced her to eat.

Wren: What happened to all the money Jake and I sent? She should a had enough to live like a queen.

Diana: What's that supposed to mean?

Doctor: You should have brought her in if she wasn't eating.

Diana: I took care a her! Me! My brother and sister didn't do a thing.

Doctor: That's not the sense I'm getting—

The doctor eyed the sisters, one of which was sobbing. From what I gathered, she, the doctor, didn't want to get caught in the hornets' nest of sibling relations; especially since their mother was already gone, and in fact was lying rigidly next to them; all eighty pounds. A woman perennially trying to get down to a svelte hundred-and-sixty not that long ago. Again, Wren noticed the wasting—She was always a food addict, she commented on the phone to me, after a visit only a few months after Florrie's move to Diana's—So who knows? Maybe this is her way of finally getting a handle on it. But while Wren was away and unable to visit, Florrie continued to lose and ultimately started to reject food altogether.

Diana phoned Wren to say, You might wanna get over here.

Wren: Things are hectic. Can I come tomorrow? Or better, how 'bout next week?

Diana: Florrie's dead.

Wren: What!?

Diana: Florence. She's dead.

Wren: She's dead?! Just like that?

Diana's voice was as cool as a supreme court decision, just handed down, regarding the fate of women in America. Wren remarked that when she got there the EMS were already loading her on a gurney; that seeing the thing in the room, the body, amid so much activity—she couldn't remember a time when it felt so lively; with all the coming and going; the radio voices breaking and relaying events in real time, so unlike the quiescence that reigned in the cloistered air when Florrie was alive—I'm sure she would've loved it; the break in silence.

Apparently Florrie had commented not long before, We get what we deserve in life.

Wren: Why would you say a thing like that?

Florrie: Strange for you to say. Of all people.

Wren: Ancient news.

Florrie: But I remember. That you're here is a wonder; a blessing. More than I deserve. I lost your brother. But here you are.

That was the last they spoke.

Wren reflected, She knew.

I remember thinking two things about the conversation. One is that I'm sorry is too high a hill for most people, Florrie especially; so they find a way around, one less steep; the second is Florrie remembered.

I was happy for Wren, but it left me with a rock in my side. The situation for me was different, after Harry left me with a parting gift, the realest kind in that he didn't know he was giving and I didn't know I was receiving. With Florrie it was different. Whatever resolution I've come to I got vicariously, through my twin.

Following her passing, Diana had her room cleared and the walls painted, converting the space into an office. She purchased a desk and computer and began following the market in earnest; monitoring and moving assets around; enough to make a killing; which when added to the profit from the sale of her house amounted to a bundle. Enough to purchase a lavish place in Independence outright and still have enough to hire a designer; a licensed decorator. From what I hear it put Romeo's parents' home in Laurentine to shame with its contemporary appointments; defining the American dream; all 5,000 square feet of it. She joined a wine-tasting club and stocked her *cave* below-stairs; next to the room she reserved for work-outs. She forked over the money for body modifications; a lift here and tuck there. I'm told she finally found her life partner; that the two were seasoned foodies; eating at the clubhouse beside the golf course where they took up the sport; became members. Wren said I wouldn't recognize her, that she's had her teeth done—no more gat-tooth. She only wears designer.

You wouldn't believe the place, either.

I'll never see it, so doesn't matter.

No, Jake—I mean you wouldn't be*lieve* it.

Is that a judgment?

Far be it from me.

Far be it.

Diana, it turns out, was living the American life; though as it turns out there are things the American dollar can't buy. Diana being Diana, she didn't let that stop her; nor did she waste time as the thing unfolded, letting the disease know who's boss; who'd win ultimately. And for a while it worked. With cost as no object she pulled out all the stops to defeat the very thing that took Tamara—You got to kill it, she declared. It's all about attitude. She refused to believe the illness was gaining; that while she was removing strokes from her game on the links the disease was scoring birdies, then eagles; besting Diana; reducing her, ironically, to the same slip-like figure as Florrie at the end. Or so I gathered from what Wren relayed, not having seen her myself. I never waved a flag for karma, and I won't now; that or cosmic justice; vindication; god's wrath most of all.

Fortunately for the partner, whom Diana wed in a bedside ceremony just before she passed, ensuring not just her but Florrie's and Harry's estate would pass to them, the partner—she was bequeathed a comfortable life. Last I heard they remarried and were thriving in Diana's former home, enjoying life American style.

57

You just never know.

Because of a chance run-in I began re-envisioning my grandfather, what he might've been like had he come from a different set of circumstances. He showed up ultimately, six months before he passed. I got to thinking of him that way, replacing the person I'd been taught to dislike without anyone uttering a word—not 'til I was old enough to think on my own—when my early feelings about him began to disappear. Had I not gotten that glimpse, apart from the document Sarah turned over, disliking would have been a hell of a lot easier, and my feelings for my grandfather excusable. I would have been able to hate the guy.

Now that's not possible, after experiencing the ghost that first my uncles then I encountered on the edge of the lagoon on MLK Boulevard; in a sense a gift but also a curse; landing a burden on my shoulders and theirs the way every paradox is a burden, especially anything having to do with change. Transformation. Transition. Usually life happens at birth, though for some it comes later; like justice. I know what Gramma Florrie would say, if I or anyone else would allow her to hold forth on the topic of Harry, which unlike Wren I refused to hear. I prefer a different view; anything but a saint; and in fact the opposite. If he was a creep most of his life he reserved the seeds of change, though not the halleluiah kind.

It's not unfortunate to be burdened with that kind of problem, knotty like knuckles, of letting go. In a sense it means freedom, from obligatory disparagement the rest of your life; looking down on him; because that gets old. He's more interesting to me now—I see you, Grampa. Always that walking, breathing curse, now in a different light, charged with color laid on impasto, like figures in a painting at the museum by my uncle's favorite artist.

I was bestowed a gift; a vision that only death affords; a reboot once he was gone; the opportunity to become closer to someone I avoided like covid. As with the downing of an old sycamore, after Harry passed a wide, blue space yawned in the sky, leaving room for Possibility. The realization that he was hankering for a chance to speak, there on the edge of Rockefeller Lagoon, which even Florrie was blotto to—was it he couldn't face the idea that she was as bad, or worse, than he; that she'd poohpooh the idea after so many years? Even my mother resisted what it might mean: Harry changing. Forcing her to redraw the map on him as well. It was easier to imagine Florrie his victim; the wife; which was always her line. When I mentioned it to Wren that Grampa Harry found me, on afternoon walks in that serpentine park along the boulevard; where my father and I used to ogle birds migrating from the north, on many afternoons; that I'd seen him and was thinking about giving the guy a chance; of meeting him on my and my father's turf; her response was, Whatever. Until she exploded. He could have come to the door! He knows full well where we live, having been here a million times! He doesn't need to go skulking around behind my back, scaring the bejesus outta you! I let the comment slide, exasperated as I was in a way. He might a felt some compunction—about you! she railed. Forget about me!—he could have kept his distance.

I think compunction is the thing, I pleaded. I mean—I shocked myself, that I was acting as his advocate. We chatted about—you! What would a been the right thing to do.

Well, the clock is running out.

Don't be that way.

I earned it. If you only knew—

Which got me to pondering sanctity a bit, the rail my father said my mother balanced on.

She complained, It's like you're always being indicted, no matter what you do. Why was it not me he sought out, instead of you—the coward! It's me he should apologize to first. There's something weird about it, don't you think? I mean, you never even met the guy! You were never on his radar—you were just a child! How could he think you could ever *possibly* care to know him after that?

I had a hard time squaring Wren so nakedly un-Wren, like I'd never seen her; especially when you consider how she was with Florrie; as if Gramma's victim-act worked. The poor-me routine, stuck under Harry's thumb. Florrie who actively, in some way consciously and adamantly, refused to acknowledge her role in what happened to my mother, regarding her expulsion and marriage to my father.

In my mind at least, Harry came about as close as a person could to treading toward that terrible, awful admission that you're human; never mind he never actually copped to it; said the words. Not in any direct way. To falling off the high promontory of pride and certainty into a lake of unknowing; revision; regarding everything; like you were a land animal and morphed into a sea creature, moving in a fluid world. I wondered if Florrie, nailed to her spousal, her gendered cross, wasn't the bigger nut to crack, if you'll excuse the metaphor, all the more interesting because she was the christian as everyone in the world knew, and Harry the heathen. He'd long ago become Florrie's charity case, which she pled before the divine at Mass every day—he made a point of telling me flat out he was acting on his own and not on behalf of some goodie-two-shoes deity who coaxed him to it. Maybe that's why it was possible in the first place, seismic as it no doubt was for him and everyone involved, directly or indirectly, I realize the older I become: he was unburdened by religion but burdened by humanity. Unlike Florrie who stuck to the book, to a god beholden to norms who'd apparently signed off on her position toward Wren and me both; never mind my father. Jake too, now that I think about it, for so many years; decades really. Where did it leave her? With Diana's warm heart to console her.

Harry, I disliked you, and in many ways still do; as I learned to do without anyone saying a word. But I feel you. See you in my mind's eye. Do you see and hear me?

I mean the world of Laurentine is a receding dream. A bigot's utopia and to me a no-place. I've had other things to deal with, peopled with individuals a good deal smarter and more educated than that lot there; just as messed up too.

My father considered my uncle a lightweight, a whiner who thought he had it worse than everyone, who paid a too-tall price for the way he was; something he had nothing to do and was born with; while my father couldn't get past the notion of this white dude, of all people, establishing a pecking order of victimhood. Bigotries. I tried several times to drill the point home that I got both sides, that you fools are both wrong. It ain't like one is light, the other heavy—they're both shitty, just in different ways.

To which my father replied, That's bullshit. He can hide and I can't. To which I shot, In what universe can Jake hide it?! And daddy, what about me?

What do you mean, What about you?

I let it slide because it was still early days. There they were in the same city—my father was brought in to pen an article about Jake of all things, after his editor discovered the two had a connection, random as it was. It was Tomás who divulged to me that they'd seen my father and Tamara holding hands around town, and not a few times; as though they weren't trying to hide it; hide Uzuri once Tamara started showing. When I confronted him, asked, What in the world are you thinking? All he could muster by way of reply was, It's complicated, little g—.

—Little G my ass.

It's my business; it has nothing to do with you.

I couldn't help inquiring, Isn't it Wren's too?

I was struggling to avoid judging, because it's one thing to declare it as a philosophy and another thing to exercise. It was one thing for religious hypocrites—they'd been judging everyone for millenniums—but it was at least supposed to be, constitutionally, another thing for me.

Going back to Harry, I overheard Jake float the idea by Wren one time that maybe he entertained a secret life. Harry who didn't have friends to speak of—Florrie was the tzarina of human relations in that family. Harry had a BFF, apparently, an OG friend, a man who lived on the Gold Coast in a thirtieth-floor apartment in Lakewood, overlooking the lake. Though the guy and my granddad shared similar roots, having both come up from the streets—nothing like the life of my grandparents, Lloyd and Delma, in the Cotton State—unlike Harry, his friend, Clarence, wheedled his way up in ways Harry never seemed capable, in part because he had mouths to feed; while Clarence was single. From time to time, I was told, Harry would disappear for a weekend; remark he was going to spend time with his buddy whom everyone knew through Aunt Midge and not Florrie meant Clarence; even though no one in the family ever met him, except in a few yellowed photos. That is no one but Florrie had made his acquaintance, the first time being when he stood best man for her and Harry; when Midge stood maid of honor.

One year the visits stopped cold turkey; after Harry was used to skipping out two, three weekends a year for a few days at a pop; returning a different person in the sense that, one, he drank more, and, two, he seemed irritable. It wasn't long after the visits stopped, I'm told, that Florrie read aloud in the paper that Clarence died.

What do you think did him in—just like that? she wondered. I mean you saw him a few months ago—did you notice any change? Did he seem ill? My mother had already been eighty-sixed from the family home by then, so it's my uncle's account I'm going by.

No, he wa'nt sick.

Weak or sluggish?

No.

Then what could it be? Papers always give the cause a death—

—I have no idea—why don' you just let it be?

—Well don't you wanna look into it? He was your friend. Let it go!

My uncle said it wasn't until my grandfather met him and Tomás on the side of the lagoon that time that he began to query it in his mind some; that it all came back to him. I mean, how many married men spend nights at their friend's home? he wondered. And a single guy at that. Then drink like an unsaved sailor when they return.

You're gossiping! Wren protested.

You shady, added Tomás.

I'm neither gossiping nor shady—why can't it be?

Because your padre isn't here to defend, whined Tomás. And you know he wouldn't have liked what you're—

—But he gave me—and you too—a kiss on the lips!—in a way that seemed so normal! Like no big thing!

It was a mafia kiss, suggested Wren.

It was a kiss, insisted Jacob. How many men do that?

It says he was complicated, niño.

That we didn't know him. Or his friend. The two a them together. I mean, maybe Florrie was on to something—what does it mean when they don't offer a cause a death?—

HIV.

Yeah, that—or?

Or what?

When it's HIV they say rare cancer. That shuts the gossips up, the way it gave Bradford cover. But if it's—y' know. There ain't no sugar-coating. To say a person killed themself. The question is why.

Round and round the three went, regarding the propriety of it; speculation; as though Jake morphed into Florrie all of a sudden; fitting out her imagination, but mostly entertaining the idea that Grandpa Harry had secrets; ones he took to the grave the way Tamara did; flying under the radar until she didn't. Until a disease took her and delivered a Zen slap to my father and my mother; expropriating her from paradise, foisting on her a rude reality.

I could go on. And I may sometime; I'm not sure. About not just my father but mother too; grandfather; because the more you follow someone the more there is that jellies out; strings hanging loosely that lead to who-knows-what kinds of connections if you unwind them long enough; if you allow your brain to follow them; toy with Possibility; knowing things. After so many deaths my sense is the field of knowns and unknowns, never mind the can't-says, only expands, at least for the living; unknowns Serge and I contemplate; riding in a modern prairie schooner, this casita in Eldorado, while we live out our days.

58

No one says what happened in diesem land, historians most of all, because it would mean rethinking germans, and how can you feel sorry for a kraut? How can you not hate him and seine sprache both? A kraut's leid or pain is nichts because unlike other people he deserves it. All krauts are bad as jeder or everyone knows—there's no such thing as a good kraut, in Waldstadt or anywhere, because they're all nazis.

What that thinking doesn't answer for is what has gone on in this country before the germans arrived. The things people do and say; my own sons too. Going on about this person and that, the shit that comes out their mouths. When they were young I slapped them for such scheisse, such filth, until they were big enough to strike back. You can do everything in your power to pass on the wisdom of your eltern, from your melting pot of a dorf in the Old Country, the Banat, what it means to live next to people different than you like they're family, zigeuner and jüden, serbs, czechs, slovaks, italians, croats, spanish, romanies, and hungarians, but if you live in a racist country like this it's a fight, even with your own. A virus too powerful to control. A bully that knocks your door down. That's inside before you know.

In Frühling they didn't care, even about people like Mutti und Vati in time, about differences of most kinds, once they had time to adjust. They married each other. Wie ich habe gesagt as I said, if you were there to place a stone on a tomb in the friedhof you'd find a star and cross embracing on the marble. It wasn't til governments stepped in that the doors of eden were thrown opened and we were pushed out. We had a church, synagogue, a mosque, and only one friedhof. In this country I wonder how my sons would respond if they would meet Mutti and Trina, Vati und Zimmi, their own flesh and blood; never mind Flora.

Try telling the truth of it to your kids in this country. Warped by what they hear. They call it cave life, barely living, where I'm from. Try telling them you were cured by a gypsy, that life there was a thousand times harder and better than what they got. They say, Are you kidding old man? My eldest told me when he was little he heard zigeuner were possessed and could climb buildings like demons. My other told me I was lucky I wasn't sold off because that's what they do, steal you and trade you into slavery. No matter how many times I stamp my foot, say Flora was family, that I'm alive because of her, Niko too, they refuse to believe.

I fear for them. I mean the things I heard from their mouths. How can this country not end up under a monster like the one in the vaterland given the way it's going. The way people want to be told by the wrong people what to think. The way they avoid finding things for themself.

It was against Mari's mind that we become Irish. My kids were coming up in the world while my people were going down, starting with the erster weltkrieg WWI when they lynched our kind on the street. How could I bear watching my own treated like monsters when all they did was be geboren, born. I didn't want to saddle them with grief and at such a early age. My three oldest come with us on the boat but so young they had no idea about anything. They grew up American. If it weren't for them I wouldn't be able to write this because I learn English from them.

If I ever said one of the things to Mutti or Vati that come from their mouths I would have been knocked across das zimmer the room, my head and body traveling in different directions. It's true I had bad feelings about Vati and Zimmi doing what a man and woman do, but I kept my mouth shut, unlike my boys, who say such terrible things about that. What's to become of a country where people feel free to say bad things about each other? To say anything no matter how hurtful. If it comes in your head then just say it. Mutti taught me about mouths, the inner and outer one and how to know the difference, what you can and can't say.

A few Sundays ago Hank's kid come to pay a visit aus heiterem himmel out of the blue. I admit I felt bad for the boy, losing his Vati at eight, then his Mutti not long after. He and the misses come with the three kids a girl and zwillinge twins. They look scurfy, as rough as Mari and me when we first arrive from the Old Country. When I ask the kid, Henry his name is I think, what he wants to do with his life he looks at me like what a stupid question. I wanna eat; come to think of it his name's Harry. The whole lot a them look thin as grass, though the wife, Flora I think is her name, like the zigeunerin, she come across better fed. Harry looks twice his age, giving me the sick feeling, like the rest a my people. Like the Frühling curse track him down. When I ask him if he has a job he says Three. I got three.

The family sat on the sofa like sparrows on a wall. I could tell they done their best to clean up though little good it do. The girl floats on the sofa in a ratty coat, bonnet and muff, I could see the hem of her dress peeking out. She was old enough to speak though I think she was trained to keep her mouth shut, making me wonder if I could a done that with Mari's and my brood. When I address her directly, ask if she has anything to say, she says You're old. The parents rush to scold her for manners, and the wife is it Flora like the gypsy woman? tells her she better watch her mouth or she'll get a spanking when they get home. She forces her to apologize and I says Leave the kid be. All she done is tell the truth. I'm too old to wanna be around. Do you know how many ninety is little girl? I'll be more than that soon though I don't know why. To live past the death of a child's a terrible thing, as bad as Harry losing his Vati.

This kid is skin and bones and a part of me wants to take him under my wing. But I know I'm not here for long and fact is he got to find his way no matter what life throws. How did Mari and me make it if it wasn't for Mutti und Vati, Peter und Anna, getting us by with their lessons for living, coming from nothing but mud and cow shit to this house here that everyone seems to want a piece of, which as they'll find out soon enough is spoken for; already in our daughter Louisa's hands. No one needs to know while we're here, including Harry and Flora who I assume come for some other reason than to pay their respects. To visit people they don't know from Adam. They mostly sat there Harry with that shock of curls testing the air like a barometer, his too lose belt, and Flora with her sizeable breasts and midsection. The three kids. The twins look like toy animals against the corner of the couch; I feel for them. Wonder if it wasn't the curse of their blood that kind of self-control. I thought shouldn't they be tearing around the place like fledermäuse, bats, breaking and spilling things. Irritating their parents and the order of things most of all, but not the way my boys mouths irritate me. Whose fault was it that Harry's kids weren't allowed to squirm and fuss the way kids should. That they were too well behaved, like there's no middle ground. As Mari brought chips and pretzels, plates, glasses and napkins back and forth from the kitchen only the parents spoke. That put the kibosh on my chance to sit on the rug an play with the twins.

I ask the parents what they do for fun and the two look at each other. What do you mean? Flora asks. In the old days we use to go boating in Rockefeller Lake but we don't go there no more. Harry adds too many niggers. Too many *what*? I says. You know. No I don't. Is that what your daddy taught you, my own son?

I wanted to push them out on the spot in aller wahrheit. What feeling I had for them flew out the window. I thought, not another one. Then I remember my friend Lennie saying it's bigger than me or anyone, that it's dyed in the fabric of the country. Which doesn't unhang Harry from the hook. How to set the boy straight; as though one talk will do. I let him know that was no way to talk in my house und besonders or especially in front of the kids; that they didn't know nothing unless he and Flora put it there. She says, Florrie, my name's Florrie. Or Florence actually. If he feel free to talk that way in my house, I says, in front of my wife there was no need to come back, I says, and the guy just looks at me puzzled. When I recover myself I notice he watched what he had to say after that but the attitude was there, inside him and the missus both like a snake.

You ask us what we wanna do she said picking up the conversation after a silence. Maria heard Harry's comment earlier just as she was coming into the parlor and as if the moment were planned she spin around on a nickel and returns to the kitchen, taking the tray of refills with her. I'm not sure what she hates most, having to sit through so much kwatsch or fearing my reaction, though in that moment I decided what's the use. Flora repeats you ask us what we wanna do, never mind it wasn't exactly what I asked. We wanna get enough money together to move from where we are to the suburbs, to a brand new division call Laurentine. What's so special about it, I says. What's wrong with where you live now? Flora and Harry look at each other, I could see her shaking her head to Harry slightly.

It's changing. Changing how? Jus' changing I guess. Plus we want more room than we got in our apartment, isn't that what everyone wants, more room? Everyone where, I says out loud. Where I'm from, two families live in a one single room, two if you count the hayloft in the barn. So you're in an apartment, how many rooms you got? Four I guess, maybe five. And you're saying that's too small. I was never happier than the one room I grew up in; at least we had a room, even if it wasn't our own. We didn't own a thing except the land where we stand, the ground under our feet. Is there any greater freedom than that? Look where you live now, spouts Flora, and then catches herself as though she went too far. Where and what is here? I says. The Forest City? This house, Harry says plainly. We were almost sixty when we bought it, I says. I married Mari when she was what, fifteen? And you're what? Eighteen? Nineteen? How could that be possible, Flora protests. It's preposterous, she complains. It's not even possible to have a baby at fifteen.

We're in our twenties, Harry protests. We don't wanna wait til we're old as you to buy a place. We wanna get one sooner than later, adds Flora. We got dreams. I says Florentina or whatever the suburb you dream of moving to could never offer more, besonders for the kids, than the neighborhood they live now. Harry says out loud there were too many damn Jews, as though that were more OK than his earlier comment. Not them, I says. But they're leaving and, you know, *other* people are moving in. The Jews is going to Miami or god knows where. Maria spoke for me. What a shame son. A smile comes to her face and mine. I says, Kid, you're a damn nazi. He says well I can't be one a them 'cause I'm Irish.

I had nothing so say to that, though there was enough in me to keep them plastered on the sofa til the end of days. You wanna live in a place where your kids grow up to think that's OK, to say such things? Like it's the real world? You got the world at your fingers where you are. The park along Liberty, which you can walk any day; even in winter; have a barbecue outdoors. You got people speaking more languages than I know of. The museum and botanical garden. The music hall. And you wanna be in a scrubbed world where everyone's the same. There are jobs where you are, schools. What more can you ask?

I ain't ever takin' my kid to no museum, says Harry. He don't need it, he says. A botanic garden. It ain't gonna put food on no table, and I don' wan' my son growing up to be no fruit.

That's when I says I gotta lay down, but what I think is I wanna kill myself. I'm thinking these two would a never lasted a day in Frühling with their attitudes. It's true I got out, same way these dreamers look to some white eden. But it ain't the same.

I ended the visit, slipping the two a twenty as they passed the door. You'd a thought I spotted them a million. After their rattletrap disappeared down the drive I broke into tears, worrying about the kids, what they'd encounter and what kind a world they were in for, in the suburbs most of all. If they'd even make it. I remember reading about the place in The Press, the whites flooding the suburbs. I fell into a senile sob because I saw the mouth of Mutti in the younger girl, set like stone. And the boy remind me of Vati, I swear. I know it's blöd or stupid but I'll say it; I saw it clear as day. I can't remember if I ate fruhstück this morning but the memory of Mutti und Vati come flooding back as though I still lived in that house, before the donut talk and the thing with Zimmi; when everything was grand. They rose up to meet me in the twins, across thousands of miles and so many decades. Making me wonder if I'm going verrückt. Senile. The chance of ever going back even for a second. Zum nackten leben zurück. I'll die a foreigner in a foreign land with big words about everything, freedom and opportunity; but for who. In a country that flatters itself. Where white ministers in pressed pants, dress shirts, and bow ties run the place, where for all their talk they and everyone else worship nothing more than a dollar.

59

Everyone's a victim, asserts Wren

After hailing the visit and the impending return to the Forest City, in whose place Cinthia and Debra will take over residence of the house the two couples co-own, across and slightly down the street from my uncles, an arrangement friendly and financial, familial too—after toasting her and Donald's stay in the City Different Wren repeats, We're all victims in this culture. Ha! returns Donald, glancing at Wren. As if you knew the first thing; you and your brother both. Give 'em a break, I shot. It's funny, ain't it bro, asserts Donald, glancing at Charles. The way they end up the victim? I mean, this guy here—he elbows Serge. As for victimhood, I know a thing or two, challenges Seth. You're on, bro! returns Donald. Are we talking numbers? That's old school, replies Seth. I'm talkin' method. Intent. The will to wipe out a people. There are a million ways to do it at scale, returns Charles. With the bible for your defense. They all do that, insists Seth. The book on how and why to hate; in unimaginable numbers.

Oh my god, you two, deadpans Skye. Just pull it out and get a ruler.

Skye, what would you know about victimhood? wonders Tommy.

Nothing I could ever imagine—could you?

In my field, trauma studies are the thing these days, informs Charles. Everyone has one to write about. 'Cept

266

these two, Donald persists, pointing in two directions. Comin' from Laurentine. From what? returns Wren. I been married to you all these years, sister woman. I saved you from an insane father, a mother-enabler. What a reason to marry, mutters Wren.

I couldn't help myself. Mom!—Dad! Stop it! I'm not really a crier, but I was starting to see the room go bleary.

A better question would be why I stayed.

You mean after you shacked up with that woman? Over how many years?

Mom!—Dad! I couldn't believe it was happening, after so many years; why it took so long to come out, and here in Eldorado of all places; under these circumstances.

Over three years to be exact; we had an agreement. You and me both.

Three years I know nothing about, whines Wren. Still! Except one thing. The fact she died—and the girl—that's two.

We were packed around the table in Jacob and Tomás's dining room, in the glow of floor to ceiling windows that admitted a diminishing, raking light, casting shadows on the landscape, the high mesa at sunset, on the occasion of a celebratory meal, to have us all together here at once, the last time for a while, before Wren and Donald returned in the spring; hopefully. The two of them, in the event that everyone would make it, stay alive—the next time extra chairs needed to be brought in.

Wren, comforts Carina. Can I get you anything? Dude, help me here, appeals Donald, peering at Charles. Three years! repeats Wren. About which I know nothing. Do you really want to do this? queries Carina. At this time? On this occasion? I do! Wren brushes Carina's hand away. Three years! I took the kid in as my own.

Holy Wren.

For which you never once thanked me.

Wren, dear. Skye reaches her hand across now, but Wren pulls her own away. I known you both forever—what is it, forty-some years?—all a way back to when I was stranded at my father's trailer in Monument Valley, after he went an' took my car and left me; all them times when we visited the Forest City, and never before have I—

I think what Wren's trying to say is it's a struggle, for everyone, counsels Beverly.

It's men, asserts Debra—sorry Donald—you know I love you. Jake, Tommy. Serge. OK you too, Charles—and Seth. You gay boys get off easy 'cause you don't make babies when you put it in. And you can't seem to help yourself; putting it in.

Oh Jesus, objects Cinthia.

I wanna talk victims! insists Wren, pounding her fist on the table. At some point you get sick of hearing it, that you, your people, are always the ones. The problem! That for him it's complicated, implying it's easy for me. To the point you start to think, maybe he'd be happier with someone else his own kind.

Ha! Was that it? It's true. You never can understand; what it's like. I been married to you all these years, with all your optimism, all your energy, which only someone with privilege has the luxury of enjoying. It comes easy for you because—it's sooooo—god! It ain't easy livin' with a saint!

How original—I can never understand. Like i'm a fuckin' idiot or something. Like I'm blind and didn't see, so many things, in so many circumstances, day in and day out, living with you over so many decades—Jake! I feel it. D'you? In my bones—I feel it, though according to him I shouldn't.

Feel what, my dear. Skye reaches toward her.

I don't know. Harry. He happen for a reason. Wren lifts herself, as if in a panic. I can't take this! I'm suffocating—I gotta get outta here—I can't breathe! Skye pushes her chair back, stands and pursues Wren out the door near the end of the table, along the portal to the driveway—Toby slipped out after them. It's past daylight and the sky has gone berserk with color, orange, red, salmon, peach, gunmetal, azure, the full complement of color.

Inside the air can be sliced with a knife.

I tol' you you should a said something, I blurted. Anything. To help her.

It ain't your business—it's between me an' her—she's an adult. She could've asked, but she's too good for that. It might mean admitting she has feelings. Jealous feelings. Which of course she's above.

Well it's everyone's business now, I blared, peering around the table. Whether we like it or not.

Can I get anyone anything? asks Carina. A glass of water?

C'mon, the night's still young, follows Cinthia.

We thought only our parents were capable of fucking things up, responds Beverly. The world—she peers at Seth. We thought our parents mucked up their lives because a what they went through, what they survived—that entire tragic mess. Tragedy on tragedy. But they passed the shit on—to us—I hate to say it, but Wren's right. Fucked up people are the end of a fucked line. The generational kind. And no one's immune.

I wonder how you break it, Carina mutters. What causes you t' miss the life you should a lived. Had things only not been out of your control.

What are you all talking about? pronounces Vida.

The comment sliced the air, causing everyone to crack up.

I'm sorry, y'all, offers Donald. Who could a planned on this?

I could! I insisted. You shoulda talked about it ages ago!

The two a you. You're both at fault.

Y'all couldn' a picked a better bunch than this, for it t' happen with, asserts Cinthia. Jake honey, go talk to her.

I would if it'd do any good. But I know better. Best just t' wait. It ain't a tragedy to feel that raw.

Jake's right, concurs Donald. She ain't her best when things have gone this far.

For some things there ain't no easy fix, counsels Debra, a counselor by trade.

Let it all out, an' all that, adds Carina. Would it be inappropriate for me to ask, Donald, not what it's all about—that's between you two. But why you stayed?

It would be inappropriate, no question. It's no one's business but mine and Wren's—not even Will's. That aside, I stayed because I wanted, and she didn't put me out—on the contrary she took the kid in. She had her affairs too, y'all—it weren't just me. She's the one who said, Maybe we should try other things, other people; I now hear because she thought I wanted it. But she got more than she bargained for. Why it's bothering her after all this time I have no idea—I mean Uzuri's grown; with a life of her own. The down side of being a saint . . . when it catches up with you. Why was she sitting on it all this time? Why let it out now? We coulda had the discussion any time, so why now.

Maybe cause she could, counters Carina.

Maybe it felt safe. Finally.

Maybe parting does that.

Funny, isn't it? replies Charles. How you think you got a handle; think, I'm cool—then—!

Time passes, along with a freight train packed with platitudes; a quote or ten, a Forest City specialty; conversational gestures; lines people unroll when there's nothing to say but you feel you gotta say something; fill the air because silence is unbearable. A half-hour goes by, with this one then that excusing themself, squeaking their chair back and rising from the table, until Jake decides there's nothing stopping him from cutting the cake; which he made just for the occasion; the group being together, finally, after so many tries; aligning schedules; the last bash before people started heading east.

The group pieces at cake with fingers and forks, engage in small talk; then the others drift in.

Jake, ventures Wren after sitting down. We were wrong to trash Harry all these years.

OK.

No, not just OK. We were wrong. There's something there, though we'll probly never know—Donald, you were wrong too; to say all the things you have.

And what about you, all those years.

I said we—*I*—was wrong—happy now? We come out of our mothers into an insane world—it never gets easier. We don't get a choice about who births us or what we're birthed into, the time or anything else—we just come out.

You're making excuses. If we did that for everyone—

—That's the point—I'm doing the opposite. Some are born in privilege and they milk it, abuse it even —look at Crumm. I make no excuses for him or anyone—not the way I did for you—

—And me you.

It's the ones born with a hand behind their back, or two, you gotta think about. Long an' hard you gotta think about them—Jake, why'd you think Harry used t' go on a bender every holiday?

Cuz he liked it?

Did it ever occur to you he never had a fam'ly, not like everyone else? That holidays are family time, the very thing he didn't have? Donald, to answer your question—I didn't know it at the time and was too blotto to think about it—I only just figured it out. It's the only way I can think about you and the girl.

Wren was looking at Donald and he was gazing back, in a way the two hadn't looked at each other for some time, maybe a decade or more, generating a palpable power, flowing two ways, like a cable transferring data.

You could hear a pin drop until Donald replies, Fair enough. But it goes both ways—for some, suffering is all they know.

Upon which note a pause ensued, long as the breath of a free-diver after going deep, for an insane amount of time, then coming up, finally, for air; after which followed in the room the slow movement of chairs, squeaking against the concrete; that and the movement of bodies away from the table.

Wait! interrupts Carina. Are we OK? Are we all OK? Let's not end this one a bad note.

Is who OK? wonders Vida.

A centripetal power morphs into a centrifugal one, like ducklings dispersing from a nest.

Until next time, comments Cinthia.

Until next time, follows Seth.

Until there's no more untils, mutters Skye.

60

THEY'RE GONE NOW, all of them. Passed like billions before them, human and nonhuman, maybe trillions or quadrillions, all of which the earth sustained because in every era it could. Until it started to groan. It's just Serge and me in the casita next to the main house, crammed with memories. Paintings. Dead space, the way museums track on as sepulchers; where things speak only when you breathe life into them. Look at and listen; until they start talking back. We're writing this together, Serge and me, we hand the pen back and forth. We're stuck here in Eldorado by circumstance, here on the high mesa. In the nation too, one petrified of change—still, for chrise sake. Just when it looks like the bigots are about to give up the ghost they come roaring back. Like it's a curse, the puritan past. We've seen enough of it to want to stay close to home. The sun comes across the sky every evening, splattering color, trailed by stars. Venus winks from above the front portal. Virgo brushes Boötes in the west this time of year. To her right stands Libra, and next to that Scorpio. Nothing can fuck them up, fortunately. After a million years they'll still be there, watching. In Eldorado we live under loaded skies, reaching to infinity.

If there were only someplace to go, some other planet, to escape what's here, where we could live in peace, unmolested, but where? Where Serge and I can be free of the zealots, what they do to your body. Eldorado isn't heaven, but it'll

273

do. The pandemic passed years ago, along with a stream of actors who came and went from the house next door. The bigots still rage against the likes of us, against rude matter and common sense; freedom most of all.

Most of the paintings Serge and I have already placed, here and there, spreading them like seeds around the country, the world, though we kept several that we visit from time to time on walls; their afterlife. There's the study Jake painted of him and Tommy, the larger version of which caused such a to-do back in the eighties, and still today. He thought three mill was a lot, then ten times that; it just sold for a hundred.

We think of Jakob, with a K. It wouldn't have worked to include the entire manuscript, but to quote him, *Thinking can wrap you in kreise or circles, which there's no saving yourself from, but maybe that's the point. Like the crossword in the Sunday paper. You know you'll get it if you stick with it long enough, that it'll fall in place, make sense. Most times. Though it takes patience.* He continues, *I'm still working on the past.*

Meanwhile Serge and I are reading a book by a woman writing how she feels speaking her mother's language, the one tainted by the terror in her country. She talks about longing for a good you only vaguely know. About nostalgia. The language of youth and youth itself, her mother tongue, which by chance is also the language of nazis. Whatever happens in a foreign tongue we can dismiss. Is that why people run from our own, because it's too close, the things it carries? So we try to fill our waking moments with noise; and nonsense.

Which is why Serge is such a comfort, carrying me out of myself, my past, putting another tongue in my mouth, little by little. The more I meet him on that terrain, replicate the language of his mother, the more he prefers English, which for him is an offramp, from pain most of all, a land animal become a water creature.

We mark each mile with another tattoo.

Otherwise we pass the pen, back and forth; the ink spills out. At night Serge tugs; removes a part of him; attaches it to me; and I enter him. I wear it for a time, for days. Until I transfer it back and he enters me. Back and forth it goes, without a home. We pass it with our tongues, trading words familiar and foreign.

Acknowledgements

I would like to thank Channing Sanchez, Hrvoje Slovenc, Chris Warren, and Linda Warren, who read drafts of *Bare Life* and sat through discussions of drafts, making smart, practical observations that have shaped the novel in unimaginable ways; including what we shared that week in Yosemite, a memory that will stay with me forever. I'd like to thank Willie too, for being my constant writing companion, and for the inspiration. You've all been there not just for *Bare Life* but the entire *Eldorado Trilogy*, including *The Lede to Our Undoing* and *Ojo,* going back to 2007 and before, when I started the project. I attribute its completion to your love and support.

Speaking of which, none of it could have ever happened without the literary and publishing know-how of Ruth Thompson and Don Mitchell, for whom I will be forever grateful. In the realm of human idols, you're mine. Thanks so much for making the *Trilogy* possible—for your guidance, insights, clarity—and generosity most of all. Here's wishing you all the best in all of your further pursuits, given you're both inspiring writers in your own right.

Thanks, too, to Sonia Sanchez-Cuesta, my guide through an ever-changing, pan-Hispanic universe, starting with the language(s) but reaching into so many complex, idiosyncratic, nuanced, and interesting matters of culture. The novel and trilogy would not have been possible without you.

I would like to extend my heartfelt gratitude to Victor Neumann as well, *the* go-to historian on all things Banat, and Romania generally, that cross-road dating back millenniums, before the Romans; for opening up to me the idea of a true melting pot, and polyglot cultures, including contemporary notions of difference, tolerance, and cohabitation. If only everyone could see the world your way. Your works, *The Banat of Timisoara: A European Melting Pot*, and *The Temptation of Homo Europaeus: An Intellectual History of Central and Southeastern Europe* made accessible not just a world but my own roots, my genealogy. There is no way this book could have been written without you; I hope you'll overlook whatever flaws you find, the liberties I've taken. I'll always remember the sustenance you provided during our visit with you in Timisoara, nutritional and intellectual both. What an honor that was.

Finally here's to the many people who live along one of several axes of difference related to gender and sexuality. You've been my teachers in your courage and fortitude, your generosity, and you were with me during every step of writing not just *Bare Life* but then entire Eldorado Trilogy. I salute you.

About Donald Mengay

Donald Mengay grew up in a suburb of Cleveland, Ohio, where he worked in a factory for a time and managed a bookstore. He began writing fiction in his early twenties.

He taught Queer and Post-Humanist Lit at the City University of New York for over thirty years, as well as English at the University of Paris, Nanterre. During his years teaching he published several articles of queer criticism in academic journals that include among others *Genders, Genre,* and *Minnesota University Press.* He also co-published a book entitled *Dis/Inheritance: New Croatian Photography,* from Ikon Press.

The Lede to Our Undoing, his debut novel, was the first in the Eldorado Trilogy; *Ojo* was the second, and *Bare Life,* the third. He lives in Santa Fe, New Mexico.